MADELINE HUNTER

New York Times Bestselling Author
of *The Counterfeit Mistress*

THE

Accidental
Duchess

He's more than she bargained for...

JOVE

ISBN 978-0-515-15131-2

EAN

9 780515 151312

5 0 7 9 9

The Counterfeit Mistress

continued . . .

The Conquest of Lady Cassandra

"Another stellar Regency-set historical romance that hits all the literary marks. Hunter's effortlessly elegant writing exudes a wicked sense of wit; her characterization is superbly subtle, and the sexual chemistry she cooks up between her deliciously independent heroine and delightfully sexy hero is pure passion." —*Booklist* (starred review)

"Intelligent and memorable . . . as smart and sharp as the best of Regency romances can be. With its tangy dialogue, *Pride and Prejudice* themes, bits of mystery, and nefarious characters, readers may be reminded of Jane Austen." —*RT Book Reviews* (Top Pick)

The Surrender of Miss Fairbourne

"Imbued with a deliciously dry sense of humor and graced with a striking cast of characters . . . A masterpiece of wit and passion." —*Booklist* (starred review)

"Hunter's unique talents for blending sensuality and suspense along with the color and atmosphere of the era are what make her a fan favorite . . . Another fantastic read." —*RT Book Reviews*

Dangerous in Diamonds

"Hunter's flowery centerpiece will suit every romance table. Highly recommended." —*Library Journal*

"Hunter . . . masterfully weaves a sensual web . . . Fans will be delighted." —*Publishers Weekly*

Sinful in Satin

"Hunter deftly sifts intrigue and exquisite sensuality into the plot of the third book in her exceptionally entertaining quartet."
—*Booklist*

Provocative in Pearls

"Hunter gifts readers with a fantastic story that reaches into the heart of relationships and allows her to deliver a deep-sigh read."
—*RT Book Reviews* (Top Pick)

Ravishing in Red

"Richly spiced with wicked wit and masterfully threaded with danger and desire, the superbly sexy first book in Hunter's new Regency historical quartet is irresistible and wonderfully entertaining."
—*Booklist* (starred review)

Jove titles by Madeline Hunter

RAVISHING IN RED
PROVOCATIVE IN PEARLS
SINFUL IN SATIN
DANGEROUS IN DIAMONDS
THE SURRENDER OF MISS FAIRBOURNE
THE CONQUEST OF LADY CASSANDRA
THE COUNTERFEIT MISTRESS
THE ACCIDENTAL DUCHESS

Specials

AN INTERRUPTED TAPESTRY

The Accidental Duchess

MADELINE HUNTER

JOVE BOOKS, NEW YORK

THE BERKLEY PUBLISHING GROUP
Published by the Penguin Group
Penguin Group (USA) LLC
375 Hudson Street, New York, New York 10014

USA • Canada • UK • Ireland • Australia • New Zealand • India • South Africa • China

penguin.com

A Penguin Random House Company

THE ACCIDENTAL DUCHESS

A Jove Book / published by arrangement with the author

Jove Books are published by The Berkley Publishing Group.
JOVE® is a registered trademark of Penguin Group (USA) LLC.
The "J" design is a trademark of Penguin Group (USA) LLC.

For information, address: The Berkley Publishing Group,
a division of Penguin Group (USA) LLC,
375 Hudson Street, New York, New York 10014.

ISBN: 978-0-515-15131-2

PUBLISHING HISTORY
Jove mass-market edition / June 2014

PRINTED IN THE UNITED STATES OF AMERICA

10 9 8 7 6 5 4 3 2 1

Cover illustrator: Aleta Rafton; vintage lace texture © D_D/Shutterstock.
Text design by Laura K. Corless.

The Accidental Duchess

Chapter 1

Lydia stared at the cascade of raw silk and muslin falling over Sarah's arms. She barely perceived the colors of the cloths. Her only alert sense had become one of touch, specifically of the texture of the letter crumpled in her tight fingers.

"Which will it be, milady?" Sarah thrust the muslin forward. "The earl always liked this blue one. Since he will be there, it would be a good choice."

The blue dress in question looked like something a girl would wear during her first season. Since Lydia was almost twenty-four years in age, it did not suit her. Her brother, the Earl of Southwaite, did favor it, but then her brother still saw her as a girl and would continue to do so until she married. The likelihood of that ever happening decreased with every year that passed.

Thank goodness.

She blinked away her distraction and smoothed out the crumpled letter on her lap.

Her fist had smeared the ink, but she could still read the words. Once more they sent a chill up her spine. This time, however, instead of heralding shock, the chill collided with the white heat of indignation when it reached her head.

> *It is in your interest to meet me at Mrs. Burton's this evening to discuss some shocking information regarding you that has come to my attention. I am sure that if we put our heads together, we can find a way to spare you great scandal.*
>
> *Your servant,*
> *Algernon Trilby*

The scoundrel had sent her an overture to blackmail. What nonsense. Would that she had something in her past interesting enough to provoke such as this! The stupid man had probably made a mistake.

She pictured bland Mr. Trilby accidentally addressing this to her, and mistakenly sending an invitation to one of his boring magic demonstrations to the real quarry of his extortion. If not for her interest in sleight-of-hand tricks, she would have never come to know him well enough to attract his attention.

Sarah shook both dresses, causing their fabrics and embellishments to make faint music. The maid's crescent eyebrows almost reached her dark hairline due to her exasperated impatience.

"Neither," Lydia said, waving away both dresses. She stood and walked out of the dressing room. In her bedchamber she settled into the chair at her writing desk. She quickly penned a note while she called for Sarah.

"Bring this down and have it delivered to Cassandra by one of the footmen. Then prepare my green evening dress."

"The green silk? Lady Ambury said it would be an informal dinner, you told me."

"I am not going to her dinner. I am begging off."

"This is rather sudden."

"Sudden, but necessary. I must go to Mrs. Burton's tonight."

Sarah's mouth twitched with an expression of disapproval. Lydia tolerated such familiarity because she and Sarah had played together as children at Crownhill, her family's county seat, where Sarah's father still served as a groom.

"Speak your mind," Lydia said while she walked back to the dressing room. "I cannot bear it when you do so with your face instead of words."

Sarah strolled in behind her and set the two dresses down. "Surely you can miss an evening at the gaming tables to be with family and close friends. I believe Lady Ambury and Lady Southwaite have been planning this dinner with some care."

Lydia pawed through her jewelry box. "That means

they invited some man for me to meet. All the more reason to go to Mrs. Burton's instead. Cassandra will add her aunt to balance the table, or Emma will bring one of ours instead. My absence will cause no serious awkwardness."

Sarah opened a wardrobe and took out the green silk. "They only want you to *meet* him, if you are correct about their plan. A mere introduction is hardly an imposition. As for Mrs. Burton's—how much fun can you have now that your brother requested that promise from you?"

"Southwaite requested nothing. He demanded it." That conversation with her brother had been recent enough that she still smarted from the insult.

"He only wants what is best for you," Sarah muttered.

Of course he did. Everyone did. Southwaite and his wife Emma, Cassandra, and her two aunts all wanted what was best for her to their collective mind. Even Sarah did.

"He knew it was just a matter of time until your luck turned," Sarah went on.

Except it hadn't yet. That frustrated her brother. Her uncanny ability to always come out ahead at the tables seemed immoral to those who believe one reaps what one sows. Her small fame as a result of her luck smelled scandalous to them.

So Southwaite, after waiting in vain for her to get her comeuppance with a big loss, had interfered to ensure such a loss never did happen. If she ever risked more than fifty pounds in one night, he would cut off her allowance and make sure every gaming hall in town learned of it.

"Perhaps he was also concerned that the excitement had captured you too much." Sarah kept her gaze on the green dress while she examined it for damage. "That is known to happen to some people. It gets to where they can't stay away, much as a drunk can't put down the gin." She reached for her sewing basket. "They pass up other entertainments, even evenings with family and friends, to return to those hells. Even if they use their winnings in the best ways, the thrill can be too alluring in itself."

Lydia glanced in the looking glass at Sarah's concentration on her needle and thread. They had played in the mud together as girls, and remained more friends than they were lady and maid. Lydia had defied both of her aunts to insist that Sarah remain at her side, even though it meant two years of supervision and training by a more experienced servant.

Lydia, however, did not much like this indirect warning from Sarah. Too many people felt free to warn her, direct her, scold her, manage her. She was a grown woman, for heaven's sake.

"Do you fear I am such a person, Sarah? Drunk on the excitement? Unable to stay away? Doing it for the thrill instead of a means to an end?"

"No, milady. I would never—" Her face reddened.

Of course she would. She just *had*. "Rest assured, I am not changing my plans tonight in order to gamble."

"Yes, milady."

"The truth is—and promise you will tell no one—I am going to Mrs. Burton's in order to meet a man."

She glanced again in the looking glass and noted with satisfaction how Sarah's eyes bulged with shock and curiosity.

"Please bring that letter down now, then help me prepare quickly."

Clayton Galbraith, the Duke of Penthurst, believed that a man, no matter how elevated his station, could not claim good character if he did not show patience and politeness to the older relatives of his family. He therefore sought equanimity while he attended on his aunt Rosalyn while she gambled at Mrs. Burton's gaming salon.

She had requested he escort her. He waited for her to reveal her reason. Thus far it appeared she merely sought his company so she could share a month's worth of gossip.

She did not need to drag him here for that. She lived in his house, as she had all his life. She had never married because, as she liked to explain, for the daughter of a duke to marry often led to a loss of status and precedence. He suspected the real reason was that marriage would remove her from the ducal residence, and infringe on her ability to meddle in the lives of its inhabitants. Since he was the only other person living there now, that meant him.

Her fashionable evening dress, the color of an iced lake, complemented her white skin, gray hair, dark eyes, and regal bearing. She lost her money at a very leisurely pace between her *sotto voce* confidences. The whole table's gaming slowed as well, to accommodate her. One by one the others excused themselves until he and she sat alone. Which, he suspected, had been her intention.

He slid the dealer a guinea by way of apology while his aunt squinted at the new hand she had just received. As age thinned her face and sharpened her features, he and she looked more and more alike. He had not realized the similarities until one day, when seventeen, he had visited her while she was sick and seen her without paint or smiles or distracting wig. The same chestnut eyes and winged, straight eyebrows, surely, and perhaps even the same wide mouth, although her feminine version of the features appeared less severe.

"It is too bad about Kendale," she murmured while she studied the cards. "He waited too long, of course. The older a man gets, the more likely some young flirt will turn his head."

Penthurst debated whether to defend his friend Viscount Kendale, or pick up the challenge just thrown at his feet. Damnation, if his aunt had plotted this evening in order to broach the tiresome topic of his lack of a wife, he would make her be blunt and not smooth the path for her. "He appears very happy, and very much in love. Would you wish less for him?"

"Kendale in love? Whoever thought to see the day."

She *tsked* her exasperation, then called for a card. "She is not suitable. Everyone knows it, including him. He should have married correctly. If he is very much in love, he did not have to deny himself."

"He is too honest for that. And you should hold now. You are likely to break twenty-one if you take another card."

"Honest? Is that what it is called when a peer indulges in romantic notions better suited to a school-girl? I hope that you have much more sense than that kind of honesty."

"Rest assured, I am so ruthlessly practical with my women that no one will ever pity me as you do Kendale."

She called for another card despite his advice. It put her over. "Yes. Well, at least he *did* marry, didn't he?" A note of aggrieved censure sounded. "She is very lovely, I have to admit. And, despite her birth, she has some style."

He refused to humor her. He turned his attention to the ballroom that served as a gaming hall in this May-fair home. Mrs. Burton ran the most polite place in London aside from gentlemen's clubs in which to gam-ble away fortunes, and perhaps the only establishment that ladies could visit alone without raising eyebrows. There had been some official moves against other gam-ing salons run by well-bred women in their homes, but Mrs. Burton's aristocratic clientele afforded her a spe-cial dispensation.

"Speaking of lovely girls," his aunt said while the

dealer slid away her money. "Did I mention that Lady Barrowton's niece is coming up to town? Her beauty is said to be celebrated."

"Said to be? Has no one seen for certain?" Only a corner of his mind heeded the conversation, since the rest already knew what it would hear. Most of his attention had riveted on the entrance to the ballroom. A dark-haired, soulful-eyed woman had just arrived. Lydia Alfreton.

That was odd. He was certain Southwaite had mentioned that his sister would be at that little dinner party being held tonight at Ambury's house. Yet here she was, ready to press her considerable luck at the tables instead.

The green dress she wore flattered her dark hair and very pale skin. She appeared happy. She only looked like that when she gambled, unfortunately. If one met her during the day, her eyes stared right through you, opaque and unseeing, and her face remained expressionless.

"Of course some have seen her niece. Otherwise she could not be celebrated. However, she has never been to town before. She is coming for her final finishing prior to coming out."

"A child then. All children are lovely. Sweet too. And boring."

"Hardly a child. A fresh, innocent girl. I would like to introduce you."

"I am not interested, but thank you."

The proximity of the dealer suddenly discomforted

her. She dismissed him in an imperious tone that had him backing away at once, leaving a good deal of money unattended. She turned her whole body. She angled her gray head so her next words would not be missed. "You must marry eventually, and this girl sounds perfect."

"I told you long ago that I would not be managed in this. If you think I will be more amenable because you raise the matter in a public place instead of at the house, you are mistaken. And, surely by now you know that I will have no inclination to marry a fresh, innocent girl when the day comes that I marry at all."

She heaved a sigh of forbearance. "I have never understood your preference for older women."

"Haven't you?"

She flushed and looked away to avoid acknowledging the question. Something distracted her. Her brow furrowed. "I suppose I should bow to your preferences, since your instincts proved so wise regarding that one there. Her poor mother must be turning over in her grave."

He did not have to look to know she spoke of Lydia Alfreton. He did anyway, in time to see Mrs. Burton greet Lady Lydia and escort her to the hazard table.

"I had no instincts regarding her. I had an understandable annoyance at you and Lady Southwaite deciding whom I would marry before the girl was one day old. Such prearranged pacts are antiquated, lack any legality, and are not to be tolerated." Upon inheriting at age fifteen, disavowing their ridiculous arrangement had been among the first things he did. No one but his aunt spoke of it anymore. He doubted anyone else even remembered it.

"Celeste was my dearest friend, and so sweet and good. Whoever expected her daughter to—well, to turn out like that." Her hand gestured at Lydia, who had just won a throw. People had gathered around to watch her. Perhaps her reputation for winning drew them. Maybe her vivacious excitement did. Eyes afire with lights that normally the world never saw in her, she raised her gaze and her arms upward while she laughed after each win, as if thanking Providence for once more favoring her wagers.

His aunt clucked her tongue. "During the day she is a sphinx, and unknowable. Here at night she is like a bacchante drunk on wine. She is going to ruin Southwaite if he does not rein her in. Everyone says so. She will ruin herself, and him, and that whole family."

"She wins. If she keeps at it, she is more likely to double the family fortune than ruin it." That was the problem. Southwaite was sure that if she would lose even once, big, that would end it.

"I am not talking about the gambling."

That got his attention. "You cannot be talking about men."

"Can I not?"

"She has no interest in them. Gambling, yes. Horses, yes. Art and literature, yes. But if there are rumors about that other kind of ruin, they are not accurate."

"You heard this from Southwaite, no doubt. As if he would know!" Her eyes narrowed on the other side of the chamber. "She has befriended a number of men while she games, and is hardly demure in her conversations with them, I am told. Her aunt Amelia is most distressed about it." She shook her head. "My dear, dear Celeste. Perhaps it is just as well she did not live to see it."

He swallowed the inclination to repeat that the gossip was inaccurate by a mile. In the end, what did he know? Southwaite certainly worried about his sister. If more than her gambling had become a problem for the family, Penthurst did not expect to be informed.

As if to underline his aunt's whispers, a man approached the hazard table. He squeezed himself through the crowd so as to stand by Lydia's elbow. Penthurst angled his head to have a better look at the fellow's face. He could not prevent a laugh from escaping once he recognized the man. Algernon Trilby? Trilby and Lady Lydia? He did not think *that* likely.

"What is so amusing?" his aunt demanded.

"I am chewing over what you just told me, and could not suppress my reaction."

"Laugh all you want. The *on dit* is rarely wrong on such things." She beckoned the dealer and returned to her cards.

Their conversation turned once more to his introduction to the sweet, innocent niece of Lady Barrowton. He sidestepped any commitments to meet her. While they carefully placed their feet in their dance of interference and resistance, he found himself looking on occasion to where Lydia seemed to be winning nicely with the dice.

She appeared to know Trilby. She spoke to him several times. Whatever she said had the man flushing. Finally Trilby peeled away and went to watch the faro play. Lady Lydia appeared to know how to shed unwelcome attention with grace but finality.

He almost pointed that out to his aunt, so she might spare his friend's sister unnecessary gossip. Just as he was about to speak, however, Lydia herself left the table. No longer bright-eyed, but wearing the aloof, blank expression that caused his aunt to call her a sphinx, she walked directly to the terrace doors and slipped outside.

Twenty steps behind, Algernon Trilby followed.

"You must excuse me. I think I will retreat for a short spell, then you can take me home." His aunt held out her hand so he might help her to stand.

"I will come and find you in a few minutes," he said.

"Not too few. The best gossip will be in the retiring room."

"I will wait until you have your fill."

She sallied forth. She left thirty pounds on the table, as if returning them to her reticule were too much a bother. For a woman supported her whole life by dukes, it probably was. He gestured for cards.

With his aunt's removal, others came to use the table. Spirited play ensued. During the fourth round, he looked around the chamber and realized that neither Lydia nor Trilby had yet returned.

There had been no indication that Lydia had planned an assignation, but with each passing minute more people would assume that to be the case. He pictured Trilby out there now, annoying her at best and importuning her at worst.

He threw in his cards, stood, and walked toward the doors. If she were his sister, he would expect Southwaite to keep one eye on her, after all.

Chapter 2

Lydia held the sheet of paper under the lantern and read the familiar words. She glared over at Algernon Trilby. "To send me the letter you did, and demand this meeting, was inexcusable, and now you dare insinuations about this page you brought me. Are you mad?"

"Are you?" Even in the lantern's light she could see him flush. He mustered haughty indignation to mask his discomfort. As soon as he had come through those doors she had met him with as much anger as she dared display in a spot that anyone might see if they chose.

"I was shocked to read that," he went on. "Shocked, I tell you. For you to take such risks. To compromise your family's honor—"

"Do not be a fool. Where did you get this?" She shook the paper in his face.

"I bought it. I paid a good deal of money for it, to spare you the scandal of it falling into the wrong hands."

"It is removed from a larger text. Much larger."

"Indeed it is. The journal that is its context hardly does you credit. Nor does it explain away why you were keeping detailed accounts and records of the ships lying at Portsmouth, and their movements, less than two years ago. It looks as if— Well, it appears that you were—" He raised his eyebrows and pursed his lips.

She stared at the list of ships. It appeared as if she were keeping track of the naval fleet for all the wrong reasons.

In a rational world no one would ever entertain the notion that she, of all people, had been spying on the fleet for the French. The world was not rational at the moment, unfortunately. It was full of people worried about invasion coming soon and French agents lurking amid them. Even her own brother spent a good deal of time defending the realm from such things.

What a muddle! And for this to fall into the hands of such a fool as Trilby— She took a deep breath to calm her chaotic emotions.

"It is not a journal. It is a *novel*, written in the first person." Not a good novel. A very rough first try. A fitful exercise in romantic artistry while she waited for something wonderful to happen. Just remembering the manuscript called forth sad nostalgia, and a spring season when she still harbored dreams.

She had not even seen those pages in over a year and a half. Not since the day she knew nothing wonderful would happen after all. Ever. She had left the manuscript in her aunt Amelia's cottage in Hampshire, unfinished.

Or had she? So many memories from that time had been swallowed by the dull, gray cloud in which she lived for so long afterward.

Trilby clasped his hands behind his back, and peered down his nose censoriously. His fair hair formed a widow's peak from which high arches of his receding hairline sprung, and the effect lengthened his already narrow face. The scoundrel dared to act superior, and examined her as if forming judgments.

Whoever guessed this unremarkable man had it in him to cause so much trouble? He had come up to town six months ago and found introductions through a cousin who was the younger brother of a baronet's wife. No one would have given him the time of day except that some hostesses thought his sleight-of-hand tricks an amusing way to fill an hour in their drawing rooms. Lydia's own interest in those tricks, for her own edification, had led her to form an acquaintance.

She crumpled the sheet of paper in her upraised fist, right in front of his face. "You must give me the rest of the manuscript. At once. It is dishonorable for you to withhold it."

He looked at her fist and squared his shoulders. "There is more where that came from. Keep that if you like."

Her mind raced through the "more." The amateurish way she had padded the novel's length with lists of banquet dishes, or ball gown descriptions—or ships at anchor—marched through her memory. The last had been an attempt at local color, much like her enumerations of the militia organized along the coast near her family's estate of Crownhill.

Oh, dear. That would look as bad as the ships.

The characters in her novel reformed, as did the details of their romance, which was based on little experience, but a lot of fantasies.

Some of the more intimate passages between the hero and heroine finally forced themselves to the forefront of her thoughts. One scene in particular, written during an especially lonely and lovesick night, played out in her head—

Good heavens.

She stepped away from the lantern so he might not see her reaction. There were chapters in that novel that would make this page pale in comparison, should they become known. And if it were assumed it were a *journal*—

"Have you read it?"

"Not all of it. I did not think that proper."

"No, it would not be proper, although it is a *work of fiction*. It is so poorly written I could not abide anyone reading it. That I thought such a literary endeavor should include lists of the ships observed from that hill is proof enough of its poor quality."

"Or of something else," he murmured.

"I repeat, it is merely a novel. You must return it to me. You know you must."

He scratched at his receding hairline while he pondered that. "I went through a good deal of trouble getting my hands on it. To spare you, as I said. I am not a rich man. I should like to be reimbursed."

Now they were down to it. "How much trouble did you go through, Mr. Trilby?"

"Ten thousand pounds' worth of trouble."

Her breath caught. Was he mad? She doubted that he had paid more than a hundred at most. Where would he get ten thousand in ready money?

Where would *she* get it, for that matter?

The outrageous amount disheartened her. Trilby apparently understood the value of what he had found. She did not think she could bargain him down, although she had to try.

"I cannot possibly reimburse you all of your expenses right away."

"Just go in there and throw the dice or play the cards. I've seen your talent with it."

"And if I lose? I will be so far down I could never pay you, not for years. I'll find a way to get you a good amount of it, and promise to pay the rest later. You will be fully reimbursed in the end." It would kill her to gamble in the future just to pay off this blackmailer. She had much better uses for the winnings, and it would break her heart to neglect them.

He crossed his arms and pouted. "If you can't see your way clear, perhaps your brother can."

The notion of Southwaite seeing that novel, and

heaven forbid. reading *that scene*, almost undid her. "If my brother learns of this, more likely he will call you out and kill you for daring to try to blackmail me."

He took a step back at the threat, but stood his ground again fast enough. "Blackmail? I seek to protect you from the worst speculations regarding your character and loyalty, and you accuse me of such a thing? I am wounded."

"You are not wounded. You are impatient and greedy."

"Such insults are not to be borne. If Southwaite won't cooperate, I'm sure I can find another use for it all. There's those who pay smartly for such things." He gestured to her fist. "The rest of that list there, for example. Maybe the government would pay to see it."

"No one will reimburse you for all your trouble except me. Would it not be better to have part of the funds soon and the rest later, than all of a much smaller amount right away?"

Still acting insulted, he thought it over. She turned away from him and crossed her arms to wait. It was then that she noticed a man standing against the house, as if he had just stepped through the French doors. He looked around until his attention settled on her. At that very moment she felt a touch on her shoulder, as Mr. Trilby called for her attention.

The man at the door noticed that touch, she was sure. He seemed to grow taller. He strode forward and the lamps' illumination caught him. Impressive in height, he wore a distinctive midnight-blue frock coat that sported discreet but expensive gold embroidery along its edges, as if its owner had relinquished the more fanciful costumes of the past with regret. The tiny glints of reflection off those gold threads told her who it was.

"Lady Lydia, can I be of service?" The voice confirmed his identity just as his face became distinct. The Duke of Penthurst's deep-set eyes did not look at her so much as at Mr. Trilby behind her. Golden, brittle lights showed in those eyes as he neared, making him appear dangerous. Trilby froze in surprise.

Penthurst glared more directly. "Sir, unhand the lady, please."

"You had better do as he says, Mr. Trilby. His Grace on occasion kills men in duels over minor matters such as this. Being a duke, he is allowed to."

Trilby snatched his hand away as if her shoulder burned. He took two long strides away from her. "I— That is, I—"

"Penthurst, it is always a pleasure to see you." She curtsied. "Do you know Mr. Trilby? We happened upon each other out here and he was confiding how he does one of his tricks."

"We have not met, although I have heard about the tricks. I did not know they involved importuning women."

Trilby's mouth gaped. "Impor—? No, never, sir. I— I—"

"Hardly importuned, sir. A mere tap on the shoulder, to indicate the trick was ready."

"More than a tap, I'd say."

"You might, but I do not. Had you not startled him, I am sure it would have been a very brief tap indeed."

Penthurst's severe expression did not soften.

To divert the confrontation into something less dramatic, she made introductions. Penthurst did not appear glad for that. Trilby could barely contain his relief. He sputtered and fawned for half a minute, making disjointed conversation, which the duke did little to help.

"Well, I must— That is, I should—" All but tripping over his own legs, Trilby took his leave.

Penthurst looked out to the garden, his profile limned by the lamps' light. Lydia took a step toward the doors too.

"Did I interrupt something, Lydia?"

She pivoted. "Only a conversation."

"You appeared angry when I first came out. Was that man imposing on you?"

"Only with his boring talk."

"His hand was on you."

"He sought my attention, that is all. He is a bit of a fool, I am afraid."

"It appeared you agreed to meet out here with him." He turned and looked at her. "It was noticed."

"By you, obviously."

"And others. Such things always are noticed."

"How careless of me, then, to indicate I needed some air in front of him. Although I cannot be responsible for who wants air at the same time as I do, can I? If you followed in order to save me, it was not necessary. While the gesture was gallant, I am not your concern."

"As a friend of your brother, and of your family, and as a gentleman, I could not allow you to be the victim of a Trilby or of the possible gossip that might result from his pursuing you out here, even if your own behavior invited it."

That last bit sliced at her already frayed composure. Due to him, she still had to settle things with Trilby. As for Penthurst's manner—she possessed a grievous dislike of the duke for several excellent reasons. One was that he really *did* fight duels with lesser men, and get away with it. The other was this proud way in which he spoke to her from on high, but also with too much familiarity.

The latter had to do with their very long history. He had been Southwaite's friend for years, and in the family's circle ever since she could remember. He had never liked or approved of her, however. Even when she was only a child, if she got into a scrap that her brother and his other friends thought amusing, Penthurst would often have a more critical view of it, and, like now, offer an occasional correction.

The way she saw it, maturity had a few benefits, and one was not having to suffer the Duke of Penthurst more than absolutely necessary anymore. She had no intention of indulging his arrogance now, on a day when a very big problem had entered her life.

"How good of you, sir, to remind me of my failings so I can improve. I am honored that you troubled yourself on my behalf. Now, lest there be gossip about *us*, perhaps we should return to the salon." With that she marched to the doors.

He reached them first, and opened one. "Why are you even here? I thought you were to attend a dinner party tonight."

"I am sure you are mistaken." She breezed past him and reentered the chamber.

He fell into step at her side. "Your brother mentioned it in passing just this afternoon when I saw him. A small informal dinner at Ambury's, he said, with you and a few others. Did you forget the date, or has the lure of the games gotten the better of you and you could not resist it even for one night?"

She considered agreeing with the second reason. That would probably invite another scold, much as everyone else scolded her for her gambling. However, she could hardly explain she had begged off the party to meet with a blackmailer.

Faulty memory it would have to be.

"Oh, dear, I believe you may be right. Perhaps I *did* forget." She blinked hard and pretended to be dismayed. "For some reason I thought that dinner was tomorrow night. How horrible of me. I will have to write to Cassandra in the morning and beg her forgiveness."

He pulled out his pocket watch. "You can still make it. You will be late, but excusably so."

"I do not think—"

"Wait here. I will collect my aunt and call for the coach, and take you there on our way home."

"That is not necessary—"

But he was gone, striding across the chamber.

She almost stomped her foot. Now she would show up at the dinner, after begging off, which would only provoke questions from her brother and everyone else there. Penthurst should mind his own business.

She spied Trilby. She caught his eye. He pulled at his collar, grimaced, then smiled. He acted as if they shared a conspiracy that had just had a close call.

At least he did not look insulted anymore. Hopefully that meant he would wait on doing anything rash, like approaching her brother. She pantomimed the action of writing, then pointed from herself to him, to indicate she would send a note soon. When she returned home, she would put her mind to just what that note should say.

With Mr. Trilby appeased for the time being, she aimed for the door, to find Penthurst and his aunt.

Ambury's house lay no more than five blocks from Mrs. Burton's. They were, Penthurst decided, the longest five blocks he had ever ridden in his life.

To say his aunt was displeased by Lydia's company would be generous. If given the opportunity, she would have refused to allow it. He therefore presented Lydia as a fait accompli. Now his aunt sat beside Lydia, face pinched and eyes flashing cruel lights while she took stock of her young companion with critical sidelong glances.

"It is a dinner party, you said when you collected me. Is that so, Lydia? Are we taking you to a dinner party? It is quite late for that."

Lydia remained motionless and expressionless, her dark eyes opaque with indifference. Her face displayed no reaction to the continued examination. She might have lost the ability to hear, she sat so impassively.

"Will this dinner party not think it odd if you arrive late, wearing that silk? It is far too elaborate, and not suitable for much other than a ball."

"I am sure they will think it odd," Lydia roused herself to say. "It might be better if I return home instead. Perhaps, Penthurst, you would direct the coachman to go to the other side of Berkeley Square so I can do that, rather than bringing me to Ambury's side."

"I fear Lady Ambury would never forgive me, or you, if I helped you jilt her," he said.

"Lady Ambury?" Self-satisfied comprehension settled on his aunt's expression. "Ah. Of course."

That brought the sphinx to life. Lydia turned her head and caught the disapproving glance aimed her way. "Of course *what*, Lady Rosalyn?"

His aunt sniffed and raised her chin. "Nothing, nothing."

"I entreat you to tell me. You are fair to bursting with the desire to do so, it appears."

No glance this time, but a direct, astonished stare. Her deep-set eyes went deeper yet beneath a furrowed brow.

He knew that look. "Aunt Rosalyn—"

"Please do not interfere. The girl demanded that I burst forth, so I shall." She turned her whole body in order to meet Lydia's challenge head on. "Your friendship with Ambury's wife does you no credit. Your brother forbade it once, and his friend's amorous adventures should not have dissuaded him from that sound judgment. Since they did, and you are now friends with her again, *of course* you are going to dress in thin silk and visit a gaming hall alone. Her influence on you would have distressed your mother to no end, and I would be remiss in my duty to her memory if I did not say so." The flourishing gesture with which she ended her speech managed to encompass not only Lydia's dress, but her entire character.

He felt for his handkerchief, ready to comfort Lydia when she began weeping. He gave his aunt a hard look of disapproval. Her ability to reduce women to tears was infamous. This was hardly the time or place, and Lydia was not her ward.

Lydia did not weep. She did not even show anger, except for the way her eyes flashed. "You do not approve of Cassandra, I can see. Or of me, I deduce. You would have preferred if we both lived ordinary lives, rather than embrace a more worldly independence. You are correct that she influenced me, but all to the good. I rather wish she had not married Ambury and become domesticated so I would have her company as I go to the devil."

His aunt's mouth gaped.

"Selfish, willful girl," she sputtered, patting her chest as if her heart palpitated. "Your mother was my dearest friend, and this is not worthy of her daughter. Go to the devil, indeed! Amelia confided her concerns, but clearly was too timid to admit the worst of them."

"My aunt Amelia barely knows me. We have had little time together for almost two years. When my brother requires a gaoler for me now, it is Aunt Hortense."

"Hortense! As if she is of much use! She is formidable in manner but empty of resolve and judgment. She is so certain she is shrewd, but she would not even notice if a merchant shortchanged her. I am sure you lead her on a fine dance on those occasions when she chaperones you. Did you ask for Hortense so you could run wild right under her nose?"

"Now you insult my aunt. Are you finished, or are there others on your list?"

He looked out the window. Another block to go. There might be fisticuffs by then. "Ladies, I believe it would be best to end this conversation before you both need salts."

His aunt turned her fury on him. He met it with a steady gaze. She swallowed whatever she intended to say.

Lydia did not. "I think it was very unkind of you to drag my mother into this at all, let alone use her as an excuse to upbraid me. You can have no duty to her that includes insulting me."

His aunt fairly rose out of her seat. "Can I not, you bold, bold girl? She and I were of one mind where you were concerned and in everything else. It grieves me that I am actually relieved I was spared my duty by my nephew's stubbornness. At least when you go to the devil, you will not drag down my family too!"

With an outraged huff of finality, his aunt faced forward and dismissed Lydia's existence. Lydia angled her head quizzically.

He realized that she had never been told of that old pact between her mother and his aunt. He had never wondered whether she knew or not, but it made sense that she remained ignorant. She had been five years old when he disavowed it.

The coach finally stopped. More than glad for a bit of fresh air, he stepped out and offered his hand to Lydia. Inside his aunt remained an imperious statue of stone staring straight ahead.

Lydia looked across the square to her brother's house. "It would be less embarrassing to just go home."

"No one will mind, surely."

Their arrival flustered the footman who opened the door. He looked over his shoulder toward the sounds in the dining room, confused. He excused himself and ran off.

"I told you I should have gone home," Lydia said. "I am causing a scene coming this late."

The footman returned with Lady Ambury. Dark-haired, blue-eyed, and too voluptuous for her own good, the former Cassandra Vernham greeted Lydia with delight. "I insisted on coming out, so you would know you are still welcomed." She gave Lydia a kiss, then turned those blue eyes on him. "I see you had a prior rendezvous, Lydia. How good of the duke to share you with us, and deliver you before the first course finished."

"Not a rendezvous," Lydia said, her color rising. "I— That is, he—"

"No need to explain to me, darling. At least not until after dinner. Would you like to join us, Penthurst? You can balance the table."

"Regrettably, another lady awaits." He took his leave of them, and returned to that lady, steeling himself for the ride back to Grosvenor Square.

Halfway there, Lady Ambury's last words penetrated the endless stream of indignation spewing from his aunt. *You can balance the table.* That meant Lydia had unbalanced it, which meant she was not expected after all. She had not forgotten the date. She had begged off, in order to go to Mrs. Burton's.

To gamble? Or to have an assignation with Algernon Trilby? Not the latter, he hoped. If she wanted to go to the devil, she could find a better devil than that.

Chapter 3

"Why are we walking so fast?" Sarah hurried to keep up with Lydia's purposeful strides.

"For the exercise. A bit of flush is healthy, Sarah. We are too indolent in our habits."

They were also in danger of being late for her rendezvous with Mr. Trilby. After due consideration, she had concluded it would be unwise to make any reference to her novel in writing, and therefore had only requested he meet her this morning in the park for further discussion.

"If you needed to work up a flush, we could have walked around the square three times," Sarah grumbled. "You said we were going to enjoy the early morning air, not conduct a foot race along the Serpentine."

"Here I arrange for you to get out and enjoy a fair

day, and all you do is complain. Next time I will leave
you at home."

"So I can be scolded by your aunt Hortense? No
thank you, milady. She burned my ears for a good half
hour when she learned you went to the bookstore alone
two days ago."

Reference to burning ears reminded her of the argument with Penthurst's aunt in the carriage two nights
ago. There would be a scold coming about that, she
was sure. It would arrive after circulating through the
family until someone was designated the agent to apply
some corrective persuasion.

Who would it be? Not her brother. He had to be
highly provoked to address her on her behavior. Aunt
Hortense? Her lessons had not stuck well in the past,
so consensus might turn elsewhere. Emma? Her brother's wife would not scold as such.

At least Emma recognized that she was not a child,
unlike the others. However, Emma's very forthright
manner of speaking might be more discomforting than
a scold. One can ignore scolds, while it could be difficult to dodge Emma's direct gaze and questions.

No one would blame Penthurst's aunt, of course. She
was a bulwark of society, and the whole world deferred
to her. No one would believe she had attacked someone's
character, her upbringing, her behavior, and her virtue,
all in the space of six or seven sentences. Those who did
believe it might well assume it had been deserved.

She strode on, feeling aggrieved. The situation with
her family reminded her of this new one with Mr. Trilby.

People assumed the worst of her, when she had never even had the opportunity to be bad! Somehow she had become the problem sister of Southwaite, simply because she avoided marriage and wanted a bit of—something different. Anything less predictable. A touch of adventure every now and then. A reason for excitement. Was she so wicked for desiring some experiences out of the ordinary ones decreed for a woman of her birth?

Her gaze scanned the park as she led Sarah deeper. A citizen's militia drilled as they did almost every day. Some gentlemen rode their horses in the distance, taking advantage of the early hour and dearth of visitors to get in some hard riding.

Ahead, behind the militia, she spied Mr. Trilby pacing back and forth, hands grasped behind his back. It did not appear he would have the sense to walk her way, so they could meet as if by accident.

As she guided Sarah around the militia, one of the citizen soldiers noticed Sarah and gave her a winning smile. Sarah pretended not to see him, but she blushed.

Lydia walked on another fifty yards so they were a respectable distance away. "Why don't we catch our breath here? We can watch the drills. Do you mind, Sarah?"

Sarah shrugged, but watched the drills closely. Especially the movements of a certain tall, sandy-haired young man with nice blue eyes. Every time he turned to face them, he flashed that smile again. Sarah got redder and redder.

Trilby took the hint, and walked in their direction. Before he got too close, Lydia waved, and eased away from Sarah. Standing beside Mr. Trilby, she continued watching the militia.

"Did you bring the money?" he asked.

"Do you think me a goose? How would I bring it here? In my reticule?" She held up the small, drawstring pouch.

"I thought a bank draft—"

"I cannot do that, even on my portion, without my brother learning of it. You have clearly never lived as a woman, Mr. Trilby, and know nothing of our limitations."

"I should hope not."

"You should indeed hope not. I did not ask to see you in order to hand over ten thousand, it should go without saying. I would have demanded that you bring the manuscript then, would I not? I asked to meet you so we could discuss this further."

Trilby threw up his hands, walked away a few paces, then turned in exasperation and strode back. "There is nothing to discuss. The journal cost me—"

"Novel. It is not a journal."

"The *novel* cost me ten thousand. I must see that much out of it. Within the week, Lady Lydia. I am strained by this purchase on your behalf, and cannot wait beyond that."

Her mind raced, trying to calculate how much she could raise in a week. Not ten thousand, that was certain. Not if she pawned every jewel and sold every silk. "It is not possible in a week."

"Make it possible. Tell your brother a story he will

swallow. Borrow from friends. You live a privileged life and should be able to put your hands on that amount with ease if you only give it some thought."

Mr. Trilby was displaying more confidence and spine than he had on Mrs. Burton's terrace. She wished Penthurst had not interfered there. She might have negotiated less money, or more time, if this man had not had two days to fortify his courage and practice his lines.

He raised his chin in the direction of the militia. "Such as them would not look kindly on your keeping watch on the fleet, no matter who your brother might be. They would take even less well to the descriptions of their kind on the coast. Oh, yes, I read that too, while I awaited word from you. Could be you might have to flee to France whether you were spying or not if those pages become common knowledge."

She did not need this man to describe the mood abroad in the country, and the misinterpretations that might arise from it. At the dinner at Cassandra's house, the men had talked a lot about the war, as everyone did. Her own brother, as best she could determine, was involved in an unofficial system of watchers on the eastern coast, in the hopes of keeping agents from infiltrating.

Even if she did survive the worst Trilby threatened, there would be enough whispering to taint everyone— her brother, her aunts, Emma. And that was before anyone read those other chapters, the ones that would be considered shockingly descriptive of the arts of Venus.

What had she been thinking?

That no one would ever see any of it, of course. Yet Mr. Trilby had. Only him?

"The manuscript was stolen. If not by you, how did you get it?"

"I cannot say."

"I want to know how many have seen it. Unless you are the thief, it came to you from another. How many hands passed it before it arrived in your own?"

"Better you should be thinking about how to have it now passed to your hands, it seems to me."

"If half of London has already paged through it, why would I pay to keep it private? Put yourself in my place and you will understand why I need to know."

"Not many hands passed it. You do not need to worry about the discretion of those who had it before me, either. I promise you that."

The promise of a blackmailer should not reassure her, but she hoped it was the truth. She wanted it to be. And truth or lie, she remained in the same predicament.

"A week, Lady Lydia. I require a message from you before the end of seven days, informing me of where you will reimburse me. I remain at my cousin's house at least until then." He walked away on those words.

Lydia strolled back to Sarah, whose gaze had never left that young man. "Have you caught your breath, or lost it entirely, Sarah?"

"He is a fine looking fellow, isn't he? Tall and strong and quite handsome."

"He has a very nice smile. What is his name?"

"How would I know?"

Lydia laughed. "Are you saying you have spent the last quarter hour flirting with a complete stranger? Really, Sarah! I am shocked."

"I didn't mean to. I sort of lost awareness of where I was."

"Aunt Hortense will be horrified," Lydia teased. "She will insist we put you on bread and water for at least three days."

Sarah puffed out her cheeks and rolled her eyes. "Only if she hears of it. I doubt you will be telling her. If I am quizzed on my behavior, I might find myself explaining how you spent that quarter hour while I was so negligently distracted."

Another blackmailer. Sarah could be forgiven for playing that ace, however. Too many people put demands on her, most of which, if she obeyed, would require her to betray Lydia's trust and privacy. She did not envy Sarah and the way she had to juggle so many mistresses.

She hooked her arm through Sarah's, so they walked the way they often did when girls. "You will probably want us to walk in the park every morning now."

"I do not think the same company musters here every morning. They take turns, I believe." She glanced over her shoulder for one more look. "There's probably a list somewhere of which citizens' militia uses the park each day. The sort of list that someone like an earl might be able to see."

"I will put it to my brother, but I will have to explain why. Otherwise he may conclude that I lost my breath this morning, not you."

"Which you did not do, since you mention it. If anything, you looked vexed. I hope you will forgive me for saying, but between my strapping soldier and your pale, thin gentleman, I think I had the better morning walk."

V iscount Ambury reined in his horse alongside Penthurst's when they crested a low rise at the back of the park. Their mounts showed sweat from the hard gallop, and stepped high with excitement.

They proceeded at a more leisurely pace, inserting themselves into the riders and walkers who also sought some morning refreshment. Few did, which was a pity, and even those who had ventured out now streamed toward the gates as dark clouds moved in, heralding rain.

They stayed to the side of the carriage path when they reached it. A few rolled past. One caught Penthurst's eye. The man inside looked like that Trilby fellow. A woman faced him. He only glimpsed her, but saw enough to know it was not Lady Lydia.

"How did your dinner party proceed, Ambury? With good cheer, I trust."

"It was deemed a success, despite the unexpected arrival of Lydia."

"That sounds more unkind that you intended, I hope."

"Damn, so it does. She had sent late regrets, is what

I meant, so her attendance was peculiar. Since it was mostly family and close friends, that was not too awkward. And it resolved the pressing question neatly and quickly, and exactly as I expected it to."

"What question was that?"

"Whether Lydia would favor a certain gentleman. Cassandra is playing matchmaker."

"I suppose someone has to."

"My wife's sentiment exactly. Since Southwaite lacks subtlety on such matters, and his two aunts' tastes are hardly those of a young woman's, Cassandra has turned her own attention to the duty. As a result, the only person at that table who was not family or close friend was a man invited for Lydia's better acquaintance."

Which man? He almost asked. Cassandra had ended up with Ambury, who had loved and left many before her, so her own tastes might not be appropriate either. Not that it was any of his business, of course.

"Then, after all of Cassandra's arrangements, Lydia begged off at the last minute. Said gentleman—a Scot of good blood and vast wealth of the MacKinnon family—came expecting to impress the sister of an earl, and ended up sitting next to Cassandra's dotty aunt Sophie. So while also awkward, Lydia's late change of heart was a relief for Cassandra."

"And a fine dinner was had by all. Did he impress her?"

Ambury laughed. "You know Lydia. Making her better acquaintance these days is like dragging a cart through mud. She was polite. She favored him with three smiles, I believe. Yet I fear the poor fellow thought he was talking to someone half dead. I do not understand her. No one does. She was such an imp as a girl. Now, the ladies say they see life in her all the time, in private. The rest of us, however . . . As for that poor dinner partner, it must have been a very long meal for him."

She *had* been an imp as a girl. Animated, loud, and often naughty. Very different from the Lydia she showed the world now. Unless she was gambling. Otherwise she hid behind that aloof mask and cloaked herself in a hard shell. He wondered why.

"Did you mind that you were not invited?"

Ambury's question startled him out of his thoughts. "Why would I mind?"

"We were all there otherwise. I just thought you—"

"Since you were all there otherwise, that means Kendale was too. While you and Southwaite have forgiven me in your own ways, he has not."

An awkwardness descended, such as always did when any of them broached the subject at hand even obliquely. The truth was that a year ago he and Ambury would not have been riding together, let alone discussing social niceties. They had all been friends for many years—he, Ambury, Southwaite, Viscount Kendale, and Baron Lakewood. But everything had changed the day that Lakewood died—at Penthurst's hands.

"There was much about that day that surprised me," he said to Ambury. "The matter that brought Lakewood and me to that field was not worth being killed over."

"I am relieved you speak of it, finally," Ambury said. "I know more than you think." His remarkable blue eyes, usually filled with sparks of humor, now flashed colder lights.

"Have you been investigating?" Ambury had a talent for such things. He had even conducted investigations for pay, very discreetly, when his father, the Earl of Highburton, had severely restricted his income.

"I have resisted the temptation. However, let me say that I now understand what you meant when you once told me Lakewood was not what he seemed. He could be opportunistic, and even dishonorable, I am sorry to have learned."

A few drops of rain fell now. They did not spur their horses, however. This topic, finally opened, begged for more airing.

"Southwaite now believes that Lakewood put himself in the way of your shot," Ambury said. "He thinks it was a kind of suicide, so his name might never be sullied."

Penthurst had come to the same conclusion after reliving those moments hundreds of times. He had deliberately aimed wide, so Lakewood would have the chance to stand down still. Instead it appeared Lakewood had moved toward the aim.

"As I said, the accusations I made hardly warranted suicide. They were dishonorable, but not damning. He could have survived it. Other men have."

"Perhaps there was more to it than you think."

"I have long suspected that there was." There had been a few halfhearted attempts to find out, none of them effective. The man was dead, and it felt wrong to muck around his history just to relieve one's own curiosity or sense of guilt.

"Do you want me to poke around a little, to see what turns up?" Ambury asked.

"I do not think so. I will let you know should I decide differently." It would be better if Ambury and the others did not even learn what he knew already, let alone what might be found with an investigation.

More drops now. A fine rain drizzled, with heavy clouds promising more. They moved their mounts to a trot. A minute later the sky opened.

"Hell, here it comes." Ambury pushed his horse to a canter.

Their speed did nothing for their sight as they sped for the park's entrance. Even so, Penthurst noticed the two women running toward a tree for some shelter. A lady and her servant from the looks of it. He glanced to the sky, and doubted that tree would keep them dry for long.

He turned his horse toward the tree. Ambury noticed and did the same. They reined in only a few moments after the women had ducked under the branches.

"Lydia!" Ambury said. "It is an odd time to be taking a turn in the park."

"It seemed a good idea an hour ago."

"I will go tell your coachman to bring the carriage here."

The maid plucked off her bonnet and shook it fiercely. "We walked the whole way." She gave her mistress a resentful glance.

Lydia did not react to that, least of all to put the servant in her place. Penthurst thought that generous of her. Perhaps she felt some guilt for dragging the woman here on foot.

He dismounted. "It does not look like it will end soon. We will take you home. You will still get wet, but the misery will be shorter." He shrugged off his frock coat and swung it around Lydia's shoulders. While she remained startled by that, he lifted her onto the saddle of his horse.

Ambury did the same for the servant, who froze into wide-eyed silence.

He swung himself up behind Lydia. With her feminine legs dangling down the side of his horse, he reached around her for the reins. She stiffened.

"Forgive me," he said. "There is nothing else for it."

"Of course."

"Grab on to something to steady yourself, or I will be obligated to become even more familiar by holding you in place."

The sphinx blushed. She clutched at the front of the saddle so hard her knuckles whitened.

Ambury ducked under the branches and rode off, fast enough that the servant let out a squeal. Lydia did not make a sound as Penthurst followed.

Chapter 4

Lydia tried not to move in the slightest way, but it proved impossible on a cantering horse. Seated sideways like this, her legs dangling and her rump threatening to slide off, she kept jostling back and forth. The forth did not concern her, since it shifted her body toward the horse's neck. The back, unfortunately, bumped her up against the formidable chest of the Duke of Penthurst.

She looked straight ahead and pretended that did not continue with a regular rhythm that mortified her. Why couldn't Ambury have taken her on his horse? Up ahead all she could see of Sarah were her shoes, swinging to the horse's gait.

Bump. Bump. At least the thick frock coat over her shoulders and arms cushioned her so it did not become too intimate a connection. Penthurst's shirtsleeves, gleaming white and pure in the rain, circled her rather too closely, however, and there was no thick wool on them.

The rain poured down. Her escort seemed not to notice as it soaked his hair and those shirtsleeves and the waistcoat a few inches from her nose. *Bump.* A nice waistcoat, she noticed out of the corner of her eye. She turned her head to give it a closer study. *Bump.* Her nose smashed right into brocade the color of claret. Her face squished against the detailed silver embroidery. She even felt the warmth of his body through the fabric.

"My apologies, Lydia. There was a depression in the ground and a small jump saved you much discomfort." His voice, low and masculine, flowed into her ear.

She pulled away and tried to straighten her bonnet with one hand. A stream of water poured off the center of the brim, right onto her nose. She looked a fright, she knew. Fortunately she did not worry whether she impressed Penthurst. He was the last man in the world whose opinion she cared about.

"It is rather fancy." She pointed her nose to the waistcoat since she dared not let go of the saddle and use a finger. "You have not totally reformed your taste. You no longer wear the satins and gold braid, and you finally cut off that queue, but you will make your point anyway, won't you?"

"I do not understand the desire gentlemen have today for looking like bankers. These plain styles are only a fashion, and will pass."

"It has not been a small change, like a new sleeve.

All of you appear very different from how you appeared ten years ago. I do not believe the old ways will come back, for men at least, because this is more democratic. You do not truly look like a banker. However, the distinction between you and a banker is far less visible now than in the past."

"Do you believe that is a good thing?"

"What I believe does not matter. It simply is the way it is."

"That is a slippery answer. No wonder your brother worries about you, if you respond to his questions like that." He lowered his head so he spoke right into her ear. "Or do you have no opinions, Lydia? Is the mind as blank as the face? I do not think so. I suspect there are many opinions behind that mask, even high passions, that you dare not allow others to know. Perhaps you put up a wall to keep us all from seeing the truth in you."

His warm breath sent a shiver through her. His speculation passed close to the truth, distressingly close. The intimacy of his comments, made all the more startling by his pressing physicality, reminded her of the one other time he had spoken to her like this, as a man might speak to a woman, and not just the sister of a friend. This time it did not shock her as much, but then what he said now did not carry the same danger.

She had put the memory of that other time in a room in her head, closed the door, and never looked at it again. Now, it burst forth, bringing with it once more her confusion, then shock, then resentment. Despite the way it made their intimacy on this horse more awkward, she welcomed the memory because she realized she might have a way to find that ten thousand after all.

"It must not be a good wall that I build," she stammered, clutching at her poise as desperately as the saddle. "If you can see through it with such ease, either it is transparent, or your conceit lends your sight abilities only you can trust."

She fixed her gaze on the houses passing by her view, but she felt him there, warming her shoulder, paying too much attention. Did she imagine that those shirt-sleeves moved closer together, closing on her? Not to steady her either. As they trotted down the cobblestone street she bumped all the more, now to and fro. Her back kept hitting his arm. She had to brace herself hard to avoid her breast doing the same to the arm in front.

Finally they entered Berkeley Square. He slowed the horse to a sedate walk. They approached her house just as Ambury swung Sarah off his saddle. Sarah, who had rarely ridden on a horse, looked delighted and giddy. She and Ambury laughed about something. Then the door opened, and a tall, dark-haired man stepped out. Her brother.

He said something to Sarah. She made a quick curtsy, and darted in out of the rain. Ambury gestured up the lane. Southwaite turned and, with a curious expression, his dark eyes watched Penthurst's horse.

Grooms came to hold the horses. Southwaite stepped down to the street. "I see you found some lost baggage, Penthurst."

"Not lost so much as stranded by the storm."

Her brother reached up and lifted her down. He gave her a good examination from head to toe, shaking his head. "It was an odd morning to go for a walk, Lydia."

"I desired a turn amid nature's glories."

"People who live on squares can have that whenever they choose, without hiking all over town. It is why houses on squares are desirable." He shook his head again in the exasperated, helpless way he so often used with her. He plucked the frock coat off her shoulders. "Go and dry off, then please visit Emma. She has been waiting all morning for your return so she can share news. Cassandra is already there."

She gathered her sodden skirt and squished her soaked shoes up to the door. As she crossed the threshold she heard her brother address his friends.

"Gentlemen, come in and have some coffee and dry yourselves too. I would have a word with you both."

Penthurst and Ambury stretched their boots toward the low fire in the library. A servant handed them each coffee. Their coats dried on a nearby rustic chair brought in just for that purpose. Southwaite stood at the side of the mantel.

"This is very good of you, Southwaite, but we only brought back two women who were caught by the storm," Ambury said. "I could cross the square and let my valet relieve your servants of all this bother."

"I said I wanted a word with you."

"Yes, you did. Let me assure you that whatever Lydia's reason for going to the park today, it was innocent, I am sure."

Southwaite scowled. "Did you think I suspected otherwise?"

Ambury took his time drinking some coffee. "Your scold when she came back implied you did."

"I was simply commenting on my sister's odd behavior . . . It implies nothing else."

"Good. But if you did suspect something, rest assured that from what I could see there was no one in the park this morning whom she might have planned to meet. I was the only person there whom she probably even knew." He began to drink again, but the cup paused halfway to his lips. "Well, and Penthurst here."

A strange little silence ensued.

"Yes, well, she is home and upstairs and hearing what I want to tell both of you," Southwaite stood a little taller. "Emma is with child."

"That is wonderful news, Southwaite." Penthurst stood and clapped his friend's shoulder in congratulations.

"I'll say so. Why are you giving us only coffee?" Ambury demanded. "It may be early, but brandy at least is called for no matter what the hour."

Brandy it was, and an hour of good cheer and happy speculation. Penthurst warmed to the camaraderie that resembled what they had all shared years ago, before duties and duels had created distance between them.

He and Ambury took their leave together.

"Lydia was probably in the park to meet someone, of course," Ambury said as he settled in his saddle. "If it were a budding tendre, or an inappropriate one, she would not want to be seen in this square with him, especially in early morning."

"Then hopefully it was the former, and Southwaite will hand her off soon and be free of the worry of her."

Ambury turned his horse away. Penthurst aimed for the streets beyond the square.

Sarah barely allowed Lydia to enter her apartment before dancing forward with excitement. "It is wonderful news, is it not, milady?"

"How did you learn of it already?"

"Cook told me while I dried out by the kitchen fire. An upstairs maid told her. I think Lady Southwaite's lady's maid told the upstairs maid, and—"

"And no doubt you learned of it before I did. It is wonderful news, however. Emma is so pleased. She has known for a few months, but delayed even telling my brother until it all looked very good and sure."

"She is four months along, cook said. Why, that means there will be a baby by spring."

Sarah helped her out of her still-damp clothes. There had not been time to change before going to Emma. When word is buzzing that there is big news, one wants to hear what it is. She had dried as best she could with a linen while she, Emma, and Cassandra enjoyed a happy time in Emma's dressing room.

The excitement had pushed the morning out of her mind, but now it crowded back in, deflating her joy and returning her worries. A week, Trilby had said. It would take a miracle to find ten thousand in a week. Or one very good piece of luck.

"Sarah, do you tell others here about me, like cook told you about Emma?"

Sarah did not deny it immediately the way Lydia expected. Instead she set down the damp hose she had just removed and sat, looking thoughtful. "There have been a few times when things have slipped out. Not important ones. It is just that in a big, busy house like this, what is and is not private can become gray, can't it? I have to remind myself that I may know things your family does not."

"If I told you it was important they not know something, do you think you could make sure it never slipped out? I need to talk to someone about something, Sarah, and I cannot share this with Emma or Cassandra."

Sarah moved to sit beside her on the divan. She embraced her with one arm. "Of course I can. I always did when we were little, didn't I? I know that you are milady now, but in my heart you will always be Deea."

It was the name Sarah had called her when they were small children. Hearing it now brought unexpected comfort.

"I am being blackmailed, Sarah." She told her about Trilby and the novel, and his demands. "The situation is ridiculous, but that does not mean it is not dangerous."

Sarah reacted the way a good friend should, with

shock and concern. "He sounds too greedy to me. Such a high amount! Does he not fear you will go to your brother with this? That is your best choice now, isn't it?"

"What will I say to him? That I wrote a novel that reads like a journal, and someone got his hands on it and noticed that parts of it might be interpreted in ways that paint me as disloyal? So hand me a fortune so I can buy him off, please?"

She had not told Sarah *everything*. She had left out the parts of the novel that crossed the lines of propriety regarding romantic events. Just remembering the explicit nature of that chapter made her face warm. No respectable novel contained such things, but she had never really believed her manuscript would be published.

She needed to make sure it never was.

"Perhaps we can steal it," Sarah said. "We will learn where he lives, and sneak in, and find it and—"

"Even if we learn where he lives, there is no guarantee the manuscript is there. I fear that I must find a way to get hold of the money and buy back my stupid words."

"Have you not accumulated some from your gambling? By now you should have a good amount, I would think."

"You would think so, wouldn't you? Unfortunately . . ." She shrugged.

That money did not stay in her purse. She had uses for it. Secret ones, known only to her. She made gifts, often anonymous, to worthy causes.

She would like to claim some goodness in doing it, but she received so much pleasure that the gestures almost felt selfish. Nor were her gifts only about charity. With each one she made a little declaration to herself that she had a separate life, was a separate person, and had purpose.

She wondered if the goodness of the acts was diminished by the prideful motivations, or the pleasure she took in winning that money?

Probably so.

Sarah stood and started plucking the hairpins out of Lydia's wet, snarled hair. "Can you borrow the money from a friend?"

"A lesser amount, perhaps. Such a sum, however—I am sure that neither Emma nor Cassandra could help me without going to their husbands for it. Even women like us do not have this kind of money, Sarah. Not unless it is in trust, which means unavailable."

"If so, what was he thinking in asking for so much?"

"I think he assumed I could win it at the tables."

Disapproval danced tiny steps over Sarah's face. With nary a word, she moved behind Lydia and began brushing out her hair.

"I could possibly do it that way," Lydia mused, thinking aloud. "It would take time, however. I have never risked so much, or won so much, let alone in a week. I would never dare to try to do it all in one night—that might be really pressing my luck." She thought back to her ride in the rain, and the idea that had come to her then. "Unless it were just one wager. Yes, that is how I should do it, if I try that path at all, I think. I am sure I would win then, and I could meet Mr. Trilby's deadline."

"I don't gamble, so forgive me if my question is stupid, but—if the other person puts down ten thousand, won't you need ten thousand too?"

She thought again about that odd encounter with Penthurst the first time she went to Mrs. Burton's last year. He had deliberately tried to shock her, she realized later. He had succeeded, for that night at least. Yet in doing that, he had proposed a very high wager, had he not? If a gentleman does that, he is bound to see it through if the offer is accepted.

"I would not necessarily need money, Sarah. It only needs to be something of equivalent value."

Chapter 5

Lydia held her head high as she approached the house on Grosvenor Square. Beside her, Sarah fussed with her bonnet, her skirt, her gloves.

"Stop fidgeting," Lydia scolded. It was all she could do not to fidget herself, and Sarah's lack of confidence did nothing for her own.

"You are sure he will give you the money? It will be very awkward to ask for it and have him refuse."

Lydia had only said that she was going to call on the duke to see if he would aid her, as a friend of the family. Sarah had assumed that meant petitioning for a loan. Better if Sarah did not know that Lydia did not intend to ask for any money, as such. Rather she would hoist the duke on his own petard, give him some overdue comeuppance, and finally know some revenge for how he ruined a chance she once had for happiness. She would also get the money. If she were not so nervous, she would be enjoying this.

The servant took her card. After glancing at it, he erased the critical expression he had shown upon seeing a woman at the door at eight o'clock at night.

"You are to wait here, Sarah." She pointed to a bench against the wall of the reception hall. "I must speak to him privately."

"Won't be proper, and you know it. I should go with you, and sit against a wall there."

"It is enough that you came here with me. Anyone who saw me, and I doubt anyone did, saw you too. What transpires now that we are in the door will not signify."

"He might get the wrong idea. The duke, that is."

Lydia laughed. It went far to calming her nerves. "I am the annoying little sister of one of his friends, Sarah. The Duke of Penthurst would never get the wrong idea about *me*. If he ever insinuated he did, it would be nothing more than a cruel tease. I will be safe."

She expected that to be true even if her plan did not work, but she entertained no thoughts of failure. Tonight she would be in her element. She would employ her one talent and distinction, and walk out this door with the money she needed. And Penthurst would indirectly pay for things he did not even know he owed her a debt on.

The servant returned for her. She followed him up the broad staircase built of white marble and cushioned

by a strip of richly patterned carpet. Across a huge landing they paced, until they faced deeply paneled doors.
The servant opened one of the doors and stood aside.

She entered a library the size of a ballroom. It had
stairs to a mezzanine around three of its sides, and
enough chairs and divans to seat dozens of people. Two
expansive tables held assortments of books, as if someone currently used them. Otherwise the chamber
appeared empty, luxurious, and rarely used.

She looked around, deciding where to sit while she
waited. Suddenly two hounds appeared out of nowhere.
They bore down on her at a run, baring their teeth. She
backed up, holding out her arms to ward off an attack.

Through the fog of her panic she heard a low, calm
command. "Caesar. Cleo. Sit."

The two dogs immediately lowered onto their
haunches and turned into statues. The command had
been so confident of obedience that she almost sat too.

"My apologies, Lydia. I forgot that you have never
been here. They will not treat you like an intruder in
the future."

His voice startled her. Penthurst stood behind a high
upholstered chair with its back to her. He must have
been reading when the servant brought her card.

He did not look like he planned a night of reading,
however. He had dressed for a night out, and cut a fine
figure in black and white. The lamp on the table shed
light upward on his face, carving its angles deeply, making him look very proud and stern and—disapproving.
Straight rather than arched, his eyebrows angled up

above his eyes in a way that made his gaze appear critical and intense.

He was every inch a duke and a gentleman, and
yet . . . She always thought he would look more at home
in a dark castle than a Grosvenor Square mansion. She
could picture him in the castle's great hall with his
hounds, tall and disheveled from riding, the fires of the
hearth roaring behind him.

She wondered if he could see himself that way too.
He had cut his queue, one of the last of his age to do
so, but did not favor some Roman style for his hair.
Rather it remained longer than most, its fullness skim-
ming his back collar and the sides of his face.

He did not move toward her, which left her no choice
except to walk toward him. The way he watched her
approach unnerved her to the point of breathlessness.

"Did you come to apologize?"

That stopped her, a good twenty feet away. "Apologize? For what? Getting you wet today?"

"That was my choice. No, apologize to my aunt for
the rudeness in the coach the other evening."

"The rudeness started with her."

"You provoked her, deliberately. As for her words,
she is an older woman who sought to issue a warning
and advice, and thus spare a younger woman much
grief. She is also a duke's daughter."

Any misgivings she harbored about the fleecing she
was about to visit on this man disappeared. "She could
be the queen, and I would not tolerate such insults. So,

in answer to your question, I did not come here to apologize to her."

"Then I assume you came to see me." His gaze took her in from head to toe, then shifted to the door. "Are you alone?"

"Sarah is with me."

"No, she is not."

"She is waiting in the reception hall, I meant. I did not think she should hear the conversation I need to have with you."

Interested now, and vaguely amused too, he beckoned her to come closer and gestured to the chairs. "Be seated, and tell me what you need of me."

She sat in another chair much like the one he had been using. His manner had turned tolerant and patient. She realized he assumed she wanted a favor, or a boon of some kind. As a duke, he probably had a lot of people come here to tell him what they needed of him.

He did not sit, but stood beside his chair with one arm crooked on its high back. She again noted his dress, and wondered if her visit had interfered with his departure for a dinner or some other invitation. Perhaps he intended to visit a woman. Something about him inclined her to think so. Then again, maybe he expected a woman to visit *him*. Not her, of course.

That would be awkward. She trusted the servants knew to keep his mistress somewhere else if she came while he had other visitors. Best to make this conversation a fast one.

"Do you remember the first time I visited Mrs. Burton's?" she asked. "You saw me there."

"I remember the first time I saw you at Mrs. Burton's. Approximately a year ago, wasn't it? If you say it was your first time there, I have no reason not to believe you."

"I was winning at vingt-et-un. Again and again, I won. You sat down at the table beside me after I had been there an hour. Ambury wanted me to leave, and so did Cassandra. Do you remember?"

Silence. It stretched until she wondered if he would claim his memory had failed him.

"I do. You were drunk on the excitement of the risk, as I recall."

Drunk did not describe that incredible excitement. She had felt alive, and vital, and alert to her entire person. She had spent months sleeping. That night she had awakened.

She won eight hundred pounds that night. A small fortune. Then, she had given it away to those desperately in need. In one night she had experienced resurrection and thrills, and also found a purpose.

"You proposed a wager, Penthurst. I think your goal was to shock me, and ruin my fun. It worked."

"Not for long."

"I gambled no more that night, or for a fortnight after."

"Then you began again. Better if you had taken me up on that wager. It was one loss that might have ended the fascination."

"I think I would have won, and should have been brave enough to play your game, rather than letting you interfere and ruin my evening."

"Do you now?"

"Yes. For reasons unknown, fortune smiles on me. I think I would win now too. I am sure of it. So sure that I have come here to pick up the gauntlet you threw that night."

He could not hide his surprise. It passed quickly, however. "Perhaps you have forgotten the details of that proposed wager."

"Not at all. You suggested your ten thousand against my innocence, the winner to be determined by a simple draw of the cards." She tried to sound worldly, as if she discussed such things all the time. She wanted him to know she was no longer the little fool who had been rendered speechless at that vingt-et-un table.

His goal had been to dumbfound her. It had worked too well. She could not remember if the mere proposal had stunned her to where she lost all interest in gaming, or that such a proposal had come from *him*. Well, she had more self-possession now. She knew a thing or two about the world.

"The wager was posed knowing you would never accept it."

"I know. However, it was never withdrawn either. How careless of you."

"You cannot want to do this."

"What I want is your ten thousand. This is merely the easiest way to make you part with it."

No response. Just a long, dark look. Her self-confidence started to fray. An excitement akin to the thrill she knew at the tables quickened in her core. He appeared a bit vexed, enough that his jaw firmed and his mouth's line hardened. He appeared even more handsome like that, but she worried his expression reflected a growing stubbornness born of duty and friendship to Southwaite and all those other reasons he might dredge up in order to refuse. He did not know he would lose, after all. The scandalous nature of the wager might be giving him serious pause.

If so, he should have never made it.

"Should you want to beg off, I cannot force you to follow through," she said. "Although I doubt you want to be known as a man who proposes wagers he has no intention of completing."

He glared at her as if she had threatened to tell the world just that. She hadn't, although it may have sounded as though she might. Oh, dear. How careless of her.

"I can see that you are determined to court ruin, Lydia. So be it." He walked to a small, round table, lifted it, and set it down between the two chairs. He strode to one of the bookcases and took something out of a small drawer. Returning, he set a deck of cards on the table. "One simple draw of the cards, you said. No trump or wild cards, aces high. Is that agreeable to you?"

"Very agreeable." She pulled off her gloves, since she never wore them at the tables. On second thought, she also untied her bonnet, removed it, and set it aside, since she never wore hats or bonnets at the tables either.

It might be best to mimic her appearance and state of mind as closely to what she brought to wagers as a matter of course. She was not superstitious as such, but if one has evidence of a force as irrational as luck, one tends to allow for other irrationalities.

Penthurst sat in his chair. He mixed the cards, stacked them neatly, and pushed the stack toward her. He lounged back comfortably. "You can go first, Lydia."

She sat forward so her body almost touched the table. She tried to ignore him because she never paid attention to others at the tables. Unfortunately, she could not remove him from her mind completely. Even without looking at him she felt him there, his eyes on her, his presence pressing on her as if he gave off a measurable energy. He made her nervous, and imbued this risk with more danger than she wanted to acknowledge.

What a goose she was being. There was no danger. Not from the cards, at least. She would draw, win, collect, get rid of Mr. Trilby, and burn her manuscript once she had it back.

She spread the cards into a fan. Her fingers shook when she reached forward. Hand hovering, she made her choice. She plucked out a card and turned it over.

The queen of spades.

She raised her arms in triumphant excitement while a little cry of delight escaped her. She looked down on her queen, admiring it, enjoying the thrill of the win.

A hand came into view over the cards. A very male

hand, but quite beautiful in its own way, long-fingered and leanly strong. Those fingers plucked out a card. It disappeared. She looked up to see Penthurst studying it. From his expression she knew she had won.

He appeared disinclined to throw it down with her queen. Laughing, she stood, leaned over the table, and grabbed it out of his fingers. She dropped it on the table, ready to gloat.

Her laughter caught in her throat. Her mind emptied. Looking up at her, side by side with her queen, lay the king of spades.

No. *Impossible*. What were the chances he would pull one of very few cards that could beat her? She stared at it.

Stunned, she sank back into her chair. "Did you fix it somehow?"

"Since you are distressed, I will pretend I did not hear that insult."

Distressed hardly covered it. His voice caused a pang of terror to sound through her. She forced herself to look at him. He watched her in turn.

"I do not understand," she mumbled. "I never lose on big wagers."

"If you had asked your brother, he would have told you that I do not either."

It did not seem fair that his luck should be better than hers, tonight of all nights. How was she supposed to predict such a thing? Now she had lost and he had won and— Oh, dear.

He stretched out his legs and crossed his boots. Eyes

bright with devilish lights, he tapped the table, drawing attention once more to the cards. "How should we handle this, Lydia?"

"Handle what?"

"I assume we both want absolute discretion. I would rather Southwaite not call me out, and I am sure you would rather the world not know you gambled away your innocence."

She could not find her voice to respond. Not that she had any intelligent response to give.

"Not in London, I think," he went on, giving the matter deliberation. "It is easy for you to visit your family's estate on the coast, isn't it? You should make plans to go there in the next week. Take only that aunt of yours, the one who never watches you properly."

"How do you know whether she watches me properly or not?"

"You are here, aren't you?"

"My aunt Hortense is not my gaoler. I can move about town without her. I am a grown woman."

"Indeed you are. I would never be planning how to bed you if you were not."

Bed you. That shocked her mind straight. She stared at Penthurst, trying not to imagine what that involved. Little flashes of pictures came to her anyway, of his handsome face rising above shoulders and chest that wore no clothes, and of that hand that rested on the table instead resting on her.

A new panic flushed through her, leaving her warm and confused and too aware of their current isolation.

She felt terribly vulnerable to the masculinity he all but beamed like a lighthouse in her direction. She kept noticing peculiar things, like that hand, and his mouth, and the tiny golden lights in his eyes, and the scandalous way he managed to observe her. That gaze appeared discreet enough, but she almost squirmed from how his attention communicated the implications of what would happen.

". . . I will arrange the rest," he continued. "I expect it might be an inn, but I promise it will be a good one, and the proprietors very discreet. Although letting a house might be better. I will have to see what is available."

"Surely there is no rush." She wanted to sound sophisticated. Instead her voice rang with desperation to her own ears.

He cocked his head. The slightest smile formed, and it hardly reassured her. "I am not accustomed to taking markers."

"I am not suggesting a marker as such, only—"

"Did you wager that which you do not have in your possession? Is that the problem?"

It took a moment to puzzle through what he meant. When she did, it only shocked her anew. "I am completely in possession of that which I wagered. However, a week—there is something else I must be doing this week."

That vague smile again. "Ah. You only wish a delay. A small one, I trust."

She nodded, dumbly.

"A fortnight hence, then, but I expect consideration

for my patience." He stood, and offered his hand to
help her to rise.

She gathered her gloves and bonnet. She accepted
his hand, too alert to the warm, dry sensation of his
skin on hers. She turned to leave at once.

He did not release her hand. Even when she gave a
little yank, he held firm. She looked back at him with
curiosity. His eyes narrowed and he yanked in response.
She spun back until she bumped right into him.

His other hand pressed the back of her waist. "You
forgot the consideration. I meant it in the legal sense.
I do something for you, and you do something for me."

His voice, low and soft, sent a chill up her spine.
She stared up at him, feeling even more a fool than
before, trying to swallow her astonishment at being
pressed against him in a most improper way.

"Something . . . ?"

"A small something. A gesture of goodwill, to promise you will not welsh on your debt."

"You have my word that—" The rest caught in her
throat as she realized what he meant.

His head lowered. Her eyes widened. Surely he
could not think to—

He could. He did. The Duke of Penthurst had
decided that a kiss was the consideration he wanted for
delaying her deflowering by a week.

She saw it as if she sat in one of the paintings on the
wall. She saw her own amazement even as she experienced it. Saw his dark head angling to claim her mouth.
Watched while she helplessly allowed it, too shocked

to move. A new shock claimed her, one of deep stirring within the confusion. More surprise then. The kiss moved her, when it was the last kiss that ever should.

It horrified her. Some presence of mind returned. She pressed back against his hand while she turned her head away.

He permitted it. She snuck one look at him while she walked away. That was a mistake. He watched her like a hawk might watch a scurrying mouse, with the same confidence that there would be no contest should he determine the mouse would make a good meal.

She almost stumbled in her hasty retreat. He did not laugh at her. At least not before she had left the room.

For a woman of the world, Lydia had not acquitted herself well. Penthurst recalled just how poorly while he drank some brandy. On the table beside him the queen and king of spades still lay face up.

Was she mad? To come here and demand he make good on that wager—the idea still amazed him, as did all that had transpired.

She had been sure she would win. There was half a chance she would too. And if not, she would finally lose big, the way her family hoped and wanted. That had certainly happened, hadn't it? The shock she displayed indicated she had begun to believe in her luck more than was wise.

That would end now. He would let her worry about his intentions for a day or so, then let her out of the bad bargain. By then she would have thoroughly learned her lesson.

His mind drifted to that kiss, as it had several times already. He wanted to say it had only been one more part of that lesson, but that was not entirely true. He could be excused for pressing his advantage a little, however. Considering the situation she had created, she was lucky it had stopped at a kiss. A woman should not allow a man to have her within his power of possession unless she did not mind him considering her in that light.

Consider he had. Rather explicitly. Poor Lydia had sat there, gaping in shock, while he pictured her naked on a bed. He doubted she had guessed that. She had been too distressed to imagine where his mind might be going. In the days ahead she might, however.

Damn right, he had kissed her. Partly out of curiosity, partly out of arousal, but mostly because he already knew it was all he would ever get.

He checked his pocket watch. With a sigh he set down his glass, and stood. He gazed again at the cards.

No, she was not mad. She had come for a reason, and it had not been to toy with him. Something important caused her to assemble the courage to dredge up that old wager, and meet with him alone in order to coerce him to follow through on it.

He flipped the two cards over and returned them to their deck. Money. She wanted the ten thousand. Badly enough to risk herself like this. He wondered why she wanted it. Or needed it. Whatever the reason, she had concluded there was nowhere else to get it. That meant she could not turn to her brother, or her friends, or her aunts.

Evidently, this had not been the first big loss after all. He should have quizzed her on her gambling debts, instead of succumbing to the baser urges her little game had provoked.

He left the library and went below. The butler caught his eye as he descended the stairs, and angled his head toward the dining room. Penthurst changed directions and aimed there.

"My apologies," he said upon entering. "You are so often late coming down that I assumed you would not mind if I dallied over some brandy while I waited."

His aunt's head tilted back so she could look down her nose. She stood as tall and straight as possible for the full ducal effect. That pose had made her formidable and frightening when he was a boy. It still indicated she was not pleased.

"I wonder if our hostess will understand as well as I do," she intoned.

"Our hostess will await our arrival even if we are two hours late, so should not mind at all that it will be less than thirty minutes. Shall we go?"

Working her mouth like she chewed on words that resisted being swallowed, she accepted his escort out of the dining room. "You were not only drinking some brandy. You had company. A woman."

Hell. "Did you see her leave?"

"Of course not. Upon seeing her maid, I made

myself scarce in the dining room. Why was Lydia here?"

He ushered her out of the building and toward the waiting coach. "She has a cause that she hopes I will use my influence on." He preferred not to lie to his aunt, but that did not mean he never did.

She stepped up into the coach. "She came here to request that? She has not had a civil word for you in years, as best I have heard. She treats you like a stranger, and suddenly you are to be her friend because you once offered her transport to her brother's party? Bold girl. *Bold.*"

"You don't know the half of it," he muttered as he sat down across from her.

"What?"

"Nothing."

"I trust her cause is not the slave question. You have worn out your welcome there, even with Pitt."

"As a politician and minister, Pitt is constrained by practicalities in ways I am not, but we are still of like mind on that and many other things. However, Lydia's cause is not that." Lest she pursue just what it might be instead, he changed the topic. "We must have a right understanding about tonight. One dinner and an introduction to Lady Barrowton's brother, and that is all. If I am invited again, I will decline. When I meet her niece—"

"Do not be ridiculous. The girl is not out yet. She will not attend."

"You and Lady Barrowton have cooked up some

ruse so I meet her all the same, I am sure. Understand that I will not call on this girl, and I doubt I will even ask her to dance if we are at the same ball during her first season."

"I accept your agreement." She gave him a coy look. "Of course, you will be free of it if you choose."

"I will not so choose. I am only doing this because you rashly promised Lady Barrowton that I would dine with her brother. Do not commit me like that again. I will not have it."

"I know. It was bad of me. I am justly chastised. I will not interfere in the future."

Of course she would. But after tonight, not for a few weeks.

Chapter 6

It took Lydia two days to recover from the disaster at Penthurst's house. Her pending doom occupied her thoughts and dreams. She debated all sorts of schemes to get out of making good on that wager. Calling upon his honor seemed the best choice.

If that didn't move him, she could always beg him to release her from the debt, but the notion of begging Penthurst for anything appalled her. She could hear the self-satisfied lecture he would give her if he agreed. She would prefer to simply refuse instead, only that would announce that *she* had no honor, either as the daughter of an earl or as a gambler.

On the third day she forced herself to set that problem aside. Penthurst should not be her biggest concern now. Trilby's deadline would arrive before any trysts on the coast were arranged. Her time to find enough money to appease her blackmailer was running out.

She could think of only one other way to get her hands on a lot of money. Unfortunately it was not a plan she could execute on her own.

She needed an accomplice.

That afternoon she walked across the square to call on Cassandra. She found Ambury with her. When she entered the library they both gave her peculiar looks—the kind people give when they had been talking about you in their last breaths.

"I trust all is well across the way," Ambury said. "Is Emma still radiant with delight that she is in the family way?"

"She is, although if my brother does not stop doting on her, she will forget how to walk. Last night there was some discussion at dinner that indicated he has proposed she avoid the auction house the rest of this year." Emma played a secret role still in her family's business, Fairbourne's auction house. As best Lydia had determined, Emma played the *main* role as well.

"I doubt she took that well," Cassandra said.

"Not well at all. There was not an argument as such, just evidence that no matter what she has been saying, he has not been listening. You know how men can be."

Cassandra shot her husband a sideways glance. "I know how some men can be, that is true."

"Since I am probably one of those men, now would be a good time for me to take my leave," Ambury said.

"Then you ladies can bemoan how men can be at your leisure."

Cassandra sparkled at him. "You never give yourself credit, darling. By some men, I meant others, not you. You are the reason I insisted it is only *some* to begin with."

"What a pretty lie. But I will believe it, since I would rather not imagine being the subject of your talk." He left them on that.

Lydia sat next to Cassandra on the sofa.

"He will come around," Cassandra said.

"Ambury?"

"Southwaite. With Emma. He is still in the first throes of both excitement and worry. She will negotiate more movement and freedom in a few weeks."

"I do not see why she should have to negotiate anything. She is not some child. She took care of herself well enough before they wed. She can even make her own way if she needs to, which I greatly envy. My brother should not be able to change her habits and interfere with her pleasure on a whim."

Two years ago she never thought she would have to make this speech to Cassandra, of all women. Cassandra had been the freest unmarried woman she knew back then. She had both envied and admired her, and tried to pattern her own freedom upon that example.

Not that she had ever gotten far in doing that. Someone always interfered. Her brother. Her aunts. Her own fears and lack of confidence. Cassandra possessed a lush beauty that encouraged a boldness of vision that captivated everyone, even if they did not agree or

approve. When Lydia gazed in the looking glass, she
saw a somewhat ordinary female lacking distinction,
who could never pull it off.

Cassandra laughed. She reached over and plucked
at an errant curl and tucked it back into place in Lydia's
coiffeur. "You will go on about how the world should
be, instead of accepting how it is, Lydia. As I said, your
brother will come around. Emma will see that he does.
We women are not without our weapons in such skirmishes."

She wondered what those weapons were, and what
their limitations might be. Neither Cassandra nor Emma
appeared oppressed, but that had a lot to do with Southwaite's and Ambury's characters, rather than any feminine weapons. If married to different men, they would
both be disarmed.

"At least you do not have to wait for negotiations," she
said, broaching the topic that had brought her here. "You
at least still dance to your own tune sometimes. Ambury
would not object if you went out some night alone, for
example."

"Is there any particular place you think I would want
to go?"

"Was I that obvious?"

"Only because I know you so well." She bent closer,
like a conspirator. "What are you plotting?"

"In a word, revenge. I am finally ready to give the
cheating knave who robbed you his due."

Cassandra leaned away abruptly. "Robbed me?
Lydia, what are you talking about?"

"You told me that you lost a huge amount at the tables because a scoundrel cheated. Don't you remember? I said I would turn my mind to how to extract justice."

"Darling, that was long ago. Almost two years, surely? I had all but forgotten it. Since that financial quandary led to my alliance with Ambury, I do not even hate the man anymore."

"Well, I do. He is a cheat. He has kept at it all this time too. I figured out who it is and I have been watching him for months, when I can. I even had someone teach me sleight-of-hand tricks, so I could decipher just how he pulls it off." Hopefully Cassandra would never learn how badly that had turned out. That someone had been Trilby and it was how he came to know her better than he might have otherwise. "I am ready to bring him down."

Instead of cheering, Cassandra appeared vexed. "You have been watching him for months? He only plays at the worst hells these days. Do not tell me that you have been a regular visitor of such places."

"I could hardly study him if I never went where he plays cards."

"Good heavens, Lydia."

"I do not know why you are so shocked. I told you I was going to do this when you first described the dilemma he created for you. It is why I learned the games in the first place, and practiced with cards so hard."

"Are you saying you only picked up this . . . entertainment, so you could catch him at his tricks? Pray, never tell your brother that. He will forbid either you or Emma ever speaking to me again." Her eyes narrowed critically. "Nor can you claim that was your only reason for gaming. I have seen how much you enjoy it. The first step may have been taken for this purpose, but you were only too happy to skip along after that, for your own pleasure."

This was not going as she had planned. "I am not blaming you. I do not think there is cause to blame anyone. I am only explaining why on an evening soon I need to visit a gaming hall less refined than Mrs. Burton's, and why I thought you would want to come with me when I do."

"You were wrong. Nor are you going. It is not fitting."

"That is an odd command coming from you. You used to go, when you were a woman of the world, and not a dutiful, meek bride." She regretted snapping that out in response as soon as she said it.

Cassandra looked like she had been slapped. They sat in silence. Lydia considered whether bringing Sarah would work. She could dress Sarah up to appear her companion, and sit her at the table, and—

"You are determined?" Cassandra asked.

"I am. I will do it alone if you think aiding me compromises you in some way."

"It isn't that." Cassandra took her hand and patted it. "I was hoping you would have learned from my mistake, that is all. I suppose that almost never happens, however. I will accompany you so there is not too much talk. However, you only get one shot in this duel, Lydia. Be sure your powder is dry before you aim."

On returning home, Lydia received the news that Emma had taken ill.

She rushed to her brother's apartment. He sat beside Emma's bed, lines of worry etching parentheses on the sides of his eyes. Emma sat up in bed, propped on many pillows. She read a book by the waning light of the day. She greeted Lydia brightly.

"I heard you were ill," Lydia said.

"I was never ill. I only had a moment of light-headedness."

"She almost fainted," Southwaite said.

Emma patted the side of her bed. "Sit a moment. Darius, why don't you take this opportunity to go to the garden and take some air."

"I do not need air."

Emma regarded him indulgently. "Lydia will be here, and there are two servants waiting in my dressing room should I need them. It would not do for me to worry about your health more than you worry about mine."

Reluctantly, Southwaite stood. "You are to call for me at once, Lydia, if she— That is, if anything—" He bent and kissed Emma's crown, then left.

Emma cocked her head, listening for the door to close. When it did, she sank back on her pillows with a deep sigh. "Thank you for coming so I have some relief. He watches me so closely that I measure every breath."

"Did you really almost faint?"

"I only had a moment of dizziness when I rose from my chair in the library. Unfortunately, he was there and—" She gestured to her bed. "He will sit here all night, I fear."

"I will offer to do so instead, if you prefer." The plans with Cassandra would have to wait.

"He will never allow it. I expect him to return soon and banish you until tomorrow."

"I suppose he is worried about the child. It could be his heir."

Emma could capture one totally with her gaze, with a frank penetration that could be unsettling. She did that now. "It is partly worry for the child that has him so protective and concerned, of course, but mostly he is tortured by worry for me."

"If you say so, I must believe you, because you know him much better than I do." There were days when she did not understand Southwaite at all, nor he her. "If he remains like this, however, I fear you will do him grave harm before the child comes."

Emma giggled and they laughed together. "Oh, he will not be so impossible after a week or so. Why, he left just now, did he not? Thirty minutes here, two hours there—I am weaning him away from my side. Eventually I will have a life that approaches what I normally know."

"Normal enough for your family's auction house?"

Emma's brow puckered. "I think so, but not quickly enough. I confess that I have had to resort to a little deception on that." She cocked her head again, listening, then fluttered her hand toward her dressing room door. "Go, quickly. In my dressing table drawer there is a letter. Bring it here."

Lydia entered the dressing room. Emma's lady's maid and another female servant sat there sewing, waiting to be called. She plucked the letter from the lap drawer of the dressing table.

She handed it to Emma, who scanned its contents. "Would that I had more time to write this, and could be more detailed. This will have to do, however." She began folding it. "Will you post this for me, to Obediah at Fairbourne's? He wrote asking some questions that I needed to answer regarding the next auction."

Lydia took the page, now folded small enough to fit in her palm. Obediah Riggles was Fairbourne's auctioneer. "You are still managing things there, then?"

"I am not managing. He asks for advice, and I give it. That is not managing."

"How did you write this letter, with my brother hovering?"

"I convinced him to allow me to bathe without his help." She laughed. "He stayed in here. You should have seen me, scribbling away while my maid splashed to make water sounds. Fortunately I really was in the bath when my lengthy ablutions caused him to look in to make sure I was not in need of his assistance."

"Maybe he just wanted to see you naked."

Emma leveled that gaze at her again. "You do have a talent for astonishing comments, Lydia. It is not so much what you say, but the everyday manner in which you say them that makes Cassandra and me wonder about you."

"I hope you do not wonder too much. I regret to say that the only extraordinary thing about me is my talent for inappropriate comments." She bent and kissed Emma. "I will go now. I think he is standing right outside your door, trying to appear as if he is still sane. I will post this, and come tomorrow to find a way for you to have enough time to write again to Obediah, if you need to."

Southwaite indeed stood outside the door, arms crossed, taming for a while his fear for his lover. No sooner did she step over the threshold than he strode in.

He probably would spend the whole night there. Which meant he would be unaware of where she had the carriage take her tonight.

The library beckoned. Attended by his hounds, Penthurst aimed there, planning a silent night of reading after a day marshaling all his faculties to argue against the foolhardy idea of invading France.

Such plans were proposed at least once a fortnight, but this one, put forward by a general who should know better, had taken wing and flown around Whitehall like an eagle, instead of the tiny, wounded sparrow it was. At least three ministers had convinced themselves the farmers and merchants of England would throw down their hoes and lock their shop doors in order to serve in the army.

He understood the desire for action. For anything, really, that might bring years of war to an end. Britain could not field an army large enough for invasion, however, especially now that Napoleon had begun conscripting his own people. Several voices had been insane enough to suggest Britain do the same. As if Englishmen would accept such a thing.

After choosing his books, he settled down in his favorite chair. Caesar sprawled at his feet. Cleo sat near his right side, her head positioned for any scratches he might absently reach over and give.

The table on which a losing queen of spades recently lay still stood beside him. He looked across at the other chair, and remembered Lydia's shock when she saw the king.

He had almost felt bad for her. Almost. He hoped that she was good and worried about that wager.

He opened his Roman history, but having now been distracted by thoughts of Lydia, his mind dwelled there, weighing just how worried to make her. A letter was in order, reminding her to arrange to go to the coast in ten days.

He smiled to himself as he imagined her reaction.

A small commotion interrupted. It sounded just outside the library, near the far door. The dogs immediately stood, ready to attack, which meant a stranger had entered the house. He bid them sit and they turned to statues. His chair faced one of the fireplaces, set close to it to carve a human-scaled space out of the chamber's vastness, but behind him he heard a door open.

"You poor dear," his aunt said. "Come. Sit. It pains me to see you so distraught."

A woman's weeping played behind his aunt's notes of sympathy.

What was she doing here? She was supposed to be at the theater, not intruding on his privacy.

The weeping continued. Words punctuated sobs and sniffs as another woman gasped out her misery. "So good of you. I have made a terrible scene, haven't I? I should have remained at home once I learned of it, not—not risked losing my composure in public."

"I will not have you blaming yourself. Were you to spend the night in your chambers, pacing the floor? The play was so boring I was glad to spirit you away. Now, we must put our heads together and see if anything can be done."

"Too . . . late. For the family to have such wonderful news, then have to contend with this—"

It was past time to make himself known. Wishing he could avoid it, knowing he would in the least be listening to an hour's explanation of the ruin waiting to submerge this woman's family, he stood and walked around his chair with Caesar and Cleo in his wake.

"Forgive me," he said. "I did not expect the library to be used tonight. I will take my book and go, so you can have privacy."

His aunt bent over her friend's weeping body while

the gray-haired woman wailed into her hands. Neither looked at him to acknowledge he had spoken. He strode to the closest door, to make good his escape before one of them—

"Wait." His aunt's voice rang out. Plumed headdress still bent to her friend's misery, she lifted an arm as if to block his departure. "Calm yourself, Amelia. My nephew is here. He will know what to do."

Amelia? As in Southwaite's widowed aunt Amelia, Lady Pontfort?

No one else but the same looked up at him, her tear-streaked soft face and filmy blue eyes full of hope. "Oh, Penthurst. Yes, he will know what to do."

He had no idea what to do. He knew what he wanted to do, but being a gentleman he approached them instead. He greeted Lady Pontfort with a voice and manner appropriate to her grief.

"Amelia was in the next box at the theater, with Hortense," his aunt explained. "I could see as soon as she arrived that she was not herself. Then during the first act she began weeping." His aunt gestured to Lady Pontfort, as evidence. "Of course I went and got her, and called for the coach."

"So good of you," Lady Pontfort whispered. She dabbed a lace handkerchief at her eyes.

"On the way back here, she told me the cause of her sorrow. Tell him what you told me, Amelia. If the prime minister and the prince confide in him, you can."

Lady Pontfort nodded. "When my nephew's coach was late tonight, to bring me to the theater, I asked the coachman why. His response is the cause of my distress." The last words almost drowned within a strangled sob.

He looked at his aunt in question. She lowered her lids in disapproval of what was coming.

"He was late because another member of my nephew's family required the coach. It first transported my niece Lydia to an infamous gambling hell in the City. Alone. The whole town is sure to hear of it. The worst sorts of men congregate there, and I have heard even—even—women of ill repute frequent this place. I fear my niece is going to ruin tonight."

"Or going *to the devil*," his aunt muttered. "She is speaking of that terrible place, Morgan's Club. I am sure you have heard of it."

He had more than heard of it, but there would be no profit in mentioning that. Or in saying anything at the moment. So much for Lydia learning her lesson.

His aunt gripped Lady Pontfort's shoulders. "Collect yourself now. She must be stopped. Her late mother would expect us to do something."

"What can I do? I can hardly march in there and demand this Morgan hand her over to me."

"Southwaite should be told," his aunt said.

Lady Pontfort shook her head. "He is with Emma. She fell ill this afternoon. The physician said there is nothing to worry about, but they always say that when they have no solution. Southwaite is sequestered with her in their apartment, the coachman said."

"If his wife is ill, he is hardly the person to rescue

her," Penthurst said. "It would be cruel to add to their worries with this business too."

"Then I will send several brawny footmen there, with orders they are to carry her out if necessary," his aunt announced.

He pictured that. Morgan employed a few brawny servants of his own, who were well practiced in ensuring no one disrupted his establishment.

"You will not send footmen. I will go, as Southwaite's friend."

"Oh, would you?" Lady Pontfort could not contain her relief. "Such generosity."

His aunt frowned. "I do not think that is wise."

"Surely not. I can think of several ways in which I will pay dearly. However, go I shall, since someone must."

Chapter 7

Lydia sat across from Mr. Peter Lippincott. For three hours now she had prepared to lure this sharper into her net. Thirty minutes more and he would meet his doom.

They sat at the table he preferred to use at Morgan's. Impeccably dressed in dark coats and crisp cravat, appearing every inch the gentleman he was not, Lippincott shuffled a deck of cards. All the while he chatted and looked right at her. She knew he wanted her to look back, and not at his soft, almost feminine hands and the dastardly work they did.

A long line of gullible pigeons had visited him here over the last two hours, sure that they could win against his conjuring tricks. He allowed one in three to do so, which meant that he profited off the others. She suspected that Mr. Morgan knew all about it, and took part of the winnings.

She was not sure Mr. Morgan knew the other ways in which Lippincott cheated. The fine fingernails on those fine hands marred the cards as he used them in other play. She had stumbled upon that fact seven months ago. On some he made tiny nicks on the sides. On others he encouraged concavity. A few saw bits of damage to their corners. All but indecipherable, the changes created a code by which he could read the cards' values from their backs or from feel.

She had spent the months since then learning the code. He always used the same one.

Tonight she had already won a good deal of money. At faro and baccarat, she had turned the one hundred pounds lent her by Cassandra into three thousand by wagering boldly. She did not doubt Mr. Lippincott would be good for more. He had become wealthy with his gambling.

Cassandra hovered behind her, whispering warnings, serving as a Greek chorus. That was part of the plan. She spoke with breathless and sorry amazement at Mr. Lippincott's uncanny luck, to which her own fortunes had unfortunately succumbed. Lydia suspected Cassandra truly was nervous. She had not told Cassandra about the marked cards. She did not want Cassandra arguing with her on the ambiguous morality of cheating a cheater.

The smooth hands moved. Although she kept her gaze on his face, she paid attention to those hands sliding around at the bottom of her sight. She saw the sleight of hand that moved some cards to the top of the deck and some to the bottom.

Holding the deck, he fanned out the cards and held them toward her. "Pick one, Lady Lydia."

She did. He made a display of thinking.

"The ten of clubs."

She threw down the two of diamonds. He smacked his forehead with his palm.

He had let her win, to lure her deeper.

"Such luck you have, Lydia," Cassandra exclaimed. "Far more than I. She has become quite famous for it, Mr. Lippincott."

"I can see why." He made a face that indicated he found her luck inconvenient and costly.

He let her win again. She laughed and bounced with excitement. Cassandra cheered. She turned to Mr. Lippincott once more, to press her luck.

The third time, when she reached for a card the fan became a moving target, sliding just enough so that her fingers landed on a particular card. The one he wanted her to pick. If she had not been waiting for it, she would not have noticed. She touched her left ear with her left hand, in the prearranged signal with Cassandra.

"Why don't you both draw this time?" Cassandra asked. "It will be more exciting that way."

Lydia did not draw. "Oh, yes. Let us do it that way. High card wins."

Lippincott glanced up at Cassandra. "I would not think you would encourage your friend to that, considering . . ."

"Considering how poorly I fared against you in that game? She has much better luck, as I said. Nor will I allow her to bid as rashly as I did when I played that game with you in the past."

He shuffled the cards again, then set them out to be cut. Lydia cut them, but instead of leaving them for his hands to spread, she slowly spread them in a fan on the table. As she did so she noted the nicks on the sides of some and the subtle lack of flatness of some others. The latter would be the honor cards. By the time she had passed her fingertips over all the cards, she knew which had been marked by his system, and what cards they were.

"You go first, since I cut," she said.

"What will the wager be?"

She frowned over her stack of money, then began to move five hundred toward the cards.

"That is far too much," Cassandra scolded.

"Are you determined to ruin my fun? I am so sure I will win that I should wager it all."

Cassandra reached over her shoulder and slid three hundred back. "I am here to keep you from being reckless. Remember?"

Lydia made a face that only Mr. Lippincott could see.

He slid his fingertips along the fan of cards, back and forth, deciding on his draw. They came to rest on one of the convex cards. He flipped it to reveal the king of hearts.

"See?" Cassandra said. "This is a fool's game, as I learned to my sorrow."

Lydia plucked an unmarked card and turned it. Of course it showed a low card, a four of diamonds. Vexed, she collected the cards quickly and began shuffling them. "One more, if you are agreeable, sir."

"If it would please you."

"It would."

"Lydia," Cassandra's voice warned in her ear.

"Oh, hush." She handed the cards to Lippincott, who cut them, then fanned them on the table.

"Lydia." The whisper hissed this time. "You have attracted attention."

That was nothing new. She often did when she gambled. She never paid attention herself to those who watched her at the tables. They were only distractions. "A higher wager this time, I think. Can you meet all of my night's winnings?"

Lippincott eyed her money. "You must have over two thousand there."

"No more than three, however, I am sure." She pushed it all forward.

Eager now, Lippincot agreed to meet the amount, and pushed at least half as much to meet hers, with the promise of a marker, for the rest to be delivered the next day, if he lost. She made a display of pondering the cards.

"Lydia."

Cassandra had become a nuisance, and her whispers a troublesome buzzing near her ear. She shooed the bee away, and reached for a card that she had identified as the king of spades.

Just as her fingers lowered to the card, another hand

got there first. Not Lippincott's. This new hand possessed more strength than Lippincott's, and long, masculine fingers.

She knew that hand.

She also recognized the presence that hovered at her left shoulder just like Cassandra pressed her right one.

"A simple draw again, Lady Lydia. You favor that wager. What do you risk this time?" Penthurst asked.

Go away, go away. "The night's winnings and no more."

"I am relieved to hear it. I would not like to think you wagered that which you have already lost."

Her face warmed. She refused to look at him. One more draw and Lippincott would pay dearly for having cheated Cassandra, and she would have enough to silence Trilby for a long while.

She tugged at the card. Penthurst held it in place.

"Move your hand, please."

"Who is this man?" He posed the question to Cassandra.

Cassandra stepped to the side of the table, distancing herself from the duke. "Allow me to introduce you to—"

"I requested no introduction. Only his name."

Lippincott shrank back into his chair.

"Mr. Peter Lippincott."

"Tell Mr. Lippincott that this particular pigeon will not be playing further tonight."

Cassandra did not have to say a word. After a sweep of the table to collect his money, Lippincott departed.

Lydia almost wept with frustration. She had been so

close. Ten more seconds and— She pushed back her chair, right into Penthurst. She stood and turned on him. "How dare you interfere."

"I dare as your brother's friend. He has larger concerns tonight than chasing after an errant sister."

"Did my brother send you?"

"I chose not to worry him further with tales of your rebellion. I do not need his request to act in his stead."

"Without it you have no authority here. However, you have done your duty as you saw it, and are well finished. Good evening to you, sir."

Cassandra emitted a tiny gasp at the blunt dismissal. Lydia trusted it would be enough to get the duke to depart. She turned her mind to calculating how to win a great deal fast without the convenience of Mr. Lippincott.

Penthurst's eyes narrowed. "You forget yourself, Lydia. No doubt it is the excitement of the games that accounts for your rudeness. Much like a lover thwarted while in the act of passion, the lack of completion of your wager appears to put you severely out of sorts."

Another tiny gasp from Cassandra.

"What were you thinking, wagering so much?" He gestured to the money still on the table. "I thought Southwaite had tightened the reins on you, but if this week is any example, you disobey him with impunity."

Exasperated, she looked at Cassandra, who had become annoyingly demure and quiet. "We were close. If *someone* had not ruined it, we would both be richer and satisfied."

Cassandra opened her mouth to respond, but her

gaze slid to the duke. Whatever she saw had her silent again. She grabbed Lydia's reticule and stuffed the money into it.

Lydia took the bulging reticule and cast her gaze over the patrons still at Morgan's tables. Two famous courtesans had been leading the hazard play when she arrived, but they had given up that post. She calculated how long it might take to turn her three thousand into ten if she were very lucky. Hours at Mrs. Burton's, but Mrs. Burton had limits on the bids, the better to protect herself from too much luck. Morgan, on the other hand, had a taste for gambling himself. It was why even peers could be found sometimes in these very democratic chambers. There were no limits imposed by the house.

Hazard it would have to be. Unless—

She looked at Penthurst, standing tall and severe, his dark eyes full of the disapproval she knew so well.

She glanced down on the table. Mr. Lippincott's cards still lay there.

She shouldn't. That would be very wrong.

"Does Ambury know you are here?" Penthurst turned his displeasure on Cassandra.

Her dark lashes lowered over sparking eyes. "I really do not know. I did not ask my husband for his permission, if that is what you mean. But then, I never do."

Yes, it would be wrong. On the other hand, Penthurst now spoke to Cassandra in a tone that hardly encouraged virtue regarding those cards.

"No doubt because you know he would not approve of your coming here, let alone bringing Lady Lydia with you. Was it not sufficient to introduce her to Mrs. Burton's?"

"I thought so. She did not. Ambury would not have wanted me to have her come here alone, that much I know. Do you think I should have?"

"I think you should have used your influence to dissuade her from coming at all."

"May I point out she is a grown woman? She knows her own mind, just as I do, and just as I did prior to my marriage. We neither require nor desire men, even our brothers and husbands, to dictate our lives, just as you would not want that for yourselves."

Lydia wanted to cheer. This was the Cassandra of old, the woman who had faced down society in order to live her life as she chose, the Cassandra Lydia had envied and, upon her marriage to Ambury, had mourned ever knowing again.

She looked again at the cards. Very wrong. However, he had become insufferable. He had just ruined her chances to take care of Mr. Trilby's threat very neatly, so making him pay instead of Lippincott had delicious appeal. And, as she never forgot, Penthurst could use a little taking down much as Mr. Lippincott could, for much more egregious reasons.

"Penthurst, you appear determined to ruin my evening of fun," she said.

"My only determination is to remove you from this place forthwith."

"And if I refuse?"

"I will see that you do not."

She grinned at Cassandra. "Do you think he will carry me out? I am half tempted to see."

"Lydia—"

"To avoid such an undignified spectacle, I propose a compromise. Allow me to play one more game of choice, for five minutes only, and I will leave of my own free will."

"I rarely compromise. However—five minutes. No more. As for how much you wager, I will not interfere. Your brother has counted on your being rash enough to get badly burned. Some need double lessons, so may you have the second one now."

Cassandra raised an eyebrow at the little speech. "I am sure Lydia is not so foolish as to wager everything in that reticule. Correct, Lydia?"

"If the wager is enticing enough, I may." She made a display of surveying the chamber, choosing her game.

Cassandra took her arm. She pulled Lydia aside for a private word. "Enough now. We were found out and Lippincott is well gone."

"I am not done. I intend to win much more. Off Penthurst."

"Are you mad?"

"Admit you would not mind seeing it, after the way he just spoke to you. I will invite him to take Lippincott's place, for the draw he interrupted. There is justice in that."

Cassandra glanced behind at Penthurst, then whispered. "You cannot think to use that same deck of cards."

"Why not? It isn't as if I have done anything to the cards."

Cassandra studied her. "You will not be cheating, then? Yet you expect to win."

"I almost always win. As for what I expect—only good fortune."

With that she walked back to Penthurst. "My game of choice is a wager with you. I will put up the contents of my purse, and you put up half as much, plus whatever you have won in the last week. If you scold so freely about the sin of gaming, you probably have no winnings to risk at all."

"As it happens, my winnings this week were handsome enough. Not, however, three thousand, such as you have to offer. Eight hundred."

"It is a tempting wager, then?"

"No."

What an impossible man. Cassandra looked relieved.

"However," he said, "I would be tempted if you promised to double what I have won in the last week, should you lose. The amount was small enough that you will be able to keep much of what is in your purse."

That was generous, if one ignored that he had also won *her* along with the "almost nothing."

Seeing her way out of that conundrum, and also a path for adding to her funds to put off Trilby, she sat down at the table. He took Mr. Lippincott's seat. She gathered up the cards. "Cassandra, perhaps you will mix them and lay them out."

Cassandra sat to her right and mixed the cards.

"One moment," Penthurst said. "Are those Lippincott's cards?"

"I think so."

"The man is suspected of being a sharper. The deck may be marked. I can't have you accusing me of cheating." He twisted, caught the eye of a servant, and called for another deck.

Her heart sank to her stomach. Normally she would assume luck would favor her, but—

Penthurst smoothly mixed the cards, his handsome hands appearing quite expert. He handed them to Cassandra to cut and fan. Cassandra did so, but her gaze locked on Lydia's and her eyes communicated her offer of retreat again.

"Why do you hesitate, Lydia? The wager favors you financially in all ways," Penthurst said. "I will add one more thing. If you win, I will never tell your brother about tonight."

Did Cassandra notice the way the duke looked right now? How golden lights flickered in his dark eyes, and how his vaguely amused expression made one's breath catch. He managed to appear predatory, but in a most attractive way. She could not ignore how her nervousness quickened her pulse. His attention created an almost appealing excitement.

It was all there in his eyes—what she really wagered, and what she now owed. He regarded her like a woman he expected to possess. The money was the least of it.

Double or nothing on her carnal debt had become the real wager, right here under the unsuspecting Cassandra's nose.

Yet was it really double? One only loses one's innocence once. After that, it would be a different sort of loss, and much smaller. Indeed, one might say that after that there was nothing much left to lose at all. And if she won, she would be free of that debt, and up another sixteen hundred.

She did not have a choice, anyway. Not really.

Penthurst waited. Lydia watched him, her complexion slightly flushed. Despite her impassive expression, she did not appear so confident now.

Had she intended to cheat him? She claimed on Mrs. Burton's terrace that Trilby had been showing her his sleight-of-hands tricks. She may have learned how to misuse that, along with other sharper tricks like marking the cards.

Someone had marked those other cards. Surely not her. All the same he could not deny that her hesitation seemed odd for a woman who had made the challenge to begin with.

She averted her eyes, and looked at the table, her color higher now. Perhaps she had seen more than he intended. As he teased her about the last wager, and dared her to double it, some vivid pictures of collecting his winnings had entered his mind. Lydia probably had no idea how often such thoughts occupied men, even when the woman was not an appropriate object of desire.

She looked rather pretty now, wide-eyed and indecisive, fighting to keep her aloof reserve in place. Not nearly so bold. He almost felt sorry for her.

Her back straightened and her tapered, slender fingers stretched toward the fan of cards. He could practically see her calling forth the goddess of fortune, and willing her fingers to land on a high card.

She abruptly pulled one and turned it over. The ten of hearts.

"You have a better than even chance of winning, Lydia. That was well done," Cassandra said.

He looked at the cards, deciding. Suddenly it did not seem so much a game, or even a way to teach Lydia a lesson. Instead, while he waited for his own luck to more than even the odds, he found himself giving a damn which way it went. That was his vanity at work. And his pride. And, he had to admit, the dark side of his soul that had fantasized too often this week about making Lydia pay up.

He plucked a card and flipped it.

Cassandra sighed. Lydia stared.

"It does not appear to be your night," he said, gently tapping his queen of hearts. "Again."

Her gaze turned up to him. Luminous. Alert. Curious. Astonished. Then the life left her eyes and they turned opaque, as she donned her sphinx mask again.

"Let us go now, Cassandra." She plucked at her

reticule's strings. "I owe you sixteen hundred, Pent-hurst."

"It is not necessary to count it out now. I know you are good for all that you wager. I will write to you and make arrangements for the settlement." He stood and offered his hand to her, then Cassandra. "Did you have your carriage wait for you, Lady Ambury?"

"A footman waits. He will procure a hired carriage for us."

"I assume you bribed him well, so he would not gossip in the household about this adventure."

"To no avail, since you have witnessed all."

"While I might have a friend's obligation to report your doings to Ambury in some cases, this is not one of them. Unless he asks me directly, my discretion is yours if you want it. Rather than wait while a carriage is procured, allow me to deliver you and Lady Lydia home."

His coach stopped at Cassandra's house first. Along the way he and she chatted. Cassandra's mood turned merry. Perhaps she forgot how this man had scolded her. Or maybe relief that he promised discretion prompted her good humor.

Lydia thought it very careless of Cassandra to alight from the coach with nary a pause to consider that she would be leaving Lydia alone with the duke. Cassandra said her good-byes, and took her footman's escort to her door. The coach rolled along toward the other side of the square.

Lydia gazed out into the night. She examined her gloves. She took inventory of the coach's embellishments. She did everything she could not to look at Penthurst sitting across from her. Even so she saw him, especially whenever they passed a street lamp and a sudden flash of golden light came in the window. Each time he turned from a dark form into a man under sharp light that found angles and shadows and details. So she saw his eyes, watching her. And his hands, settled by his sides on the cushion.

More than that, however, she felt him. He filled the coach. Not only his size cramped her. The rest of him— that presence that had caused her discomfort since she was a girl—did too.

"I will be discreet regarding your visit to that hell too, even though you lost the wager," he said.

She should thank him, she supposed. Only she did not want to admit life would be more pleasant if Southwaite did not know. The notion of accepting favors from him did not sit well with her either.

"If you employ discretion, do so for him, not me. He would worry far more than he needs to."

"You do not care if he knows?"

"Not at all. You will spare me some tiresome lectures, that is true. However, my brother is enlightened enough to know that a women of my age cannot be chaperoned like a young girl."

A flash of golden light sliced across his face, showing the lower half and revealing his vague smile. "He only accepts that because he does not know what you are doing. He sees that blank stare you turn on the world, and he wonders if there is any mind behind it, let alone a clever, scheming one."

"Clever? Scheming? Do you intend compliments or insults?"

"Only the truth as I see it."

She felt his attention boring into her through the dark.

"You were going to cheat me tonight, weren't you? Those cards were marked. I saw and felt enough of it as I handed them off to Morgan's servant."

"They were not *my* cards." She put her face to the window to judge how much farther they had. One could almost throw a stone from Cassandra's house to hers, yet this ride never ended.

"One does not set aside honor because circumstances not of one's making present the opportunity."

Pique turned to hot anger in a blink. "How dare you lecture me on good character. It is laughable for you, of all men, to do so. I might as easily say to you that one does not use honor as an excuse to kill a friend, just because circumstances present the opportunity."

Silence. A heavy atmosphere settled between them, one so thick that it might rain blood. They passed another lamp. This time the slice of illumination showed his eyes. His expression made her breath catch. She doubted she had ever been the object of such direct anger and—something else, something poignant that she could not name.

"You are referring to Lakewood. I remind you that the lords acquitted me."

"You are a *duke*. Of course they acquitted you."

"Your own brother acquitted me too."

Yes, he had. Not only had Southwaite voted thus at the trial, but after almost a year of refusing to speak to Penthurst, her brother had ended the estrangement. So had Ambury.

She could not believe it! A man kills a friend, and his only punishment is a year of silence from the other friends in that circle. Even dukes should face more justice than that.

A fury of disappointment and resentment choked her breath. Beneath the anger a deep grief stretched her heart. These men never considered that Lakewood had been *her* friend too. She had lived in the margins of the entire episode, not even an afterthought. They left her out of the grief and the anger, then out of the decision to reconcile. Southwaite, Ambury, and Kendale had each other as they accommodated that loss. She only had herself and whatever comfort Sarah could give.

She faced Penthurst now as she had learned to face the world in the dreadful months after that duel, with her grief hidden behind a face that reflected nothing.

"I stand corrected. Once more you point out how my behavior, and even my thinking, is in error. Having been acquitted on the basis of your own word that a good man's death had been a matter of honor, you must now be spared any reference to it, and we must all accept the rightness of your actions."

The coach mercifully slowed. She threw open the door as soon as it stopped, and kicked down the stairs, then stumbled down the steps into a footman's hurried attendance and rushed to the sanctuary of her chambers.

Chapter 8

The sun burned off the early morning mist while Penthurst rode into Surrey. On a lane two hours from London, he turned up a drive to a stone cottage surrounded by thatched outbuildings. He dismounted and led his horse to the stable in back. Shedding his frock coat, he removed the horse's saddle, rubbed him down, and set him into a stall with some hay.

Rolling up his shirtsleeves, he aimed for a field behind the stable. Two men worked there, one quite young. The older one noticed him and stopped the ox that pulled his plow. Boots loose and muddy, he walked over, wiping the sweat off his brow with a handkerchief.

"You be early this month, Your Grace."

"The day looked to be fair. Maybe I will avoid the rain this time, Mr. Gosden."

Mr. Gosden chortled. "Looked like a drowned dog, you did."

"A mud-covered drowned dog, as I remember." He gestured to the plow. "You are turning up this bit here, I see. I'll finish it, unless you require me elsewhere."

Gosden's small pale eyes narrowed on the field. "Lots of rocks in there. Been avoiding it for years, but figured I'd give it a go. We got out the worst of 'em, but if you plow there, you be careful."

"I will try not to break your plow."

"It's your head you should try not to break. Or a leg. I'll leave it to you, though, since you are of a mind to break a sweat at least instead. We have some planting of winter wheat we'll tend to, and be glad of the help here."

Mr. Gosden walked away, collecting his helper as he went. Penthurst took the plow and began churning the ground. Man and beast fell into a rhythm as old as agriculture, silently playing their roles in coaxing crops out of the earth.

Penthurst welcomed the humble labor. The exercise and the fresh air provided the clarity he sought regarding the matter occupying his thoughts.

Lydia's accusations last night had surprised him, but mostly because they came from her. Undoubtedly many people held the opinion she expressed. *The law is different for lords. They take care of each other, and expect the same for themselves in turn.*

But her scathing, furious directness in speaking of it had been startling. No one flung such accusations at him. Not even Southwaite and Ambury. Those friends had cut him, but they had never spoken their minds.

Perhaps they thought he would call them out over it, and kill too. He saw that calculation in men's eyes sometimes now. *If I press this point with him, will I find myself dead at dawn?*

He wondered now if it had been a mistake not to pursue his suspicions about Lakewood. For over a year now it had eaten at him, that a man would choose to die to avoid what would be a survivable scandal. That suggested more had been at stake.

Guilt had kept him from finding out. He had taken Lakewood's life. What good could come from also taking his good name?

Today, however, as he walked the turned earth, Lydia's accusations rang in his head. He had not liked hearing that view of his character. Especially coming from her. He was beginning to realize just how costly it had been to protect Lakewood's name.

The plow suddenly jerked to the left while a good-sized rock flew to the right. He cursed as the rock barely missed his knee.

A shout went up from the end of the field. Mr. Gosden, who had been returning, broke into a run.

"Did it hit you?" he called as he neared.

"A miss, fortunately. It was my fault. I was distracted."

Mr. Gosden wiped his face and caught his breath. He kicked the rock aside. "Distraction be easy enough on a fair day, but not so wise, Your Grace. A plow is a serious thing." He bent down and examined the ox's legs, to make sure the more valuable partner in the labor had not been hurt either. "You be done now, sir?"

"Do you think I should be done?"

"Do I think? Not for me to think, that I know."

He did not only defer to his betters with his answer. Mr. Gosden paid much less to be a tenant than normal, because he allowed a duke to work here on occasion. It was not for him to approve or disapprove, or to draw fine lines around how long that duke should stay.

"If I am ever hurt, you will not be blamed, Mr. Gosden. That will be laid at the feet of my eccentric habit." He smiled, so perhaps the farmer would not look so worried. "When they hear of it, everyone will think my doing this was as strange as you find it."

Mr. Gosden shrugged, and grinned. "Strange enough, I expect. If I was a duke, I'd never work a plow. What good is being a duke then?"

There was an explanation, but not one that Gosden would understand. What had started as a punishment long ago had continued by choice. There were times when this duke, at least, needed to remove himself from the title and its privileges, and this was as far away as he had ever found. Working the soil of the estate proved a respite of the most elemental kind, and provoked the kind of thinking that often resolved dilemmas.

As it had today.

"I will leave the plow to you, Mr. Gosden, and hope my few hours here were more help than hindrance." He gave the ox a firm pat on its rump and walked away.

"Will you be coming again?"

"Oh, yes. The usual day, however."

Feeling more himself, that evening Penthurst dropped in on one of his clubs. He paused inside the door to Brooks's subscription room, to see who else had sought refuge here. He spied Ambury sitting with Southwaite and Kendale.

Ambury gestured him to join them. Since Kendale did not turn stone-faced, Penthurst settled into a chair at their table and accepted some brandy. "Is your wife feeling better, Southwaite?"

"She says she is."

"Do you not believe her?"

"He was just telling us that he should not have come tonight, and needs to leave very soon," Ambury said.

"I explained why," Southwaite said firmly, his dark eyes reflecting displeasure at the teasing note in Ambury's voice. Unlike Ambury, who lounged in his chair like a man content with his world, Southwaite appeared distracted and preoccupied, and unlikely to be good company.

"Emma was looking a tad pale when he left, he said," Kendale offered, deigning to join the banter, which was unusual for him.

Kendale had been in the army prior to inheriting upon his brother's death. Stiff, hard, and a social disaster, her green eyes tended to see the world as divided into a series of halves. Right and wrong. Duty and self-indulgence. Bravery and cowardice. In such a world view, Lakewood's death had been murder.

That Kendale even tolerated his company tonight probably reflected his improved humor due to his recent marriage, and not any true accommodation.

"She should have rested another day."

"Did the physician advise that?" Penthurst asked.

"I am thinking I need to replace him."

"I assume that means no such advice was given," Ambury said. "If women take to bed for two days every time they are light-headed, we will have a lot of invalids."

Southwaite crossed his arms and looked petulant. Penthurst guessed the jokes about this had been going on for a while before he joined them.

"I cannot wait to hear your cool logic at work when it is your turn, my friend," Southwaite said to Ambury.

"She is probably restless," Kendale said. "Your wife

is a woman of purpose and action, Southwaite. You will drive her mad if you try to make her into anything else." His military posture straightened even more as he issued this opinion on the subject he understood least—women. No doubt his recent marriage misled him to think he had acquired sufficient experience to give advice.

"The philosopher speaks," Southwaite muttered. "However, she insinuated much the same thing, if you must know. She all but threw me out of the house."

"She is probably annoyed that she missed the fun the other night with Lydia and is in no mood to indulge your notions of protection further," Ambury said, his attention mostly attached to a servant who had brought over a cigar he had requested.

Southwaite looked over sharply. "What fun?"

Ambury's perennial, affable smile froze. He watched the servant prepare his cigar and paid heed to nothing else. Definitely not to Southwaite.

"*What fun?*"

Ambury took his time with his first puffs. "A little outing, that is all. My wife and your sister spent the evening together. The ladies do that sometimes, of course. Not at all unusual. Emma probably heard of it, was all I meant, and felt left out."

That appeased Southwaite. He even appeared a bit chastened. "Where did they go, that she would have felt left out? I will take her myself, to make amends for my overbearing worry."

Ambury frowned amid the smoke he made while he pondered the question. "I'm not sure Cassandra ever said. Let me investigate my memories."

Across the table, Kendale tapped his chin. "Cassandra and Lydia out and about together, free of their cages. Hmm. Where might they have flown? Hmm . . ."

"Wherever it was, there is no reason to think twice about it, so you can stop making trouble," Ambury said to him. "They were delivered home safe and sound by Penthurst here, so were hardly walking hell's streets if they met up with him."

"Lady Ambury had brought a footman too," Penthurst added. "Rather than have the servant go for a carriage, I transported them home."

"Good of you to look out for them," Southwaite said.

"Very good," Ambury nodded.

The topic was mercifully passing. For everyone except Kendale, who lacked good instincts when it came to social conversations. "You are right, Ambury. If Penthurst was there, all kinds of hells can be eliminated. Gin houses, for example. He would never go to one of those."

"The taverns near Covent Garden too," Penthurst said. "I never visit them at night."

"Almack's," Ambury added. "You hate it. Not that either lady would receive a voucher even if she wanted one."

"A male brothel can be eliminated as well," Kendale offered. "He'd never have cause to go to one of those."

That got everyone's attention. One brother and one husband shot dangerous stares at Kendale.

Penthurst laughed. "I can confirm that I did not meet the ladies at a brothel of any kind."

His effort at levity did not work.

"What is wrong with you, to imply that Cassandra and Lydia might have visited a male brothel?" Ambury asked.

Kendale looked honestly confused, and annoyed to have had his rare attempt at humorous small talk turn around and bite him. "We were itemizing where they could *not* have gone. How does my saying they could not have been there mean they might have gone there?"

"To even reference such a thing is enough to get you thrashed, in the least."

"By you? I don't think so."

"By both of us."

"Let's kill him, Ambury," Southwaite said.

"Two against one? Hardly fair."

"If it is the only way you finally learn to watch what you say, two against one it will be."

"Gentlemen." Penthurst tried his most ingratiating tone. "Kendale was attempting a joke at my expense, not the ladies'. Weren't you, Kendale? Such wit requires some practice, I think you will agree. He is new to the game and is bound to commit some unintended errors."

Ambury's hard expression broke first. He sighed in acknowledgment that Kendale would be Kendale for a long time to come.

Penthurst decided to turn the conversation elsewhere. "You have been gone several weeks, Kendale. I trust you enjoyed the country with your wife?" The marriage to the French émigré Marielle Lyon had been recent enough for Kendale to still be in the throes of new passion, to the extent he succumbed to such things.

"Very much. Fortunately, she prefers it to town, as I do."

"Did you start any private wars while you were away?" Kendale had served in the army, and at times acted as if he still did. That had created a few dramatic adventures in the past. "Or has Mars been disarmed by Venus?"

"Venus would be disappointed if I laid down all my weapons, I think."

Penthurst laughed. It took the others a five-count to join in. Kendale so rarely made bawdy jokes that they had almost missed this one. Kendale's unbending posture might have had something to do with that. He had sat in his chair the whole time as if he rode a horse in a parade.

"His current private war is here. He has brought Marielle back to town for more skirmishes with society," Ambury said. "You will have to allow Emma out of bed if only to help out, Southwaite."

"Yes," Kendale said. "Marielle will need what friends she has by her side. We both will."

That was another unusual thing for Kendale to say, making this a rare day indeed. Normally he presented a face that denied any lack of confidence, let alone the kind that anticipated the need for friends. However, even before marrying an inappropriate wife, Kendale had hardly gotten on well in society, so these battles would take place on unfriendly ground.

"Let us all go to the theater on Friday," Ambury proposed. "You and Marielle will be my guests in my family's box, Kendale. You must come, Penthurst. It will make all the difference."

He waited for Kendale to object to that last point.

"I would not miss such a display of social independence as you will present in that box. A phalanx of it. You will give the matrons apoplexy," he said when no such objection emerged.

"You can bring your current mistress, whoever she is. Then all of us will be with unsuitable women."

"As it happens, there is no current mistress."

Southwaite roused himself from whatever distracted him. "There is no current mistress? What became of Mrs. Ca—"

"That has been over for some time. I can be as discreet about my private life as you can be, if you are wondering how you did not know."

Southwaite's eyebrows went up. "Then the ladies

will balance the group another way. It is decided, then? We will all await your invitation, Ambury. I promise not to imprison Emma since it is such a worthy cause."

Chapter 9

"If it rains again, I may cry," Lydia said while she and Sarah once more trod through Hyde Park. It was already damp enough without any rain and the air carried a frigid bite, such as autumn days could do unpredictably.

"If it does, do not blame me."

"Why not? We came this morning so you could flirt."

"I think we came so you could talk to that pale, thin gentleman again. He is waiting up ahead."

Algernon Trilby indeed waited, much more conspicuously than the last time. He stood cockily, propped up by a walking stick angled away from his leg in a strong diagonal and locked in the hand of one outstretched arm.

The militia paced through their formations. Lydia had not asked her brother to obtain the schedule of which militias used the park which days. Rather she had approached his secretary, and confided Sarah's infatuation. The sandy-haired citizen soldier now bestowed one of his smiles when he noticed her.

Leaving Sarah to gawk, Lydia walked a further hundred feet to Mr. Trilby. She did not allow him a greeting before she launched into her rehearsed speech.

"I have a good amount of what you require, Mr. Trilby. Not on my person now, of course. However, things are well under way, and we only need to reach an understanding and I will hand it over, and set about obtaining the rest."

He pivoted his walking stick to and fro while he gazed out on the park. His eyes narrowed beneath the brim of his hat. He shifted his weight, placed one hand on one hip, and looked like a man pretending to be in a fashion plate.

That made her notice his garments. They appeared new, and a cut or two above what he normally wore. His yellow waistcoat bordered on flamboyant. The scoundrel must be spending freely, based on his expectations of fleecing her.

"I think not," he finally said. "I am sorry. I misspoke on the amount."

Overcome with relief, she almost hugged him. "I knew you to be a decent man. Ten thousand pressed your advantage rather steeply. Even a thousand would, although of course if that is what you want I will—"

"You misunderstand. It was not too steep. Rather it was too low."

"Good heavens, have some sense. There is no point in demanding more than I can ever lay my hands on."

"I have been contemplating that conundrum. I have hit upon a way to ensure you can pay it."

"I trust it is a fair solution."

"Fair and generous, I believe. As I pondered the question, an idea came to mind. Your reputation for luck at gaming kept presenting itself to my thoughts. Combined with my own at magic tricks, we might make a good partnership."

He meant that he and she could cheat in partnership. He would use sleight of hand to stack the decks, but she would win. No one would question if she did, since she always won. Almost always, she corrected herself.

"Not here, of course," Trilby added. "One of the spa towns, I think. Buxton, for example. It is far enough from London, and not too fashionable. We will not be well-known there."

His intentions revolted her. His clear delineation of his plan surprised her. He had thought it through with distressing thoroughness. Buxton's wells and spa attracted the right sort of people. The sort who gambled after a day taking the waters. Being up in Derbyshire near the Peaks, it did not attract the same circles that spent most of their time in London, however.

She would not do this. She would find a way out of it. For now, however, she needed to appease him rather than anger him.

"If you are determined, I agree that Buxton would do," she said.

"See how already our partnership is productive? We should each go there next week, I think. Why, in two days you should find your luck has created untold riches."

"The week after would be better."

His lids lowered. "You are the one who demanded a rapid settlement. Shall we agree to both be in Buxton by Thursday? We will spend a day discussing strategy and plans, then get to it right away."

She agreed, then walked back to Sarah and dragged her maid away.

Whenever she thought she had found a resolution to Mr. Trilby's threats, she only ended up in more trouble. She was supposed to go to the coast next week. Penthurst would be writing with the plans any day now.

She would just have to put Penthurst off again. *My Lord Duke, I regret that my deflowering will have to be postponed another week or so. I need to help my blackmailer cheat innocent people out of thousands of pounds on the day you have in mind.*

She might as well actually write that. It was so absurd he would never believe it, anyway.

Lydia had spent the last year restless, almost frantically so, and dissatisfied with her very ordinary life. Suddenly it had turned extraordinary in the most bizarre ways, and she rather longed for the old predictability and lack of even minimal drama.

So it was that the invitation to the theater appealed

to her. A night surrounded by family and closest friends would be a respite.

Then she learned that Penthurst was coming too.

"Why is *he* going to be there?" She and Emma sat in Cassandra's dressing room discussing the evening, and Cassandra had tacked on that unwelcomed name after rattling off the usual ones.

"The whole purpose of the party is to help Kendale and Marielle, by showing the world they have friends who accept Marielle despite her birth. If a duke is in the box with us, and that duke in particular— It will do more than the rest of us can hope to achieve in years of effort," Cassandra said. "I coached Ambury for an hour on how to propose the evening in Penthurst's presence and try to have him included."

"But Kendale does not even approve of Penthurst."

"Kendale did not object, so why should you?" Emma pointed out. "The duke might be doing it as a peace offering, or to at least put Kendale in a more friendly frame of mind."

That left her with no alternative except to sulk. "It will not be as much fun as I anticipated. Now I regret putting off my visit to Crownhill."

"Do not be a goose. Aunt Hortense said that she could not accompany you until Monday," Emma said.

"I fully intended to travel to Crownhill by myself."

Cassandra became engrossed in unsnarling a silver chain that lay on her dressing table. Emma chose that moment to pull over a footstool and prop up her feet.

124   Madeline Hunter

"Without a chaperone," Lydia added.

Her friends looked at each other. Cassandra sighed and let the silver chain drop to the table. "Lydia, the truth is most everyone worries what you will do if allowed to go about on your own."

"For all we know, you would become a pirate," Emma said. "Or a highwayman. You ride well enough for that."

Cassandra swallowed a giggle. "That smuggler that Southwaite knows asked after you once, and Ambury told me your brother almost killed him. Ambury said he thought Southwaite suspected the fellow had a partner's interest more than a lover's. A peculiar notion for a brother to entertain, so he clearly fears what you are capable of."

"Like going to gaming hells like Morgan's," Emma said.

Lydia groaned. "How does he know about that? Penthurst must have told him! He promised he would not. See? Penthurst is not a man to be trusted or admired and—"

"No one told him. If anyone had, I think you would be on your way to a convent in France, and damn the war," Emma said. "I learned of it, but your brother did not."

Cassandra's guilty expression showed who had done the telling.

"Cassandra was with me," Lydia pointed out. "I did not go alone. And that hardly means that if left to my own devices, I will become a pirate or a highwayman."

"I speak metaphorically, Lydia," Emma responded.

"Replace pirate with anything thrilling, daring, romantic, and of questionable legality."

Like being a sharper with Algernon Trilby.

Cassandra, instead of defending her, picked up the silver chain again. "So, it is settled. You will tolerate Penthurst, and he you, and we will all have a wonderful time while we help Marielle brave it out in that box."

Penthurst found Lydia's efforts to avoid him at the theater comical. He only needed to shift his weight to set her moving, seeking spots where at least two people served as a barrier from him.

On the few occasions they acknowledged each other, her color rose fast. That had just happened, and now Lydia spoke with Lady Kendale, keeping all of her attention on the bride, pretending the wall they stood beside were not less than fifteen feet from the wall where Penthurst stood.

Kendale's wife probably was the loveliest woman in the box, if one judged by the strictest external qualities. Willowy, and blessed with delicate, elegant features and luxurious golden brown hair, Marielle made as good a viscountess as she had made a spy. Not that she had actually been a spy. Or so Kendale believed. Her French accent, long suppressed, still colored her inflections when she spoke, and French insouciance still touched her manner.

She had sought a few private words with Penthurst

when he first arrived, and spoken with disarming honesty. "My husband, he tells me that he gave you a little book that I brought out of France, and that you made arrangements for it to go back, to men who are trustworthy. He tells me that you reported all worked as planned, and that the contents of the book were used to bring down he who threatened me. Thanks to you, I am safe now, forever."

She had taken his hand then, in an unexpected gesture. Holding it in both of hers, she had kissed his ring.

Kendale, noticing, had stepped in and gently extricated hand from hand. "We do not do that here, Marielle. He isn't a Catholic bishop."

Marielle proved incapable of embarrassment. "However the gesture is made, you have my gratitude forever."

"He simply saw that justice would be done," Kendale said.

"A fine and fair justice it was," she said, her eyes gleaming with gratitude.

"That is the only kind," Kendale said, taking her away.

The look Marielle shot over her shoulder as she left indicated she knew justice often came with ambiguities, even if her husband did not agree.

Now Lydia spoke with Marielle about something that animated them both. Yes, objectively Marielle was the lovelier, but he preferred Lydia's appearance. Tonight her dark eyes did not stare like opaque disks but showed depths with lights and thought. Her pale skin did not appear ghostly, but fashionable and touched with healthy little flushes high on her cheeks. Her pale yellow dress flattered her height and, he realized, her figure. Her breasts swelled in perfect high mounds above the beribboned high waist and the soft fabric flowed around a lithe, long-legged womanly shape.

His imagination followed where these observations led, and soon Lydia stood there naked except for her headdress and hose. He liked what he saw. Enough that he watched while she moved again, walking to the front of the box to chat with the other ladies, her gently curved hips swaying just enough to be provocative, her bottom beautifully and erotically swelled.

He tore his gaze away, thinking it was a damned shame that honor demanded he let Lydia out of that debt. As he shifted his attention, he noticed that two pair of eyes had been watching him.

One pair belonged to Ambury who watched so blandly he might not have detected the thoughts behind that long gaze at Lydia. Except men always knew when other men were thinking such things, and Ambury surely had. He displayed no curiosity and no surprise as he returned his attention to his wife. Ambury more than most would know that carnal calculations enter men's minds all the time, and often for little purpose.

The other pair of eyes, however, belonged to Southwaite. There had been surprise in Southwaite's expression in that moment when Penthurst caught him watching. Confusion too, as if he had never considered his sister a potential object of lust. Then again, perhaps

Southwaite merely wondered what if anything he should do, and how much trouble this might herald. Their world generally agreed that a man did not seduce a friend's sister, aunt, or—heaven forbid—mother, but that did not mean it never happened.

Feeling guilty for his friend's dismay but not for the reason, Penthurst walked to Lydia.

It was time to let her know that he would not hold her to the wager.

As he approached, he overheard her speaking to Emma.

"I will wait on Aunt Hortense until Monday, but not a day later. I will be at Crownhill by week's end with or without her."

Emma noticed him behind Lydia. Lydia turned with a start. Seeing no escape, she collected herself and greeted him, finally. Meanwhile Emma turned aside and became immersed in a conversation with Cassandra.

"The play is humorous, don't you think?" Lydia asked, choosing to look at the stage rather than at him.

"I would not know. I have not heard a word the actors spoke thus far."

"This playwright is known for humor, however."

"Then humorous it must be." Out of such inanities were conversations made. "I could not help but over-hear that you intend a journey to the coast next week."

She tried to become a sphinx, but the mask would not form. She flushed from hairline to neck, and sneaked worried glances at him. He was about to launch into a quick, merciful announcement of clemency, when she managed to collect herself.

"I do intend that journey," she said, looking him straight in the eyes. "However, not for the reason you may assume. The purpose you have in mind will have to wait . . . due to this other engagement that I have. I am so sorry."

His good intentions disappeared in a blink.

She displayed no sense of obligation even though the wager had been at her insistence. Instead of simply asking for his mercy, she meant to put him off indefinitely. It was damned well safe to say that if she had won instead of him, she would have demanded the ten thousand in gold bullion within the day. Having lost, however, she treated the entire matter as her prerogative to ignore.

So much for learning her lesson.

"I think not, Lydia."

"You think not that you will have to wait? There can be no choice on that, I assure you."

"I think not that you are sorry. I think not that you have another obligation. And, yes, I think not that I will wait."

"You are calling me a liar on two counts."

"I am calling you too sly by half. Had I known there would be all these delays, I would have demanded more consideration than I did."

She glanced around, to see if anyone watched. He did not bother to check too. Should any of their friends notice this conversation, they would see a duke smiling graciously and a woman holding her own well enough.

"I cannot believe you speak of any of this here," she hissed quietly.

"I will arrange to take you home after the play. Then we can speak of it in my carriage. When we are alone, you can explain this new obligation that interferes with your paying up in full."

She just looked at him, her eyes wide and her lips parted in astonishment. She appeared much as she had after that kiss in his library. Enough so that he actually began calculating how he really could arrange that ride alone with her.

Her self-possession returned. "You will do no such thing. My brother will never allow it. I will return in his coach just as I came, of course. As for all this talk of paying up and considerations, I know that you are toying with me, just as you did that very first night at Mrs. Burton's. You only seek to worry me, so that I will understand the foolishness of that wager. You can stop it now. You waste both of our times with this game."

It was all he could do not to drag her away, and pull her outside the box. He moved enough to reposition them both, so she backed against the wall and he faced her. Neither of their expressions would be visible now.

"You give me too much credit now, after giving me so little when last we spoke. I am a man who would kill a friend over a minor matter, remember? Insisting that you pay up will be a very small thing after that, and no game. Your assumption that you will never settle that debt tells me that you are badly in need of some discipline, Lydia. I will enjoy providing it."

That shocked the smugness out of her. She pressed the wall. Her gloved hand went to her mouth to stifle her gasp.

He stepped back. "I will see you at Crownhill, as planned originally."

It was well past the start of the second act, so the party finally sat themselves to watch the play. He made it a point to sit behind Lydia. Quiet conversation continued, which gave him cause to lean forward and remark on this or that to Southwaite, who sat beside her. He always found a way to include Lydia in the exchange. She tried mightily to avoid that, to no avail.

"Heard from the coast yesterday," Southwaite said over his shoulder. "Tarrington reports the French smugglers are getting bold, and going into Diehl. He wants to sink a few of their boats to protect his territory and was good enough to ask if it would interfere with any of our plans."

The plans involved a network of watchers Southwaite, Ambury, and Kendale had helped establish on the coast, to be alert to any unwelcomed French visitors who slipped ashore with smuggled goods or refugees. The idea had been Penthurst's several years ago, but the execution came during his estrangement, so had fallen to the others.

"Are you sending him a response through Lydia? Is that why she journeys there?"

Lydia, whose attention remained on the stage, shivered slightly, perhaps due to how his breath teased the hairs on her nape.

Southwaite looked at his sister. "I may, now that you have given me the idea. As to my sister's grand scheme, I am, as always, ignorant."

"Better to let me do it. I have some business nearby and will be there."

Lydia's crown rose a full inch as her body jolted with alarm.

"Besides," Penthurst continued. "If Lydia meets up with smugglers, she may decide she wants to be one after she sees Tarrington's lair."

"I regret to say she has already seen his lair. Isn't that so, Lydia?"

Her cool profile showed as she faced her brother. "You and I have known him and his family our whole lives. If I must repudiate everyone on the coast who has connections to smuggling, I must obliterate my past and present, I fear. As must you, dear brother, with more devastating results than I will ever know."

Whatever she alluded to, Southwaite retreated on the point. "What takes you to the coast, Penthurst?"

"I need to collect on a gambling debt that has been lagging."

"Hell of a thing when a gentleman's debt is not paid. I hope if the fellow puts you off again that you will let the rest of us know his name."

"I trust that honor will win out in this case."

"Unless he is not good for it. That happens all the time."

"This is a matter of property, not funds, so I am confident nothing was wagered that is unavailable."

"Doubly dishonorable, then. Are you listening to this, Lydia? You think I lecture too often on gambling, but wagering more than one should in the excitement of the moment often leads to uncomfortable situations like this. Now Penthurst needs to travel to remind this man of his obligations, in the hopes of sparing the fellow's reputation."

Lydia's head did not move an inch. Her dark tresses in their neat arrangement on her crown just stared at the man behind her.

"It is actually worse," Penthurst said, angling close so his mouth almost touched her cheek. "Having first wagered and lost, the wager was then doubled, and lost again."

"No!"

"Yes."

"Was this man a fool, or drunk?"

"Too confident, I'd say. Although the second time, I think—I am not sure—that it entered that desperate mind to cheat."

"No."

"It did not happen, as I said."

"Still, best you settle this soon, so the temptation does not overcome him next time around."

"That is my thinking on the matter."

"You will be doing him a favor. He will pay the wages of sin, and perhaps lose the taste for it entirely." He looked meaningfully at his sister.

"Or you can forgive the debt, and be known as a generous man." Her voice projected forward, not back, and was barely audible.

He leaned very close to her head. "I have not been asked to forgive the debt. Instead it is ignored, as if the reckoning need never happen. That does not encourage notions of generosity. One might even say it does not encourage behavior appropriate to a gentleman."

"Understandable," Southwaite said. "Of course, he *will* be a gentleman, Lydia. Some pique is allowed, however, along with strict adherence to the points of the wager in the circumstances. I hope you are learning something from this. The rules are no different for women. When women get in too deep, they too must pay up. Or else their male relatives must."

"I have never needed you to pay up for me," she said emphatically.

Southwaite sighed, like it was just a matter of time.

"I have reason to believe that your sister has never wagered that which she can't pay on her own. Isn't that true, Lydia?"

She glanced back at him. If looks could kill . . .

"Quite true," she said to her brother. "Your fortune is safe from me. Now, may I watch the play? I have half figured out what is going on, and I sat here in the hopes I would not have chatter buzzing into my ear like a bothersome bee."

That made him the noisy insect, he guessed. He rested his forearms on the back of her chair and spoke into her other ear. "If you have half figured out this farce, it is better than I can claim, Lydia. Enlighten me so that I can follow the script too."

Chapter 10

No one in her family knew the people of Crownhill as well as Lydia did. Even Southwaite did not enjoy the same intimacy. He had always been the future earl to them, while she had been little Lydia.

Her years here as a girl, her closeness to Sarah, her visits while she rode her horse to villages and farms—her familiarity with the land and people made her more welcomed in the humble abodes on their property than she ever felt in the drawing rooms of the county's best houses.

In treating her like one of their own, they covered her tracks sometimes. None of the servants really lied to her brother when he quizzed them about her activities, but they could possess very short memories. Now that she was a grown woman, a few would even deceive Aunt

Hortense on her behalf. More egalitarian than her own class, the servants thought it odd when she was treated like a child by chaperones, and were inclined to believe her doings, for good or ill, were her own business.

So it was that within a day of arriving at Crownhill, her plan for leaving had been put in place. Penthurst's stated intention to come to the coast to collect that debt had necessitated a more elaborate strategy than initially envisioned.

Did he seriously think to follow her here? Then what? He calls on her and Aunt Hortense? What could he say or do? *Your niece owes me her maidenhead, madame, so if you would kindly close the drawing room doors as you leave, we will get on with it.*

It had been an idle threat, to needle her into more worry. He did not like that she had assumed he would relieve her of the obligation, and had guessed his game. It had been a big mistake to throw that in his face.

He had implied that if she had asked for the debt to be forgiven, he might have agreed. Or he might have let her beg and plead, then refuse. A real gentleman of good character would have released her of the obligation by now without her requesting it. She already knew his character was not in truth what others thought, so she had no secure confidence in which way it would go when she did beg and plead, especially now after that conversation at the theater. It would kill her to apologize and petition for mercy now, but she supposed she had to try.

But not right away. It might shock Penthurst to know that she had larger worries than her stupid wagers with

him. Trilby came first. She needed to resolve matters
with this other scoundrel so the cloud of shame threatening to rain on her went away.

She would go to Buxton. She saw no way out of that.
Once there, however, she would not help him cheat.
She would convince him his plan was not worth the
risk. She would bring three thousand pounds with her,
to add weight to her arguments, and make him agree,
finally, to take the rest in yearly payments.

It meant diverting all of her winnings away from
her good causes, perhaps for years. Maybe forever. She
resented that deeply. One would think, considering the
two ways of spending the money, that fate would be
kinder.

After a hard ride along the coastal ridge road, and
a visit to the horse farm where her brother bred and
trained some of the finest racing horses in England,
she returned to the house on the day she arrived in time
to have an early dinner with her aunt.

They had not visited Crownhill for several months,
and her aunt had spent the afternoon collecting gossip
on anyone worth knowing up and down the coast. Tall,
buxom, and fearsome to those who did not know her
well, the physical and temperamental opposite of small,
soft Aunt Amelia, Hortense now treated Lydia to all she
had gleaned. Her expressive soliloquy communicated
her opinion of the potential scandal in each tidbit.

"Gone north until spring," her aunt said in a theatrical
tone of insinuation regarding the daughter of a respectable family several miles away. "Well, everyone knows

what that means. The chit got with child by that rake of a cousin of hers, is what. Poor thing. He'll go on preening his feathers while she is ruined. Utterly ruined."

Lydia nodded dully. She stared at the decanter of wine. The facets of the cut crystal seemed to swim. She used her handkerchief to pat her dewy brow.

"Are you unwell, Lydia?" Her aunt's eyes sharpened on that brow, then the rest of her.

"I am fine. A little warm, that is all."

"It is not warm here. It is quite cool. Come here, child, so I can check you."

Lydia rose and went over to her aunt, who pressed the back of her hand along her jaw.

"You do feel warm."

Lydia chose that moment to feel a bit dizzy too. "Perhaps I will go out and get some air."

"Heavens, no. The damp evening air will do you in if you have a fever."

"I do not think I have a—"

"And what would you know of it? I have seen many more fevers than you have, and I think it likely you do have one." She turned to the footman. "Call for her maid. Up to bed with you. I will send up instructions for your care."

"Perhaps a physician—"

"Quacks, all of them. I know more medicine than they do. If not for the interference of physicians, my dear Jonathan would still be with me. Now, up you go. Once you are abed, send that maid down so I can tell her exactly what to do."

Sarah appeared at the dining room door. She helped Lydia up the stairs. Once the door of her apartment closed, Sarah giggled. "I assume the brandy worked."

"Better than I expected. Whoever guessed it would make me flush and feel dizzy."

"You are not used to it, is all." Sarah pulled a valise out of a corner. "All packed for the morning. I would feel better if I were coming with you. Not right for you to travel alone."

"You do, whenever you come to visit your family here. You get on the coach all by yourself."

"That is different."

The only difference was society did not consider Sarah worthy of rules regarding the protection of her body and reputation. "You need to remain here taking care of the sick Lydia. Remember to have me starting to mend in the morning, then a bit better day by day. We do not want Hortense sending for my brother. Bring her regular reports, and promise to do everything she instructs. She fears catching maladies, so she will not insist on seeing me."

"I am sure that I can put her off long enough."

"I will travel by post chaise the whole way, and not stop, so I think I can finish this soon. Mr. Trilby will see the benefits of my proposal quickly."

Penthurst had a fondness for Crownhill, the county seat of the Earls of Southwaite. The grand house imposed itself on a bluff of a hill, backed by the sea. Salt sea air made upkeep a nuisance, but the inhabitants thought the bracing winds and tumultuous views worth it.

He did too. The wildness of the sea influenced the affairs of man on the coast. Society operated with slight differences. A bit less formality, even among the best families. Perhaps that was because when a bad storm blew inland, they all had to help each other, and niceties of station might get set aside for a day.

When a youth, he sometimes visited here during brief holidays from school. His own country manor sat far north, almost at the Scottish border, and too far away for short visits. Southwaite would invite him here instead. They rode along that coastal road, trying out his father's racehorses, risking their necks in contests of speed or practicing dangerous saddle tricks.

As he approached the house, he remembered the first time he came here after his own father died. Too young to be formally invested with the title, he still had become Penthurst, superior in precedence even to Southwaite's father. At school the manner of the tutors and fellow students changed immediately when that happened. Overnight he became more a title than a man, and he guessed at once that any friendship he had not already tested would never pass any test he created. Everyone wants something of dukes, even if it is only the social distinction of being friends.

Southwaite had spoken to him about that. First the father had, then the son who was not yet Southwaite. The earl sympathized, but cast it as the burden of duty. The son had mentioned it during one of those rides.

"Changes things, doesn't it?" He had said as they slowly walked their mounts back to the stables at the horse farm. "Of course, you were always going to be a duke, and that is rare, while you can't turn a corner at school without bumping into a future earl. But now that it has happened—do you mind, how it gives you authority you did not request?"

"The authority reminds me of that possessed by a tutor. Suddenly I am old before my time, seriously lacking in wit, and expected to forgo all fun."

"It could be worse. You could be a *royal* duke."

"I've heard nothing to indicate they feel obligated to behave well, so that would be better, not worse."

Southwaite had a toothsome grin then, before his face caught up with his mouth and formed something handsome. "The girls should like it, though. Hell, you can probably command them at will. Their mamas will line them up for you."

Would it have shocked Southwaite to learn then that the last duke of Penthurst had advised his son to dally not with those girls, but with the mamas in question? Less trouble that way.

"Well, I shan't defer to you, so I hope you do not grow too accustomed to it. You start putting on more than the normal number of airs, and I'll be done with you."

"What do you mean, the normal number?"

"You've always had some. Comes with the expectations, I suppose."

"I haven't!"

"You have. Last spring when you were here you even scolded Lydia."

"I did not scold her. I warned her that her governess was going to be angry that her shoes were covered in horse dung, and that it was dangerous to enter the corral with the stallions."

"She was in there with *me*, so the scold was for me too, I suppose. Don't deny it. But my point was who the hell are you to instruct my little sister? Yet no one said anything, did they? Because you were going to be a damned duke." Southwaite reached over and gave his arm a good-natured punch. "I'm used to that much. More of it, though, and I'll not be bowing to it, is all. You are not liking it now, but it could become a habit, having everyone grovel."

No one had said anything partly because they thought he was supposed to marry little Lydia of the dung-covered shoes. Southwaite did not know that Lydia herself had not taken that scold in stride. Oh, her eyes had grown wide and her face had lengthened to the point shy of crying, but as he turned away he had seen her stomp one shoe back into a pile of dung, deliberately, and stick out her tongue at him.

In a manner of speaking, she had done the same thing at the theater last Friday, hadn't she?

He pulled up his horse at the front of the house. Two grooms appeared at once, as if they waited for him. They led the horse away while he presented himself at the door.

The servant took his card away, then returned to escort him into the library. Lydia's aunt Hortense, formally Lady Sutterly, widow to Sir Jonathan Sutterly, waited for him.

Like a ship's figurehead, Lady Sutterly led with her bosom. Ample and broad in any style, it all but overwhelmed the current dresses. A discreet gauze covered the skin above her bodice, but that shelf of femininity announced the formidable personality in the head rising above it. Gray-haired and given to viewing the world through opera glasses attached to a long wand, "Aunt Hortense" appeared every inch a woman who did not suffer fools kindly.

"My dear duke!" Lady Sutterly performed a low curtsy of remarkable agility. "We are honored. Are you passing through the county? Are you in need of hospitality for the night?"

He had not intended that, but the offer opened all kinds of possibilities. "That is generous of you, if it will not inconvenience the household."

"They will manage perfectly, as my nephew's servants always do. The majority are in town with him, of course, but our comforts are met well enough." She sat, and told the footman to bring brandy. "Lydia will be so distressed that she cannot come down for dinner. I am sure you would have enjoyed her conversation more than you will ever be amused by mine."

"You are a most amiable hostess, and famous for spirited conversation, so I can have no fears about a dull dinner."

Lady Sutterly smiled a smug acknowledgment of the rightness of her reputation.

"However, why will Lady Lydia not join us?" he asked.

"She took ill yesterday. She is on the mend, but must remain abed, of course."

"Should not a physician be called?"

"To what end? To bleed her, or administer some tonic? She developed a small fever, but her maid reports that she is somewhat better today. I have seen such minor illnesses often in her. With several days of bed rest, all is well."

"Does her brother know of these illnesses?"

"They pass so quickly there is no reason to write to him. Such things are easy to misunderstand from a letter's description too. I would not want him to worry unduly, or to leave his wife to ride here. By the time he did, Lydia would be out riding herself, an instant reminder that he had wasted his time, if not his brotherly affection."

She spoke as though all of this were a regular thing—Lydia turning ill, then sleeping it off in bed, and Southwaite never informed. Perhaps she believed that if Southwaite knew, he would not allow the aunt and niece to journey here together, alone, and her frequent respites near the sea would end.

They chatted awhile, then he left to make arrangements for his horse. With Lydia quarantined in her apartment, the evening promised to be far less fun than he had planned. Instead of goading her into a sweat about her debt, he would be listening to Lady Sutterly confide the local gossip.

Crownhill's horse farm sat on distant property, across the main road. The manor house had stables too, however, and he assumed his mount had been brought there. Rather than send for his valise, he walked through the gardens and across the small field to the building.

Hay was being put down in the stalls. His horse appeared rubbed down and content to munch his dinner. Lifting the valise from where it had been set outside the stall, he turned to see an older groom laughing with a young woman with dark eyes and high, half-moon eyebrows. They sensed he watched and fell silent. The groom jerked his thumb at the woman. "Best get back to her."

Walking out, he remembered where he had seen that woman before. "That was Lady Lydia's maid, wasn't it?" he asked the groom.

The fellow set his attention on repairing some tacking strewn across his lap. "So she be, sir. My daughter Sarah does for the lady. Has for, oh, five or six years now."

"It is convenient that Lady Lydia visits here often, then. You are able to see your daughter frequently."

"Her mother and I are grateful for it."

"I am told Lady Lydia is quite a horsewoman."

The man's teeth glistened against his sun-browned skin. "Took to it as a child. As fine a rider as you will see. Better than most men, and I do not think I am favoring her in saying so. That's her horse in there, the white one. Not a mare either. Helios she calls him."

He strolled back into the stable and along the stalls until he found the white Helios. She had named him after the Greek god who dragged the sun on its path through the sky by his chariot. Helios had been bred to race, that was obvious, and was not a large horse. Still, he did not appear the sort of horse accustomed to quiet, sedate walks.

The horse appeared clean, relaxed, and neatly groomed. Rather too neatly. He looked much like Penthurst's own mount, and lacked the evidence of hours in the stall.

Still carrying his valise, he returned to the groom repairing the tackle. "Was Helios ridden today? I ask because he appears recently groomed."

The man kept his attention on the bridle he inspected. "Might a been."

"Yet I was told that Lady Lydia is ill."

"Could be he was exercised, sir, what with her being ill."

Could be. Mighta been. In his mind's eye he saw Sarah skipping back to the house, and to the apartment where Lady Sutterly assumed she cared for Lydia.

Some game was afoot here. Perhaps this was how Lydia escaped her aunt's supervision. She claimed illness, took to her chamber, then snuck out to ride where she wanted and could do as she pleased. Or, perhaps, the pending visit of a certain duke to whom she owed a debt had led her to use the ruse of illness to avoid him should he indeed visit.

He strode back to the house, and handed off the valise. After the servant showed him up to a chamber, he waited for the man to go. Then he toured the upper floors of the house. In the wing opposite the one where he had been put, he crossed paths with a scullery maid bearing a tray of food. Pausing, he watched her deliver it to a door where Sarah took it from her hands.

Once the way was clear, he in turn presented himself at that same door. Sarah's eyebrows arched with shock on seeing him.

"How does your lady fare?" he asked.

She licked her lips. "Well enough. Better, that is."

"But not so well as to come down to dinner."

"No. Not so well as that."

"And yet she has been riding today." He did not make it a question.

Her face reddened. "Riding? I don't— That is, I am sure that—" Flustered, she stepped through the doorway and closed it behind her. "I must go to her aunt and report now, Your Grace, if you will excuse me."

"Not yet. You should stay for a few minutes more."

"Why?"

He pushed the latch and threw open the door. "I would not want to cause a scandal by visiting her while she is alone."

Sarah lunged for the door's latch, but he had already crossed the threshold. He strode into the apartment, expecting to see Lydia reading or writing letters, fit and hail after a few hours of exercise.

Instead the sitting room was empty. Feeling half foolish, very suspicious, and mostly concerned, he turned to the door that must lead to her bedchamber. Sarah darted ahead and threw her body against the door. "This is very irregular, sir. I cannot allow my lady's privacy and modesty to be intruded upon, even by such as you."

"You do that very well, Sarah. You are a credit to your lady."

"Thank you, sir."

"I will pay my respects and offer my wishes for her speedy recovery, and be gone."

Sarah pressed herself against the door harder. "I— That is, she is sleeping."

"Sleeping so soundly that you could leave her and go visit your father, you mean? If you did that, I do not believe she is very sick at all. Now, you will step aside, or I will move you."

Her mouth gaped, then grimaced. With a sick expression, she moved away from the door.

He entered a bedchamber full of light from large windows facing the sea. Awash in blues and greens and white, it appeared a chamber that might be found underwater. He noticed a few details in his quick appraisal of the space—the tray of uneaten food on a table, the nightdress folded over a chair. Drapes the hue of a robin's egg surrounded the bed.

He did not have to look to know Lydia did not recline within that blue bower. Her absence had been palpable as soon as he entered. He had even sensed it outside the apartment.

Sarah stood silently, head bowed, fingers interlaced. "Where is she?"

Sarah did not move or speak.

"I do not want to cause trouble for you. If she will return shortly, tell me. If a bigger game is at work, you must let me know. Whatever has happened, you are complicit and her brother will not be rational or quick to forgive if something happens to her. Even an accident will result in blame."

She balled her hands together and raised them to her mouth. A long sigh made her body sag. "She will not be back shortly, I am afraid. Not for several days."

"Yet her horse is back."

"She rode him, that is true. With one of the grooms, who brought the horse back. She rode to Diehl this morning."

He debated whether to question her further. Lydia must have arranged a rendezvous in Diehl. A friend could have met her there. Or a lover. The latter possibility snaked into his thoughts, bringing more disappointment than he would have expected. Because if she had assignations with a lover, she had lied about that wager, boldly so.

No, that was not the source of the thickness in his chest. The very notion of a lover caused it. That and the possible evidence that Lydia had a full, unknown life that occupied her, and placed him even further on the edges of her world.

"Is she meeting a friend in Diehl?" he asked.

"Friend?" Sarah puzzled the word. Her eyes widened in shock. "Oh! *No*. My lady is not—this is not what you must think. I'll not have anyone suggest such a thing. She went there to hire a post chaise, that is all."

"Where is she going?"

Sarah shook her head. "North. I cannot tell you more. What little I know was spoken in confidence, and I would be a poor servant if I revealed that which she tells me."

"Has she done this before? Played ill while she snuck away for days?"

"Not for days. It may have happened every now and then of a day, though. When her aunt bores her badly, or she just wants to ride up the coast for no purpose in particular."

He gazed out the window while weighing it all. Clouds rolled on the horizon, and the thin strip of visible sea out there appeared more gray than blue.

He did not like this. Deep inside, his instincts said Lydia headed toward trouble. That she had not dared such a thing before only increased the nagging worry.

He could probably browbeat what else Sarah knew out of her, but he guessed that if Lydia schemed at anything significant with this journey, she had kept most of it even from her lady's maid. However, there might be another way to reassure himself that she was not headed for some disaster.

"Your discretion is admirable," he said while he walked to the door. "It would be best if you carried on as your lady instructed. We will trust that she indeed returns in a few days, as she intends."

He made his way back to the stables. Sarah's father no longer sat in the sun, but the lads putting down clean hay still worked the stalls. He lounged against the entrance to one of them, watching. The young men worked harder, speeding their actions more with each passing second. Finally one of them stopped and wiped his brow.

"Can we be of service, Your Grace?"

"Perhaps. I may need my horse prepared soon."

"We can do it straight away if you want."

"Whether I want depends on whether either of you escorted Lady Lydia to Diehl this morning."

The other young man froze with an armful of hay. Then he tossed it down and began spreading it with his pitchfork. "If the earl's sister says she needs an escort, we escort. We don't ask why or wherefore either."

"Of course not. However, you also do not turn blind or deaf. I am curious whether you guessed where she intended to go from there."

The two exchanged sharp glances.

"May have," the first one said. "Not for certain, though."

"I must insist you tell me, certain or not."

They hesitated long enough for him to wonder if loyalty to Lydia would win out.

"Andrew here rode with her, and brought Helios back," the first one said. "Tell him, Andrew. He is the earl's friend, and a duke himself, and none can blame you for answering such as him."

Andrew turned red while he continued to work his fork. "I carried in her valise and heard her talking to the coaching inn fellow about getting to Buxton. Planned to take the waters, she said."

"Did you not think that a long way for her to go? She could take the waters nearby in Royal Tunbridge Wells."

"Not for me to think anything, Your Grace. She would not like that any more than you would, I expect."

From their expressions of veiled relief, he knew that they did think something, however. Both of them thought Lydia's current adventure extraordinary, and worrisome.

"I think that I will want my horse prepared after all. Right away." With that he returned to the house, to make his excuses to Lady Sutterly regarding his sudden change in plans.

Chapter 11

"If we do not concentrate, it will take us days to perfect this," Lydia said.

"You keep distracting me with your arguments. I will perform as well as necessary, I assure you." Trilby spoke with undue confidence while he dealt out the cards again.

The last few hours had proven several things to Lydia. The first was that convincing Mr. Trilby to abandon his current plan would take better persuasion than she had thus far mustered. He had shown no interest in her carefully articulated rationales regarding how he should take what she had for him now, and they would set up a schedule whereby she paid the rest.

The second thing in evidence was that Algernon Trilby was no Peter Lippincott. Despite his skill at sleight-of-hand tricks, he knew almost nothing about being a sharper. Which meant she had to instruct him, without sounding like an experienced one herself. At the same time, she needed him to conclude that this partnership was not a good idea.

"I do not mean to argue," she said, trying a new tack. "I only feel that you are trying to hasten matters with this plan, when it is not in your character to do something so dishonest. I merely remind you that there is an alternative."

"The alternative that you propose would take forever. Now, pick a card." He pointed to the fan of them on the table between them.

Nearby, four matrons from Newcastle played whist. At this time of year Buxton was not a busy spa town, and even the patrons who came were not the sort one would meet in Bath, or even Royal Tunbridge Wells. These four women were the wealthy wives of new industrialists from the sounds of them.

This card room in the Crescent was available for guests who took rooms there. Since Lydia had done so, under the name Mrs. Howell, she had a somewhat public place in which to meet Mr. Trilby. He had taken a room in one of Buxton's guesthouses.

She chose a card. Trilby made a stack of the rest, then split it and offered the top center card as a place to perch her choice. As soon as she did, he again turned clumsy.

One of the women laughed at her companion's conversation. Trilby's face reddened. He kept glancing at the whist table.

"If you fear they know what we are doing, I assure you they do not," Lydia whispered.

"It isn't that, Lady Lydia."

Of course it was. "Mr. Trilby, you can only do this if you display supreme confidence. If you appear at all guilty or nervous, everyone will be suspicious. You must practice on your demeanor even more than your handling of the cards. And I remind you not to address me as anything other than Mrs. Howell."

He threw down the cards and folded his arms. He stared at the table. "I tire of both the game and your criticisms."

"It pains me to criticize, sir. However, it is necessary if you think to execute your plan. You were not born for such as this, as I said. I urge you to take the longer view of your expectations, so we can both leave this town with our self-respect and honor intact."

He toyed with the cards, watching his fingers thoughtfully. "You are right. My goal should not be immediate reimbursement, but self-respect and honor. I have been thinking about that since we met in the park, and realized that I erred in demanding this scurrilous choice when far better ones exist."

"I knew if you gave it serious thought, you would see the risks of this scheme were too great."

"Indeed they are, and quite unnecessary. I was a fool not to address the matter differently."

"I trusted you would see things differently. I even brought the sum I have on hand already with me, so I can give it to you forthwith."

He looked at the whist table. Two of the women there looked back. "Not here, surely."

"Of course not, but while we are in Buxton."

"Tomorrow, then. Let us meet outside, on the path behind St. Anne's well. Shall we say at ten o'clock?" He began to stand.

"Don't you want to discuss the rest of it? The future payments? Your turning the manuscript over to me? I would like to see it before I hand you such a large amount."

He made a bow, to take his leave. "I am sure we will contrive to make it fair, Lady Lydia." He took her hand and kissed it. That raised some eyebrows at the whist table. "I will explain my new thinking on the matter tomorrow. I anticipate all will work out to our mutual advantage."

Even great investment cannot make a town fashionable. Penthurst considered that as he rode through Buxton. Famed as a market town, it had recently received the patronage of the Duke of Devonshire, who, in commissioning the Crescent and a few other improvements, had tried to make it another Bath. Only it was not by the sea, but high in the foothills of the Peaks, far from London, and no Mr. Nash had endeavored to provide it with the social graces that marked Bath. Thus it was that anyone who was anyone had visited Bath, but most of those anyones had never taken the waters at Buxton.

He stopped in front of the Crescent, so imitative of

the one in Bath as to be embarrassing. Unlike most of those other anyones, he knew this town fairly well. His title's county seat lay west of here. In chasing Lydia, he had almost returned home.

Within a half hour he had procured a chamber in the Crescent, had his horse seen to, drunk some coffee in the card room, and looked in on the grand salon. Deciding sleep could wait, he left the building to see what he could learn about the whereabouts of Lady Lydia.

He doubted she had used her real name, no matter what the goal of this adventure. While he paused outside to pull on his gloves, he realized that the most likely place for her to stay was the same likely place he had chosen. He considered how to ask after her without sounding like a libertine prowling after some woman who had caught his eye.

While he picked among the various ruses that came to mind, he noticed a carriage slowing across the way, near the wells. A man hopped out and walked around the tower that backed the wells. He appeared familiar. Was that Trilby?

He walked up the lane fifty feet to get a better view. The man from the carriage strode up a little rise toward a park area with paths. A woman waited for him there. One with pale skin, and dark soulful eyes.

"You are punctual, unlike most women. I am glad to see it," Trilby said as he approached. "That speaks well of you."

Lydia wanted to respond archly. She hardly needed Mr. Trilby's approval of her character. She swallowed the impulse, so that they might finally be done with this.

She patted her reticule, the largest one she owned. Even with her winnings converted to the largest banknotes she could get, it bulged. "I trust that you brought the manuscript, so I can at least see it is whole. I have twenty-five hundred here. I will manage to bring another five hundred by year's end. Then five hundred a year hence, until all is settled."

Trilby eyed the reticule. He removed his hat and raked his pale hair back with his fingers. He looked toward the wells. "I think not."

Her heart sank. Not again. "Sir, your inconstancy is such that we will never make an agreement. I refuse to have this continue in such ambiguous a way. You cannot possibly hope to gain more than you first mentioned."

"I have rethought it all since we last met in London, and concluded that I should recognize this opportunity for what it is."

This did not sound good, Lydia thought. No, this did not sound good at all.

He turned and smiled. "Lady Lydia, I do not want what is in that reticule. I should like instead to improve my station in the world. What good is thousands if I am still the mere cousin of a man whose sister married a baronet? How much better to be a man who is married to the sister of an earl?"

His smile turned too familiar. His eyes became

pointedly focused. Alarm began freezing her before she had it all parsed out, but she picked through it again because his last sentence had been too bizarre.

"You cannot be serious."

"It is the kind of marriage made all the time. One that is mutually beneficial. I am hardly going to release to the public a scandalous journal that impugns my own wife's reputation, and through her mine too. I thought you would embrace the brilliance of it, since it ensures my discretion as money never could."

This was horrible, not brilliant.

She could barely breathe. Her mind grasped for reasons this would never do. "You will find yourself far poorer this way."

"Perhaps monetarily, but rich in other ways that any man of my station values highly."

"My brother will never approve."

"You are of age and require no guardian's permission. However, to ensure he does not interfere, I propose a jaunt up to Scotland forthwith, where bans will not delay matters. We will depart at once."

She looked at the carriage. He hardly needed one for this meeting. By "at once," did he mean right now?

He had left her yesterday with this plan well hatched. Perhaps this had been his intention even when they met in the park. The cheating partnership had been a ruse to get her to Buxton, and more than halfway to Scotland.

She had been a fool to underestimate him. She had done so, however. Badly. Yet nothing about him suggested he could be this sly.

She stepped back. "You are too impatient. Let us return to London and have a proper wedding. It would be cruel to my family if I eloped."

He moved closer. He took her hand in his and raised it to his lips. She watched, aghast. It felt as if time had slowed.

"My dear Lydia—you do not mind the familiarity, do you? Since we will soon be wed, it is not inappropriate— You are a clever woman, that is certain. However, please do not assume I am a dolt who cannot see through your schemes. If we return to London, you will find ways to put me off on this as you did with the money. No, the border it will be."

He stepped back. She tried to pull her hand free without success. Trilby's smile became a thin, firm line of annoyance. He took her arm and her stupid slippers slid right over the moist grass, refusing to grip the ground while he pulled her toward the carriage.

Dear heavens, he really intended to go right now! Once in Scotland, she would have a simple choice. Marriage to Algernon Trilby, or total ruin.

She would be damned before she married this man, or even rode in that carriage with him for one mile.

Swinging her stuffed reticule at his head and arm, she screamed for help. Trilby proved stronger than his appearance would suggest, however, and in a moment she would be dragged into the carriage.

Through the blur of her vision she saw people moving toward them. Two women and a man had been summoned by her cries. Then a dark presence burst through them and surrounded her and suddenly Trilby's hold on her vanished. She fell to the ground on her rump while confusion and movement and grunts swirled above her.

Suddenly all went silent. Eerily so. She blinked hard and looked at the carriage. For some reason, Trilby's head lulled up near the top of the carriage door with his chin deep in his collar. His body hung like a rag doll. In front of him, holding him up there by a grip on the front of his coat, stood a tall, dark-haired man.

"You have until nightfall to choose your weapon," a biting, low voice ordered. "We meet on the field of honor tomorrow morning, or you will be known as the coward you are."

Trilby's eyes bulged in shock. Then he slumped to the ground as the hands released him.

Slowly the world had been righting itself. She felt the damp beneath her rump, and saw the gazes of the women and man. Her reticule had split, and the edges of some banknotes peeked out. She tucked them back in and clutched the reticule so the money would not pour out and fly away.

That dark presence hovered above her. She looked at the boots mere inches from her hip. Then up long legs. Up, up farther, her stomach sickening more with each inch. She knew who it was. She realized she recognized the voice. She had never heard it speak like that, but—

She took a deep breath and tilted her head back. A handsome, severe face looked down at her. The Duke of Penthurst had come to her rescue, and did not look one bit happy about it.

He bent down, lifted her, and set her on her feet. He took her arm and pushed her toward the street and the Crescent, not showing much more patience than Trilby had.

"I should thank you, but—"

"Not another word until we have privacy, Lydia. Not one. If you speak, I will turn you over my knee right here and give those people even more to write home about tonight."

There was one chair in his chamber at the Crescent. Lydia sat in it primly, her dress shedding grass onto the carpet.

He washed his hands and assessed the minor damage from the fisticuffs with Trilby. He had landed more blows than necessary. Lydia's scream had turned his mind black and his blood hot, and Trilby got the worst of it.

She had wisely obeyed, and not spoken. Instead she had retreated behind her sphinx mask. He was not in the mood for that right now.

"Are you hurt?" he asked while he put his coat back on.

She subtly flexed her body this way and that, checking. "My arm will be sore, perhaps. And my hand is bruised."

He took it in his own. Trilby's grip had left its mark on the back. "Are you going to tell me what happened out there?"

"You bid me not speak. I have decided I prefer not to anyway." She looked up. "You are not really going to fight him, are you?"

"Of course I am. No gentleman can allow such behavior toward a lady to stand. Whatever his reasons for being here, whatever your reasons for meeting him, he crossed a line that must not be crossed."

He waited for her to answer the unavoidable questions. *What was he doing here? Why did you meet him here?*

"I should not be here," she said.

"I should say not."

"I mean here, in this chair, in your— I have my own chamber and should go there."

"Lydia, you have just been the center of a spectacle that will be reported far and wide. You were almost abducted. The scandal waiting to drown you cannot be avoided. Being here with me is the least of our worries."

She tried her impassive face, but could not manage it. Instead she came close to weeping. She stood, but wobbled a little. "I must go all the same."

Gently, he pressed her shoulders so she sat again. The shock of the episode outside was taking its toll. He had seen that before, how a body might not react until well after the danger passes. "You will sit awhile longer."

She obeyed, fretfully. He had much to say to her, and questions she must answer, but now was not the time.

He took a flask out of his valise and poured an inch of brandy in a glass. He handed it to her. "Drink this."

She pushed it away. "I couldn't."

"Are you saying you have never drunk spirits before? Why do I doubt that?"

She reached for the glass. "I might manage just a sip."

She managed it very well. She closed her eyes afterward. He imagined the amber-hued liquid sliding down her throat, warming all it touched, calming her but also bringing a shocked alertness to her physicality. A little could center a mind and improve thoughts. From her expression it appeared to be doing that for her.

When she opened her eyes again, she appeared more herself. "I have created a terrible muddle, haven't I?"

He wondered if she understood just how big a muddle it would prove to be. "Better a muddle than being that man's victim. Although one might say that entertaining a friendship with him began the muddle."

"You would make a good vicar. You scold so well."

"I am not scolding. When I do, you will know it."

She stood again. "I will go before you are tempted to show me."

He did not stop her this time. "We will talk in a few hours, Lydia. After you have recovered. If I am going to duel with a man, I would like to know the reason."

She lay on her bed and tried to sort out just how big a disaster the day had been. Had there been a way to stop Trilby short of screaming for help? Could she have persuaded him to give up his shocking idea of marriage? What if she had traveled to Scotland with

him? Along the way, would better sense have pre-
vailed?

She doubted it. His plan's boldness stunned her, but
she could not deny its brilliance too. Why not parlay
his hold on her to demand marriage? He could dine with
dukes and better himself in a snap. If her income did
not match his monetary ambitions, no doubt he could
insinuate himself into investments and other financial
plans, making use of what income she did have.

She could hit herself for not seeing the danger of
him lighting on the possibilities. She had spent so long
unmarried, and uninterested in marriage, and spurious
of any suitors, that she had lost sight of the fact that
she would be a good catch, and to men far better born
than Trilby.

His behavior had been unforgivable. Brutish. That
did not speak well for the happiness of any woman he
did marry. All the same, she could not allow Penthurst
to duel with him. She had only recently recovered from
the last time Penthurst killed a man, and this time it
would be all her fault.

A knock on her door interrupted her racing thoughts.
She opened it to find a serving girl, who said his lord-
ship requested she would join him in the card room.

She dusted the residual grass off her skirt and put on
dry shoes. She gave her reflection a passing glance in
the looking glass. All she saw were dark eyes peering
back at her, and dark hair piled a bit haphazardly atop
her crown. She poked a few errant strands back into
place, then made her way down.

The chamber was full of the Crescent's visitors. Of course it was. Why take the waters when great theater unfolded in one's hotel? Conversation broke fitfully when she appeared. No one stared, but everyone glanced at her.

Penthurst sat in a small armchair against one wall, his long form casually lounging with one booted leg extended. He appeared to be reading something. When he noticed her, he stood, and greeted her formally.

She sat in the chair facing his, feeling conspicuous. "We could have met in the garden. Or taken a turn through the town."

"That would never do. You will have to brave this out, and you may as well start now." He resumed his comfortable position, and again perused the paper he held. "You should see this."

She took it. Trilby had written.

My Lord Duke,

There will be no choice of weapons, or visit from a second. There will be no duel. You have grievously misunderstood the day's events. I will endeavor to explain.

The lady is my fiancée. She agreed to marriage and met me here to effect an elopement to Scotland. When we met this morning for that purpose, she claimed second thoughts on the matter. This despite the money I have laid out in preparation of these nuptials, including letting a house in London,

purchasing a wardrobe appropriate to my new sta-
tion, and hiring the carriage that brought me to Bux-
ton and would in turn bring us both to Scotland, then
back to town.

As for my behavior as I reacted to this unexpected
lack of constancy on her part, I have no excuse other
than the shock of a man anticipating lifelong happi-
ness but instead facing the death of his most cherished
dream.

I will apologize to her if you would be good enough
to arrange a brief meeting. I trust she will understand
that, under the circumstances, I will have no choice
except to bring a breach of contract action against
her, but that is for a later day.

Your servant,
Algernon Trilby

She folded the letter and set it on the table between
them. "I never agreed to marry this man."

"I find it odd that he has an explanation for everything, while you have one for nothing."

"I *swear* that I never—"

"You do not have to swear for my benefit. I am neither judge nor jury."

She did have to swear, however. She did not want
him thinking she had been so stupid as to agree to
marriage with Trilby, then so callous as to throw him
over at the last minute. "I have had no relationship with

him that could even be misinterpreted as one that might lead to marriage. He is not my fiancé."

He nodded. "And we know he is not your lover. After all, your innocence belongs to me."

She could not believe he made reference to that in the Crescent's card room. Ever so calmly too.

"Yet he is here, and so are you." He tapped the letter. "Will you be satisfied with an apology? I will insist on the duel if you prefer. He will refuse, but the world will know him as a coward. That means more to names more illustrious than his, unfortunately. I believe he is willing to live with it."

"It is better than being dead, isn't it?"

He acknowledged as much with a tip of his head. "Are you going to tell me what brought you to Buxton?"

She pictured his reaction if she did. She would have to explain about the blackmail, and the novel she had written . . .

"I will not. I will tell you this, however. I have done nothing wrong. Nothing at all. I may have been foolish and blind, but I never believed he would claim such a lie as a betrothal between us. He has no cause to do so, and is taking advantage of the coincidence of our both being in Buxton at the same time." She almost stumbled on the tiny untruth about it being a coincidence.

"Perhaps he learned you were coming here, and followed you."

She said nothing, and prayed that supposition would be accepted.

"Your reticule this morning looked very plump, Lydia." He leaned toward her over the table and captured her gaze with his. "Did you come to Buxton to gamble? Did you journey so far from home so your brother would not hear of it?"

Whoever thought that her dreaded gambling would save her like this? Several clever retorts lined up in her head, all of them admiring his remarkable powers of perception. She did not have the heart to speak any of them. He had saved her from an impossible situation, and deserved better.

"I will only say what I have already said. I have done nothing wrong."

"Not yet, at least." He stood, and offered his hand. "Let us partake of the midday meal they offer here. Then I will write to Trilby, and arrange his apology."

She permitted his escort out of the card room. As they crossed the threshold, chairs scraped the floor as the other guests decided to dine too.

"You have quizzed me, Penthurst. Now permit me one question. What are you doing here?"

He kept her palm poised atop his hand, as if they led a formal party down to dinner. Indeed a long line had formed behind them. "I followed you. First to Crownhill, then here. You knew I would. I all but promised it." He looked around the appointments of the Crescent as they paraded down the stairs. "You chose well for us. Devonshire ensured this was a very elegant place. It would have been more than comfortable, and, but for the unfortunate events of the morning, it would have been perfectly discreet too."

Not for the first time today, she sensed that she had missed half of a conversation. "For us? Discreet?"

"For when I collected on your debt, Lydia. That is the real reason you led me all the way here, isn't it?"

That quip did not make for an enjoyable meal. Penthurst ensured she ate, although her appetite had left her. She sat across from him again, feeling the eyes of the guests on them both, hearing a few whispers that included his name.

She cleared her throat. "About that debt . . ."

"Debts. Plural. Remember?"

"I would be a strange woman if I forgot. However, you did say that you might consider forgiving them if I requested it."

"I spoke in the past tense. I might *have* considered forgiving them if you *had* requested it."

"I thought you would find that lacking in character on my part—to engage in such a wager only to beg off if I lost."

"I would find it lacking in honesty, that is true."

"Yet as a gentleman, you could not be thinking of actually—of going through with it."

"Why not?"

"Because there are rules about such things. About innocents and—such things."

"I am not sure there are any rules that cover our situation. Nor have you shown much inclination for following rules. I can't see why I should be bound by them if you are not."

"You are going to make me beg, aren't you? Humble myself. Fall to my knees and plead."

"That sounds very appealing."

"You are a scoundrel to demand that of me before you let me out of the debt."

"Oh, are we still talking about forgiving the debt?"

"Of course. Why else would I beg and plead?"

A vague, slow smile formed. "You *are* an innocent, aren't you?"

"Of course."

"I look forward to enlightening you."

"You are teasing me, and it is not amusing."

"A week ago I was teasing. Even days ago. However, I would say that your making good on that debt has become inevitable now."

"Only if you are a scoundrel."

"It will not be I who forces the issue, Lydia." He made a vague gesture to the chamber's occupants. "They have not figured out who you are yet. It is only a matter of time, however. Pretend you are one of your aunts, and a fellow gossip calls with a delicious story about a certain duke, a parvenu, a lady, and fisticuffs on the streets of Buxton. See in your mind what they all have seen, and ask the questions they are asking."

She tried to stand outside of it all, and indeed see it thus. Everyone would learn she had traveled here alone, she had to admit. They might learn she stayed at the Crescent as Mrs. Howell. They would assume she had come here to have an assignation with either Trilby or Penthurst. They would conclude the gentlemen had fought over some notion both had of rights to her. They would have heard of Penthurst's challenge, and of this time she now spent with him. Word would spread that he and she had taken chambers in the same hotel.

As she viewed the events this way and that, and itemized the likely gossip that would spread, her heart beat harder and harder. With each thump a word loomed larger in her mind's eye. Scandal.

She stared at Penthurst. He looked back, not unkindly, but with a resigned expression that indicated he had already worked out what she was just beginning to realize.

From beneath lowered lids she glanced to her right, and to the diners who had followed her from the card room. Did she imagine that all of them kept one eye on her and the duke? The low buzz of conversations roamed the chamber. *Penthurst. Yes, that is he. The woman? A lady. Do you recognize her? I can't place her, but the men addressed her as Lady Lydia . . .*

"What do I do?" she whispered desperately.

"The choices are limited."

"It isn't fair. I did nothing wrong."

"Will the reason for this journey vindicate you? Can you offer a plausible excuse that can be the foundation of a rebuttal? If so, you might try that."

The true reason would hardly save her. Rather the opposite.

"I gather the answer is no," he said dryly.

"I cannot bear that I will bring this upon my brother and Emma. I could survive it myself, if it were only me."

"No, you could not. Trust me on that. Well, the solution is clear, I think you will agree."

Nothing was clear. The more she thought of the storm forming on the horizon, the foggier her thoughts became. Perhaps as a duke he thought he could simply decree she be spared?

"My name is linked to yours in this. Assumptions will be made," he said, watching her closely. "We will marry forthwith."

That shocked her head clear. "But I do not want to marry you."

"That is unfortunate. Yet marry you will, Lydia. I'll be damned if I will be known as a man who has an affair with the unmarried sister of his best friend, and does not do the honorable thing."

Chapter 12

She looked like she faced a hangman's noose. Eyes wide. Lips slightly parted. Skin drained of color.

Shock. Shock and horror.

If he were not so insulted, he would find it amusing.

He poured some wine and pushed it toward her. "Drink some, and look adoringly at me instead of like a woman bereft of hope. Give them a show, Lydia. It will help the story."

She gulped some wine. She found some composure behind her sphinx mask. Hell, but he hated when she did that. "What story?"

"You and I developed a tendre, and decided to elope. We came here separately; to then travel together to Scotland. Trilby, a spurned suitor, followed you and tried to interfere. Maddened by the thought of losing you forever—"

"There is no need to be melodramatic."

"*Of losing you forever,* he attempted that abduction this morning, which I stopped. After ensuring you were recovered, in the morning we continued on our planned journey and wed as soon as we crossed the border."

"It sounds almost plausible."

"It is very plausible, and covers all the public facts. I should be writing novels, the plot is so neat."

"I do not suppose you could rewrite it just a bit? The marriage part. I would prefer the story unfold differently. Perhaps, after the shock of almost being abducted, I found my nerves so unhealthy that I decided it would be unfair of me to allow you to marry such a sickly woman."

"I hope you are not saying that you find the idea of marriage to me so revolting that you would prefer to live your life pretending to be an invalid." He did not miss how she had made herself very noble with this change, while leaving him the scoundrel who seduced his friend's sister.

"Maybe I would not have to pretend forever. Perhaps I could go to the Alps for a year and regain my health. That might work, don't you think?"

She glowed with renewed hope. He had never thought to find himself sacrificed in a marriage of obligation to save a woman from ruin, least of all to Southwaite's sister. However, he had definitely never expected, should that happen by some perverse twist of fate, to have the woman in question so resistant.

"You do understand that I am speaking of a legal marriage, don't you?" he asked. "You would be a duchess."

"Of course I understand. A legal, unbreakable bond. As for being a duchess—everyone will know who I am. Everyone. I will be watched by the world. Even what I have known thus far will look like reckless freedom in comparison. And, let us be honest, you do not want this either. We will have one of those dreadful marriages of duty and strained patience with each other. Of brief couplings in dark beds and ritualistic family life. If you would be content with that, you would have married years ago. You deserve better. You really do."

She spoke earnestly. And honestly. Perhaps more honestly than she ever had with him, he guessed. Her insight at the end impressed him. In a few sentences, he came to know her much better.

He wondered if there might be another way out of this for her. He could not think of one.

"It is good of you to worry about my contentment, Lydia, but do not concern yourself. I was born for duty, and you have become a part of that now. Pretend I proposed, and you accepted, and leave it at that."

The sphinx gazed at him for a solid minute before speaking. "I would have never agreed. Not ever. I am more sure of that than anything in my life. You murdered a man who was your friend, and mine too. My brother may have forgiven you, but I have not." She stood. "I am suddenly much affected by the day's events. I will retire and rest now, to prepare for our meeting with Mr. Trilby."

L ydia allowed the hotel's maid to redress her hair, then sent the woman away. She washed herself, and the water, although warm, felt like a shock. A chill had entered her in the card room. Almost at once the cloud had tried to engulf her again.

The only way to put that year in the past was to leave it alone. Yet he had stirred it all up again, with his talk of marriage. Now the old emotions plucked at her heart, and poked at her composure. She washed and washed, because once she stopped there would be nothing to do.

A light knock on her door startled her. She opened it a crack, expecting to see the maid. Instead Penthurst stood there.

He did not ask to enter. Instead he gripped the door's edge and simply moved it back and stepped inside. He did not move from that spot, but she backed away as if he did.

"We did not finish our conversation, and I do not think it can be put off to your liking," he said.

His audacity in coming here astonished her. A welcomed warmth spilled through her as her mind snapped alert to the danger and assumptions attached to his presence in her chamber.

"I am quite done with it. I promise you that you will not like the rest if you demand it."

"I do demand it, however. You hold that duel against

me, and judge me harshly, you have made clear twice now. Almost two years have passed, however. Others have reconsidered their judgments, and under the circumstances, it is time to put your anger aside."

"The circumstances require it, or do you?" She heard her voice rising. Felt her heart bursting. "You killed him. Over some stupid, little point of honor that probably could have been ignored." Her eyes stung, but she refused to wipe them, refused to admit her anger had led to tears. "So I cannot pretend you proposed and I accepted. I would have never, ever, listened to talk of marriage with you, even if somehow I could set aside that I have never liked you, that your manner toward me has always been superior and proud and you have always spoken to me as if I am a child to be instructed. That my choice should be ruin or you is a cruel joke."

His expression hardened under the onslaught of her fury. "I am, as always when that day is discussed, at a disadvantage, Lydia. There is much I could tell you, but little you would want to hear. I am not inclined to explain myself either, for what is done is done. I will say this much, and hope you hear it. First, I never intended to kill him. Second, it was not over a small, stupid point of honor. And, third, for all that we knew him so well and so long, we did not know him at all."

"Will you now try to destroy his memory too?"

"You can remember Lakewood as you choose, but I will not allow you to sacrifice your life and future out of misplaced loyalty to him. You may have never

entertained a proposal from me in the normal course
of events, but you will have to accept the one I make
now."

"I do not."

He came over and looked down at her. She almost
jumped out of her skin. "Let me be as blunt as you,
Lydia. You do not have a choice. Do I have to exact payment for that debt, in order for you to see the rightness
of it? Once I have seduced you, there can be no other
honorable conclusion of the affair except marriage."

"You wouldn't dare."

"Wouldn't I?" He strode to the door. "We will meet
Trilby at five this afternoon. And we will set off for
Scotland in the morning."

Panic swelled. Lydia stared at the door after the duke
left, and wondered if she should try to move a
heavy chair against it.

Forcing some composure, she took a long look at
her situation. Penthurst spoke of scandal as inevitable,
but with a little fancy dancing, could she avoid it, and
also this marriage of obligation he proposed?

She feared that nothing less than the full truth would
stand against the image of Trilby trying to force her
into that carriage. Since the full truth meant explaining
that stupid novel, and the blackmail, and her agreeing
to meet Trilby in order to cheat Buxton visitors at cards,
she did not think even the truth would put her in a better place.

This was all Penthurst's fault. If he had not followed her here . . . Lydia sighed. If he had not followed her here, she would have been at Trilby's mercy once she was in that carriage. Who knew what he might have done to ensure she exchanged vows in Scotland?

Nor could she ignore the fact that Penthurst had only followed her because she had gone to his house and forced his hand on that wager.

She really wanted to hold someone else responsible for her impossible situation, but no matter how she viewed it, the finger of blame pointed right back at her. Even that novel that had started it all—what had she been thinking?

Try as she might, she could not put herself back into her state of mind during those months when she wrote it. Between now and then there existed a murky period that swallowed memories and time. She thought that a good part of her had taken refuge in a walking sleep, because being truly alive brought too much pain.

And now she was faced with marriage to the man who had killed all of her dreams.

She could not stop thinking she had dared the devil in demanding the wager go through, and now the darkest powers laughed at her.

Hardly becalmed, and not at all at peace, she turned her attention to horrible Mr. Trilby, who still possessed that damned manuscript of hers. Perhaps she could use his outrageous behavior to demand a final agreement this afternoon, so he did not complicate her life even more than he had thus far.

* * *

Algernon Trilby had the brass to appear aggrieved
when they met him at five o'clock that afternoon
near the wells. Lydia wanted to hit him, but she instead
greeted him formally. Penthurst did not. In fact, the
duke managed a cut direct while standing right in front
of the man.

Nothing else was said until Trilby spoke. "I apologize sincerely for my behavior this morning. It was
inexcusable."

"By *inexcusable*, do you admit that you had no cause
to believe I would journey with you to Scotland, or to
anywhere else? I cannot allow your claims of an
engagement to stand, let alone be aired in court," Lydia
said. "If your apology does not include that admission,
I do not accept it and you can have that duel or stand
down as a coward."

Trilby's expression twisted and twitched. He
appeared a man taking the worst-tasting tonic against
his will. "Since you now demand it, I will add that I
may have misunderstood your intentions."

"And there was no engagement. Say it outright, sir,
lest you later claim you never said it at all."

Trilby glared at her, then at the duke who would
serve as the best witness in the world. "I declare without qualification there was no engagement," he said
between clenched teeth.

"Then I think we are done here," Penthurst said.

"If you will indulge me, I would like to speak to Mr. Trilby alone for two minutes. No longer, I assure you."

Penthurst eyed her with curiosity, but shrugged and stepped aside. Lydia walked to Mr. Trilby and kept on pacing, trusting the scoundrel would fall into step with her. Side by side, she guided Trilby out of the duke's hearing.

"You have created a fine mess, sir. Except for my willingness to hear your apology, the duke would be cleaning his dueling pistols right now."

Trilby's mouth thinned. "His challenge was excessive under the circumstances."

"He found you twice with your hands on me. Furthermore, you are a despicable blackmailer. Ongoing avarice led you to devise plans to cheat at cards, then force me into marriage. Just thinking about my list of grievances against you makes me think I should not have interceded with him on your behalf, but let you face him at his worst."

Trilby's face twisted into an ugly sneer. "You may have a duke as your protector, but I still have that journal. That is why you accepted my apology, and let us not pretend otherwise."

"How good of you to mention that. I am quite done with the trouble it has caused me. I brought twenty-five hundred with me, as I told you. I have packed it up, and given it to the manager of the Crescent. Your name is on the package, and he will hand it to you when you apply for it. I suggest you take it, and let it suffice for a good, long while."

It was the plan she had brought with her to Buxton to start. After all she had been through, and would go through, he had better accept it.

He paced a good dozen steps before nodding. "It will have to do. For now. However, you will not receive the journal until I get the rest."

"And I will expect proof you still have that manuscript before you get another shilling."

She stopped walking. They had moved about fifty yards from Penthurst. She looked back to see him watching, ready to move if necessary. "We are well done. I do not expect to see you, or have communications from you, again for at least a year if not more."

They faced each other. "Good day, Lady Lydia." Trilby bowed, and continued walking in the direction they had been going.

Lydia walked back toward Penthurst.

He stood amid trees almost barren of leaves, a tall dark form with eyes concentrating on her almost invasively. He appeared very separate from the town, his hair whipped by the breeze and his stance commanding the landscape.

She looked at him hard. Looked at him objectively as she had not in years.

He was very handsome. He always had been, but she had been loath to grant him that quality, since she wanted to dislike all he was. She admitted now that nature had more than favored his face and form. If she were any other woman, she probably would be breathless at the thought of being his wife, no matter what his station might be. A lively little warmth began dancing in her chest as his gaze locked on her own.

How disgraceful that this man could do that to her, with his eyes and kisses. She looked away to end the outrageous stimulation.

"I think we can bid farewell to Mr. Trilby," he said. "After we are wed, he will not dare so much as claim to have known you."

She looked up at his profile while they walked back to the Crescent. That irritating warmth danced again. Suddenly her problems with Mr. Trilby paled beside the enormity of becoming Penthurst's wife. Perhaps she could at least put it off.

"Is Scotland really necessary?" she asked.

"My plot does not work without it."

Probably not. Only his plot required a very hasty next chapter.

He took her arm, and angled off the path. He pulled her behind a tree that afforded some privacy. "I do not think it is only your anger over the duel that makes you resistant. I also think you are afraid of the consummation. You do not have to be."

Afraid? She was a woman of the world, and they did not get the vapors over the notion of marriage beds. Had Cassandra been afraid of Ambury? Unlikely, from the little jokes that had been made about it ever since. Of course Cassandra really *had* been a woman of the world, while she, Lydia, only aspired to be. And her stomach churned whenever she thought much about this part of his plot.

"I am not afraid, but I may be sick."

He laughed quietly. His forefinger came to rest on her lips. It proved a distracting and warm, exciting little touch. "I do not think any other woman would have said that."

"I thought I should warn you. It seemed the polite thing to do."

"Then I should be polite enough to warn you too."

"Of what?"

He did not respond with words. Instead he lifted her face and bent to kiss her. It was not a very aggressive kiss. Rather a sweet one that lured more than ravished. She guessed he had a lot of practice kissing. She in turn had very little, so she allowed herself the curiosity of experiencing it. Under the circumstances, with marriage all but inevitable, it behooved her to decide how revolting it all might be.

The intimacy affected her more than the actual touching of lips, although an interesting pulsing began in hers and they became more sensitive. Nor did he just press his against hers. He prolonged the contact with gentle nips and movements that encouraged her lips to respond in a way that might be considered kissing back.

A pleasant heat flowed in her. Arabesques of delight patterned through her body. A desire to have the sensations continue woke in her, like a new voice whispering to her will. She did not object when he cradled her head in his hands and kissed again, more firmly. She sensed something in him that spoke to her instincts and urged a release of restraint. The conversation definitely dwelled on carnal pleasures.

She understood then—what was in him as a man and her as a woman, and how it had little to do with any human interaction she had known before, not even her love for Lakewood. Even when she had succumbed to her most emotional girlish fantasies, she had never guessed the potential for wildness that she sensed just beyond the edges of his kiss.

He looked down at her, his thumb caressing her lips. "Do you still think you will get sick on me?"

Strange tremors filled her. "Perhaps not."

"I will make sure you are not afraid either." He took her hand, and led her back to the path and toward the Crescent.

That night, with the memory of Lydia's cautious lips still in his head, Penthurst sat down to write a letter. Southwaite should be informed of what was about to transpire, and why. In the least it would reassure him that Lydia was safe, should he have discovered her disappearance from Crownhill.

Southwaite,

If you do not already know that Lydia left Crownhill, you will upon reading this. She is with me, and we are on our way to Scotland to marry. I will explain all upon our return to town. Ideally such an event would be celebrated with family in attendance, but that delay was not wise. She has been compromised, and I fear you will hear the tales even before you open this missive. As you know, it does not matter if such talk consists of lies and exaggerations.

I would prefer privacy until we announce this when we are back in London. If in your judgment a quicker publication is necessary, do it. I expect the nuptials to be a fait accompli by Tuesday of next week.

Penthurst

He trusted the reference to lies and exaggerations would lead Southwaite to entertain the possibility, at least, that his friend had not ruthlessly seduced his sister, and only did the right thing now because some plan of discretion went awry.

After sealing the letter, he considered whether he should write to anyone else. His aunt? He pictured her reaction to the news. Whether it came through gossip or the mail, it would put her in rare form. He set the pen in its holder. Perhaps after the wedding, he would take it up again on her behalf.

Leaving his chamber and the Crescent, he went for a walk through the silent town. His boots made their rhythms against the stones. He strode with purpose and used the exercise as a replacement for a few hours at

Mr. Gosden's farm. He had insisted Lydia accommodate the inevitability of this marriage. It was time for him to do so as well.

When she laid her fury and blame in front of him today, he had been sorely tempted to explain that duel to her, and specifically that Lakewood was far worse than Trilby, the man who had just been sent packing. It had been wiser to hold his tongue, however. She would not believe anything he said now about that. Perhaps she never would.

He had no reason to feel either guilt or responsibility for her present quandary, yet he did. Furthermore, whatever incited the reckless behavior that brought her to Buxton, and he assumed it was something significant, she would be safer with him.

He made his way back to the Crescent. Lydia would willingly journey to Scotland in the morning, and not because he had threatened seduction to ensure she agreed. She was not stupid. She knew when society had a woman's future at its mercy.

Which meant he would soon marry a woman who disliked him intensely, even if she was not immune to his kisses.

You deserve better. So did she. But they would have to make the best of what they both were getting instead.

He was almost at the Crescent when a carriage turned onto the street and picked up speed. He stepped into an alley to let it pass. As it did, the carriage lantern's light washed the side of the vehicle. The image it displayed caught his attention, but he only deciphered what he had seen after it passed and the street returned to darkness.

That had looked like Trilby's coach, the one he had used when trying to abduct Lydia. And certainly that had been Trilby's profile at the window. Of more interest had been another profile, nothing more than a silhouette barely visible inside. A woman's.

He continued retracing his path to the Crescent. Thwarted in his plan to marry Lydia, Algernon Trilby had apparently lost no time in finding other feminine companionship. It appeared Trilby's life would suffer no disruption due to the day's events, or even moderate inconvenience. It was unlikely Lydia would enjoy the irony of that.

Chapter 13

Their journey to the border made the marriage inevitable, if prior events had not. In traveling with Penthurst alone, she sealed her fate. A long night of pacing and thinking had led to the conclusion that her fate was sealed already, however. By morning she had accepted that, even if beneath the calm she still rebelled.

He showed no resentment of the accusations she had made when her emotions overcame her. He treated her kindly in every way. Initially he did not even ride with her in the coach he hired, but accompanied it on his horse. Only on the second day, as they left the coaching inn where he had procured chambers for them, did he step into the coach after her.

She occupied herself viewing the passing landscape. He had brought a book with him, and offered it to her to read. They passed the time with little conversation. She pretended she did not become more nervous with each passing mile.

"I wrote to your brother," he said late in the day. They would stop for another night at an inn before crossing into Scotland. "I thought he should be told."

"What did you write?"

"That we would marry in Scotland. That you had been compromised. It was a very brief letter. We can decide before we see him if we want him to believe my plot, or whether you want to explain it all to him."

"He will probably be relieved it is you," she said. "It could have been a much less attractive match, from his viewpoint. A pirate, or a thief."

"A smuggler, or a penniless adventurer."

"A gambler, or a gentry gentleman's ne'er-do-well third son."

"A Trilby."

"I expect if it had been a Trilby, my brother would have wondered if I had gone mad."

"And not if it had been a pirate, smuggler, or gambler?"

"A woman's head might be turned by the dash and danger of a pirate or smuggler. But a Trilby—there would not be a good explanation for him. Of course a duke is perfect. Every woman wants to marry a duke. I doubt I will need to give him any explanation at all. Emma, on the other hand, will not believe your plot. She will be the one who asks me questions."

"I hope she will not disapprove."

"She is a very practical person. She will not disapprove. She will just be curious, and skeptical." She could imagine Emma's disconcertingly direct gaze leveled at her, and hear her comment on how odd it was that Lydia would change her mind about the duke.

Undoubtedly Cassandra would be suspicious as well.

Or not. Penthurst was a duke after all. A duke. Most likely no one would question how a woman had come to be married to one, no matter the circumstances. As with royalty, notions of love sounded almost childish when talking of a duke's marriage.

Which meant that no one was going to feel bad for her or question her happiness. No one would care that she had been forced into this by circumstances she had not really controlled. Even the duke—he had known his whole life he was one of the best catches in the realm. He was incapable of mustering any sympathy for her plight, let alone a touch of guilt. If he thought anyone should be seen as the victim of fate here, he probably thought it was himself.

The more she thought about that, the more it galled her.

"Did you mention anything about the settlement in the letter to my brother?"

"I assumed we would discuss that when you and I return to town."

"I would like to address a few parts of it now, if you do not mind."

"And if I do?"

"I will have to accept your refusal, although I do not

understand why you would object. I am speaking of very minor parts. So minor as to barely be worth the ink used to scratch them onto the vellum."

"Let us strike a bargain. I will entertain your negotiations over these very minor parts of the settlement, if you entertain my presence beside you on that bench."

She judged how her rump all but filled the seat. "Won't you find it tight and cramped over here?"

"Not at all."

"I suppose, for a while, if you prefer."

He moved over. They were quite cramped, it seemed to her. Their sides pressed each other.

"Now, which minor parts do you want to talk about?"

"Regarding the settlement, I would like to discuss my pin money.

He made a face.

"Oh, dear. You find that distasteful. I thought, since we would marry soon, that it would be acceptable. Are we never to talk about money? Ever? That is good to know."

"I expect there will be times when we must, as husband and wife. I am not accustomed to it with women, that is all."

"Really? You never talk about money with women? How interesting. Do you have your solicitors do it? With the other women whom you support, for example. Your aunt. Your mistresses."

She received a long, steady look for that.

"You are right, Lydia. If we were in London, I would

be discussing all of this with your brother, without any hesitation. If you want to know what your pin money will be before you say the vows, it is only fair that you do."

That was rather nice of him. Which suddenly made this less fun.

"So, how much do you expect?" he asked.

She made some quick calculations. Five hundred a year for Trilby, damn the man. A few hundred for her private causes. A hundred or two for the actual pins and such.

"I should like a thousand a year in the least. My brother may know more about what duchesses get, and ask for more, but I want to know it will be at least a thousand."

"I will agree to that, if you agree that you will not use more than a hundred of it per annum at the tables."

"Only a hundred? You might as well say I cannot play ever again."

"I might, but I have chosen not to unless it is necessary."

"This is why marriage is an onerous state for a woman. I am a grown woman, not some schoolgirl, and have known some independence. Ideally you will go about your life as you have and I will go about mine much as I have."

"That sounds so sane. I would be impressed, and feel bound to agree, except for one problem. I think you got yourself in a lot of trouble going about your life as you have. It took you to Buxton, and it put you in this carriage. So forgive me, Lydia, if I think I will be keeping an eye on you, at least for a while."

She had no good response to this, since she could not dispute the facts. "There is something else. I also want to bring Sarah with me. She is my maid. I want you to tell your housekeepers that she is to be treated well, and not made to feel out of place or unsuitable."

"That is an easy promise to make."

"As for your aunt—"

"Before you request that which I cannot give, let me explain something. The family homes are all she has known her whole life. I promised my father before he died that I would never obligate her to leave."

That was not good news. Rosalyn had made clear what she thought of Lydia. If the two were required to live under the same roof, neither of their lives would be tranquil.

"Do not expect me to defer to her, or allow her to instruct me."

"In your duties as a duchess, she may be helpful. It will be your choice whether to accept her advice. I ask you to be kind to her. You will displace her in the household, and she will feel the difference sharply."

She did not think Lady Rosalyn would step down from mistress of those houses graciously. She had wielded power for more than twenty years now. Abdicating in favor of a new duchess might not appeal to her at all.

Penthurst would not understand the kinds of skirmishes women might fight in such a war. He probably would not want to hear about them either. Nor did she intend to be the kind of fragile, emotional bride who proved helpless when faced by a formidable female relative. Should Rosalyn not stand down, there would indeed be a war. Penthurst had been forewarned.

They arrived at the coaching inn before nightfall. Again he took two rooms. While an inn's woman helped her unpack the necessities for the night, the duke appeared at her chamber's threshold. He looked around, noting its appointments.

"This is much better than mine. More spacious and comfortable."

"Did you present yourself as the duke you are? If so, I am sure an error was made. We can trade." She gestured for the woman to stop unpacking.

"My chamber is adequate for tonight. I am glad to see something more suitable is available for you, however. I will tell them to hold it for you." He noticed the servant. "Make sure Lady Lydia is ready to travel a half hour after dawn. Good night, Lydia."

It was her turn to survey the chamber. She supposed it was suitable for tomorrow night's purposes. He would come to her here, and collect on that gambling debt, only by morning he would own everything she had and was.

When she lay down that night, she realized that even sleep would not belong to her in the future. This was the last night that she could be sure would be hers alone, without Penthurst appearing at her side should he so choose.

*   *   *

Tarduff did not have the fame of Gretna Green, which suited Lydia just fine. She thought Penthurst's decision to use this more obscure town showed some style and a good deal of sense.

Elopements to Scotland resulted in rather perfunctory ceremonies. At ten thirty in the morning she entered a small, damp church of ancient design and stood beside the duke and two witnesses. The vows sounded very distant, as if spoken in other voices in another chamber. At the same time everything she saw appeared too vivid and sharp. She thought she might remember the surface texture of the nearest stones forever, with unaccountable detail.

Then it was over. Her hand weighed heavy with Penthurst's signet ring on her finger, the only ring available this day. The vicar smiled at the duke, delighted to have performed a service for such an important man. The witnesses awaited a coin for their trouble. Finally she noticed that one person paid attention only to her.

Penthurst still held her hand and faced her. She forced herself to look up at him, half afraid of what she would see. The life she had known might be over, but this marriage affected his too. No longer would he have the choice in his wife and duchess. The reality of that might not sit well, now that it could not be ignored.

She saw no anger in his expression. No dreaded resignation either. His gaze appeared almost gentle, and even a little amused.

"The vicar is wondering why you keep looking around as if you are planning renovations to the church," he whispered.

"It is charming as it is."

"Yes, but he is waiting for us to kiss."

She turned to the vicar, who smiled expectantly and patiently. A kiss. Yes, that was in order. She swallowed a flutter of panic and looked up at Penthurst. At her husband. Not a stranger, at least. That was something. Coming here had been her choice too. That was something too. She could not deny he was handsome. Also exciting, she had learned. With a bit of time and some negotiating, they might have a bearable life together, despite the role he had unwittingly played in her life.

That pain began to emerge as soon as she thought of it. She forced it down, away. Not now. Not today. Perhaps never, if she tried hard enough. She did not know if she could live in this marriage if she allowed those memories any freedom.

He cupped her face with his handsome hands, and kissed her lips. Then he said something unexpected, in a voice so low that she wondered if he even meant her to hear.

"Little Lydia, after all. Astonishing."

For a woman who a day earlier had implied she might shoot the cat on her wedding night, Lydia's composure after the ceremony impressed Penthurst. Like the woman of the world she kept claiming to be, she did not get a case of bad nerves, or retreat into the sullen silence of the sacrificial victim. Instead rather suddenly she became animated, and spent the time back to the inn quizzing him on his properties, family, and on the formalities she should expect as she took her place as his duchess.

Only when they entered the inn's yard did her chatter pause. She looked at the building, then at him. "There are rituals to wedding nights, but I am not experienced in them. Unmarried women do not help such preparations. I do not know what to do."

"We are free to dispense with ritual, Lydia."

"I still do not know what to do."

He found her consternation adorable. "After we dine, why not call for a bath if you like. Then have the servant prepare you for bed the same as she did last night."

"Bath, then bed. That is easy enough. Then you will visit me?"

"If you do not mind too much. We can wait until—"

"No waiting. You do not tell someone a tooth must be pulled then make them wait days anticipating it." She spoke most earnestly. He managed not to laugh. "I intend to be done with this forthwith, if you do not mind."

"I do not mind at all."

She talked all through dinner. He had little need to contribute any conversation, which left him to envision the night's events to come. He suspected Lydia's loquaciousness was a way for her to avoid similar visions. She appeared dismayed when it became clear there was nothing left to eat, and the meal was done.

She just sat there looking at the tablecloth.

"Perhaps you would like to retire," he said.

"Yes. I suppose so. There is nothing else for it." Hitching her wrap higher on her shoulders, she excused herself.

He went to the public room and had some port amid the noise and commotion of the passengers of coaches stopping to change horses. All the while his mind paced out Lydia's activities above as she had her bath and prepared all alone for her wedding night.

Lydia went through her plan while the servant washed her back. Once this bath was done, she would put on her nightdress, dry her hair, and fix the chamber. One small candle far from the bed would be necessary, but these others would be snuffed. The bed's curtains should be closed too. She would lie down and wait, and do what was required when he came.

She did not know how long it would take. No more than five minutes, she guessed. There was no need for a lot of kissing and such. By such means men lured women, and the duke had no need to seduce. She was his, and he did not have to cajole her into giving herself.

There would be some pain, but Emma had once implied that too much was made of that by women trying to scare girls into being virtuous. Still, she did not expect this night to be very pleasant.

She thought about the scene of love in her novel. She had included a lot of kissing. Other things too, such as she had figured out happened sometimes. Her characters had been lovers, however. Truly lovers. Since they took pleasure in each other's company, of course they would find pleasure in physical bonds too.

Her situation tonight would be different from that. She avoided dwelling on the details, or picturing any of it. Her assumption, however, was that it should be over quickly.

The warm water soothed her. The soap made the mist smell sweet. The servant left her to finish washing, and laid out her nightdress on the chair. Then she left, the door latching behind her with a sharp click.

Lydia eased back so her neck rested on the metal tub's rim and her rump slid down. She bent her legs and raised her knees so she could submerge most of the rest of her.

"Now, that is a sight to take away a man's breath. You look like a nymph whose modesty is protected by nothing more than water."

It was her breath that caught. She noted with a fast glance that the water afforded her very little modesty in truth.

She turned her head. Penthurst stood ten feet away. He must have entered as the servant left. He had shed his coats and cravat and wore no boots. The candles' light made his white shirt a brilliant contrast to his dark pantaloons. Except for where the open collar revealed a deep V of skin.

She tried to sink deeper in the water. Her voice felt stuck in her chest. "I expected you later."

"I heard you in the bath, and decided to see just what gift fate had delivered to me."

She realized that water or no water, he could see her naked body. The fluid shimmers of the lights' reflections hid very little. Dismayed by the change from how she expected the night to unfold, she sat up and embraced her knees so some part of her might be covered.

He walked over. "I should have remained silent, so you did not become shy." He knelt on one knee beside the tub. With two fingers under her chin, he lifted her face from her knees. "You are beautiful, Lydia. I do not think you know how lovely you are."

He kissed her lips, then her bare shoulder. "Are you finished with the bath? The water has cooled."

She could not speak. She could barely inhale. She nodded and reached toward the chair and the bath linen.

His hand closed on it first. He stood and offered her his hand. To take it meant unfolding her body and rising out of the water. She would be unable to hide anything. She stared at that hand while she mustered some courage. She might be inexperienced, but she did not want to appear no more mature than a girl married off after her first season.

Hoping she looked sophisticated, and praying her mortification would not show, she took his hand and stood. She glanced down. No one, not even Sarah, had seen her so thoroughly unclothed.

He did not stare or gawk, but as he helped her step out of the tub she felt his gaze on her, sliding over her body, lingering on her breasts and legs and mound. He wrapped the linen around her. She clutched it close and tried to dry herself with its edges.

"I will do it." He took another linen off the chair.

She kept the towel around her, holding it closed in front while he dried her arms and shoulders. She continued grasping it when he knelt on one knee and began drying her legs.

"You are very composed. I am impressed." His hands moved the towel over her feet and shins.

"Well, I am not a child. Women of the world do not become madwomen just because a new experience unfolds."

He looked up, amused. "A woman of the world. Is that what I have married?"

"Not much of one, I will admit. Due to the war, I have not traveled the way Cassandra did. And due to my aunts and my brother, I have not lived independently or even with much freedom, except that which I could arrange without their knowing. Yet I aspire to be one, and have done my best under the circumstances."

He lifted one of her legs and set the foot on his knee. The towel fell away so most of her leg showed. Almost all of it. Almost up to—

"Now that you are a duchess, being a woman of the world will be easier." He used his towel to dry her leg. Except it was already fairly dry, so the effect was more a caress. Slowly, up and down his hands moved that cloth. She became very aware of how high each time. Almost to her—

She tried to ignore it, but her body could not. Her senses exclaimed with alarm each time the caress rose high. Then, after a while, another reaction joined the shock. An odd stirring made her wait for that shock, as if she wanted it.

Standing on one leg grew difficult. She had to force herself not to wobble. The duke seemed unaware of her condition.

"I would not want you to misunderstand, however. I will not allow you to have affairs, if that is part of being a woman of the world in your mind."

"I know that is out of the question until your succession is secured. I am not unschooled in how things are done."

"You should not count on my allowing it even after I have my heir, Lydia. I am sorry if that is an unexpected surprise."

Since his attention was more on her body than her face, she trusted he did not see anything to reflect her thoughts. She did not much care for his talk of allowing this or that, or not. Surely he knew that if she fell in love, she probably would not deny herself any more than he would.

It might be wise to mention that now, rather than accept this little rule he had just made. A retort formed in her mind. Then he looked up at her, and her mind emptied.

Tiny fires showed in his chestnut eyes. The natural severity of his face tightened, but not in an expression of anger. His gaze probed in a way that left her dumbstruck and trembling.

The linen fell from his hands, but the caress did not stop. Deliciously warm, subtly rough, unmistakably possessive, his hands moved over her leg and thigh. The stirring thrummed, rising to a focused vibration whenever his hands moved high under the drape of her towel.

Warmth suffused her, as if a strong fire burned in the fireplace. A small thought broke through her amazement, that an innocent should be afraid of this, and embarrassed. A part of her was both those things, but she could not look away, and the fear itself possessed a compelling excitement.

His caress stopped. She thought perhaps he intended to now dry the other leg. She doubted she would be able to keep her balance if he did that.

Instead he reached up to where she held the linen in her hands. Instinctively she clutched even tighter.

"Let go of it now, Lydia."

She did not willfully obey, but her hold loosened anyway. He took the edges from her grasp and let the towel drop.

She did not look at herself, but awareness of her exposure teased at that stirring until it quivered and moved like something alive. Her foot still rested on his knee, and she wondered if he could see that which she had never seen herself. The notion did not shock her too much. She was beyond that.

He caressed again, up the outside of that leg, all the way until his fingertips slid over her hip to her waist. His other hand did the same on her other leg, like he outlined her on both sides, until his hands closed on her waist and held her. He leaned forward and kissed her stomach.

Bolts of delicious sensation shot from that kiss. To her extremities and her heart, and down low to where the stirring continued its erotic churn.

He stood and embraced her. Covered by him, she felt no less exposed. If anything she became more naked as she pressed the hardness of his body and his clothes rasped her skin. Even the kiss stripped her more, calling as it did to the physical responses that she could not control.

Vulnerable but safe. Awake yet dreaming. Alive, so alive, so aware of details and nuances, but also dazed beyond comprehension, she could only follow and accept. Kisses on her neck left her gasping. The power of a new, invasive kiss, astonished her. The way his hands moved over her back and then her bottom startled and delighted. Pleasures small and large cascaded, leaving her short of breath. Soon they were all she thought about, and wanting them to continue dominated her instincts just as he seemed to dominate her body and will.

A caress up her side, both luring and controlling, captivated her attention. Tremors rippled in her as she waited for something wonderful. Her essence anticipated what her mind did not know. Higher that warmth came, then around her body until his hand closed on her breast. It felt so good that her whole being sighed. His thumb skimmed the tip, creating a pleasure so mesmerizing that she forgot to breathe.

"You like that," he muttered into her neck while his

mouth added to the wonders. She nodded. Those gentle flicks of touch intensified the pleasure to the point of anguish.

She almost cried an objection when it stopped. A bit of sense seeped back into her mind. Enough to hear him say, "Get into bed now."

She staggered the few steps there, and climbed up, not thinking about what he did or did not see, or what would happen or would not. His hands closed on her waist again before she lay down, while she was on her hands and knees. He held her there, she knew not why, then kissed the small of her back before releasing her.

She flopped on her back, feeling worldly and sensual, transformed into a goddess by these extraordinary physical discoveries. A bit more sense returned, and she reached for the sheet so she did not appear to lack all modesty. As she stretched to grab its edge, she noticed that Penthurst was undressing.

He noticed her noticing. "I will put out the lamp and candles." He moved toward one to do so.

"Not on my account. I have seen disrobed men before."

"Have you now?"

"Oh, yes." She spoke airily, like the woman of the world she truly had become in the last fifteen minutes.

He continued with his shirt. "When was this?"

She pondered that, her memory skipping through the fog mostly occupying her head. "Not so long ago. I was of age if that is what you mean."

"I was not aware there was an age when unmarried

women start looking at naked men. I wonder how I missed that social rule."

"Not all women. Only sophisticated ones."

"You mean women of the world, like you." He pulled off his shirt and in a minute he was naked to the waist. She stared, fascinated. How interesting male bodies were. His looked lean and hard and defined. And suddenly more powerful. Compared with his height and his strength, she would be small and weak. A bit of misgiving seeped into her confidence.

"Were you alone with him?"

She realized with a startle what he was asking her. "Oh, it was not—it was an accident, you see. I chanced upon them—"

"*Them*?"

"Uh—two of them, swimming."

"Such things are unavoidable, I expect. You immediately left, I assume."

Immediately had been an unfortunate choice of word. "I quickly left, yes."

He sat on the edge of the bed and continued pulling off clothes. "Did they know you saw them?"

"I am not sure. Probably not. Cassandra said most likely not." An outright lie. Cassandra had said no such thing.

He turned his head and looked at her. "Lady Ambury was with you?"

Oh, dear. "We were riding together and we chanced upon this spot where people swim and she made every effort to protect me from seeing more than a glimpse."

All true, but not completely accurate. "It was nothing, really. Just a moment of surprise, then it was over."

"Not really nothing, if you find the notion of an unclothed man normal and not shocking. I am relieved. I had worried about your delicate sensibilities. Since you are not only a woman of the world by your own accounting, but an experienced one in such matters, I will not concern myself with the lamps or anything else."

He stood on those words and turned around, totally naked.

At which point she did what she should have done, but did not do, when she chanced upon those swimmers. She covered her eyes with her hand.

So much for the sophisticated woman of the world. Lydia sat all huddled again, her knees up to her chin and her hand firmly pressing her eyes. He glanced down at what had made her cry out. An arousal of prime proportions stood at attention.

Patience. Patience. The litany had been chanting in his head all day, reminding him that despite her age and her claims of sophistication, she was not an experienced woman but an innocent, with all that meant.

He lay down beside her under the sheet. "Come here." He gathered her into his arms and pried her hand from her eyes. "My apologies, but you said—"

"The back. I saw them from the back."

"A small but significant omission from your story."

She set her head on his shoulder. The softness of her

breast pressed his side. The scent of her filled his head. "I hate that I reacted like a child. You must think I am tedious."

"Not at all." He doubted she would want to hear what he did think of her. That she was sensual by nature, easily aroused, and probably not too constrained by notions of proper and improper acts.

She rose up on her arm and looked down at the sheet that covered him, and the clear evidence of his erection beneath it. "This is going to end badly, isn't it? I am going to wish it had been a bad tooth that needed pulling instead."

He hoped not, but it was not something to talk about. Nor did he want to talk about anything else. He caressed up her back, then eased her back down beside him. "If you allow yourself to enjoy the pleasure, I do not think it will end so badly as you fear. I will try not to hurt you."

Her color rose. Her lids lowered. He noticed for the first time how thick her eyelashes were, and how dark. He kissed each lid, then her soft cheek, then her lips.

Immediately he hardened even more. Images entered his head, erotic ones of the pleasures he took with women who really were sophisticated, but which he would not know tonight. He would make sure she experienced desire, however, so she did not shrink from him whenever he reached for her in the future.

She parted her lips to his kiss so he could explore the warm velvet of her mouth. She trembled within his embrace again and again, and finally attempted a tentative embrace of her own. The careful pressure of her palms on his shoulders charmed him.

He looked down at her dark eyes and thick lashes and pale oval face. She was lovely. He wondered why he had not noticed years ago. Her abstract expression the last few years might have discouraged it. Tonight, no one could call her impassive. Lights danced in her eyes. She looked alert and curious and brave. She might be gambling, she appeared so alive.

He smiled to himself as he lost himself in kissing the warmth of her neck. Little sharp intakes of breath sounded in his ear, their pitch saying which kiss moved her more. When the melody quickened and her embrace tightened to a grasp, he lowered the sheet to expose her breasts.

"Put your hands behind your head, Lydia."

Eyes dazed with passion, she frowned in confusion, then released him and bent her arms so her hands lay beneath her head. The pose raised her round breasts. He touched one, then the other, and the tips hardened at once into dark, luring tips. He grazed each again and she gasped and arched her back. Each time she arched, again and again, her body begging. Finally her cries did too.

She closed her eyes as if to contain it and find control. He teased, circling with his palm until a moan sighed out of her. He pressed his hip and leg against hers to feel the way her body flexed to the pleasure and need.

"Do you want me to stop, Lydia?"

She shook her head.

"Do you want more?"

She opened her eyes and looked at him. Wild now, close to abandon, she nodded.

He lowered his head to use his tongue.

She could barely breathe from the power of the sensations. More, he asked. There could be more?

She watched his head lower and felt the softness of his hair on her chest. His kiss on her breast gave a hint of what more meant. His tongue flicked and she almost died. He used his tongue and mouth on one breast and his wicked hand on the other, and she thought she would become unhinged.

Surely if she could hold him, she would not feel so helpless to the way pleasure overwhelmed her. Offering herself this way, taking the pleasure he gave without stop, only made her want more again, and more, and yet more. Only within the more and the want a force built. A desperation pressed at the pleasure and threatened to explode out of it. Her body moved and rocked in response to it. Down between her legs she felt wetness and a throbbing that only ached for more too.

Caresses now, wonderful strokes down her body. She moved into them with sinuous, languid stretches.

He rose up on one arm, bracing himself beside her. She opened her eyes and almost shut them again. Hair mussed, jaw firm, eyes ablaze, his severity held a terrible sensual quality. An alluring one that made her want to look and look. So compelling and handsome that just the sight of him had her throbbing more and wanting more.

He stripped the sheet off her so she lay naked, her hands still at her head and her breasts still rising high. He watched his caress claim all of her, hips and legs and thighs and stomach. Then his hand slid between her legs and he touched all that was left.

She did not believe it possible to be shocked by a sensation still. She did not know that the more meant different pleasures, not only more of the same. This touch proved almost painfully direct to the center of all the others.

He did not hurt her but she still wanted to cry. He touched places of unbearable sensitivity and made the desperation build and build. Over and over he did it while he kissed her lips and body, until she wanted to scream from the need he caused.

He moved over her and eased her legs farther apart. She knew what he was going to do now but she could not think about anything except relief. With the first pressure as he began to enter her, she knew that this was the more all the rest had led her to.

He was slow and careful, but it hurt enough that she bit her lower lip to avoid crying. Then it hurt less, as if her body gave up a rebellion. She moved her hands then, so she could hold on to him should the rest hurt too.

Soreness echoed when he moved in her, but she felt no real pain. Or perhaps her astonishment left no room for such ordinary sensations. His size and strength eclipsed her and dominated her. He braced his weight on his forearms, but she still cowered beneath him, indisputably small and frail in comparison.

The intimacy of the act seemed stark and overwhelming to the point she could only accept it, dazed by the shock of being claimed and possessed in such a physical, even primitive manner. For all his care, his need would not be denied and when it found release, its power shocked her anew.

So did a singular insight that entered her mind when their gazes met near the end. She had seen the carnal side in him all along, she realized, only had not understood or given it a name. Like a fearsome spell, it shadowed his pride and lit his gaze and affected all that she knew of him. It made her uncomfortable with him, because in his presence she tasted that desperation waiting for her, and the abandon calling her name.

She wondered if she would ever look at him again without being stirred in wicked ways.

Other than her lashes fluttering against her pale skin, she had not moved a hair since he moved off her. Her legs still spread wide beneath the sheet that now covered her. As she had predicted, it had not ended well.

Taking a woman was easy. Knowing what to say afterward, if anything, had always been the sticking point for men. As if they guessed, many women, the real sophisticated women of the world, had a patter of conversation to ease the awkwardness. Tonight he knew it was incumbent on him to speak instead.

"I am sorry if I hurt you, Lydia. I never will again."

She drew up her legs and turned on her side, facing him. "I was not too hurt. A pulled tooth is probably worse after all."

He kissed her forehead. At least she did not flinch. "That is heartening to hear. I would not like it known that sharing a bed with me is more hellish than that."

Her eyes opened. Soulful now. No longer dazed with pleasure or alight with excitement, but instead revealing serious thinking and perhaps some sadness.

"I am accommodating it all. I feel a little odd. Different."

"I will leave you, so you have your privacy, if you like."

She did not respond for a long count. Then she nodded.

He dressed enough to be decent, and returned to his own chamber. He sat in a chair by the window and did his own accommodating. He did not feel odd, but different to be sure. Married, for one thing.

In the heat of passion women could be somewhat interchangeable. Tonight he had never forgotten he was with Lydia. His wife. For the first time he had bedded a woman as the law and society intended.

It changed things. The same act. The same pleasures. Yet, different.

Not different the way Lydia meant, however. This was all she knew. Her reference to different had been about herself and her life, he guessed. He had taken her innocence, and that marked a critical turn in a person's life, man or woman.

He wondered what she was thinking in that bed soiled by their joining. Did she castigate herself for allowing herself to enjoy what she could? Did she resent that he had used his skill to all but force pleasure on her? Did she weep as the reality of this marriage could not be ignored any longer?

Perhaps all of those things. Mostly, however, he suspected she accommodated that she had given him something only given once in a woman's life. Her innocence was gone forever, and he had not been a man she had chosen to receive it.

Chapter 14

Lydia truly felt more a woman of the world as they journeyed back to London. Not only because she officially now was the first part of that appellation, a woman. Rather her wedding night had explained so many things previously ill understood.

For one thing, she now comprehended some jokes whose humor had previously eluded her.

Then, the way her brother and Emma looked at each other suddenly made sense. She realized that memories of their own pleasures passed in those gazes. She hoped she did not blush or giggle when next they shared those long looks in her presence.

And Cassandra! She had never really understood the spell Cassandra cast on men. Yes, she was beautiful in a distinctive way, and her manner managed to both flatter and challenge. Now, however, she realized her appeal. Much like Penthurst, something about her spoke of carnal things, and intimated the pleasure to be had. It was a little shocking to even consider, but she suspected men became aroused by Cassandra merely upon seeing her.

Finally, her wedding night had taught her the last lesson she ever expected to learn, which was that nature had given each woman the means to feel extraordinary for a short while. That was how pleasure affected one. She had always assumed that if a woman was in love, the physical union might be very special. How alarming to learn that could happen even if you found yourself with a man you not only did not love, but never could.

Or at least it seemed it could be amazing. Since Penthurst did not visit her chamber again during their journey, possibly that only happened the first time and later it became most ordinary indeed.

She almost hoped so. After he left her bed on their wedding night, her confused heart had known its fair share of guilt. The long hours in the carriage gave her too much time to dwell on that, until a sadness lay at the bottom of her heart.

She had no intention of spending her life pining over a dead man, but it had still been disloyal to abandon herself to the duke as if she had forgotten what he had taken from her. She should have done her duty and nothing more. Surely she could have resisted the pleasure of that seduction if she had kept her wits about her.

Unfortunately, the duke's constant proximity over the long miles left her doubting she could have. He had only to look her way, or touch her for the most practical reasons, to start the inconvenient stirring again.

Upon their arrival in Berkeley Square, they found a little crowd outside her home. Three men loitered near the steps and all snapped alert when the coach rolled to a stop. One peeled away immediately and ran across the park toward Ambury's house. Another, whom she knew, bolted into the house. A third began walking away.

"Mr. Riley," Penthurst called to him.

The young man turned and came to the carriage window. "Your Grace?"

"What are you doing here?"

"The lady told me to wait here and come at once if I saw you, sir."

"I trust you were allowed to sleep at night."

"Charles took my place at night, Your Grace."

Penthurst opened the coach door, kicked down the steps, and alighted. "Do your duty, then. However, tell my aunt we may be a while in coming to Grosvenor Square. That will give her time to prepare the household to meet their new mistress."

Mr. Riley stared into the carriage at the only possible person who might be that mistress. Bowing three times, he turned on his heel and walked away quickly.

Penthurst offered his hand to her. "Shall we go in?"

"I am thinking I would rather not."

"Courage, Lydia. Besides, you are mine now. Even if your brother wanted to punish you for your careless behavior—and he never did before, so why would he start now?—he no longer has the authority. Only I do."

That might be true, but it was not punishment that she dreaded with Southwaite. Rather his disapproval and disappointment could feel worse than ten lashes with a cane.

Up the steps they trod. Into the house. It felt very quiet inside. The butler greeted them as if she did not live here. Which, she realized with a startle, she no longer did.

"Ask the earl if he will see me," Penthurst said.

"Yes, Your Grace."

"Do you think to meet him alone?" she asked.

"I do. He should have the freedom to say what he wants. He will not if you are there."

"What am I supposed to do?"

"You have chambers here, don't you? You might go to them and pack some clothes to bring with you."

Of course. She also had to pack Sarah. She wandered to the stairs, to get on with it.

She opened the door to the apartment she had used since she was a child. A pang of nostalgia throbbed in her chest. Then she saw Sarah standing at the doorway to the dressing room. Sarah's eyebrows rose high above wide eyes.

"Oh, milady, I've been bursting with pride since the countess told me. A duke, Deea! A duke!"

* * *

The butler threw open the library door and ushered Penthurst in. He announced him like this were a state visit.

Southwaite sat at one of the tables, pen in hand. He looked up then returned to his task. "Penthurst! Welcome back. Sit. I will be finished with this in a minute. It is the announcement."

"You were able to put it off."

"Yes. Barely. I had to threaten one of my aunts with never allowing her to borrow our carriages again. Even so she told your aunt, so it did spread a bit." He jotted away, then set down the pen. "How does this sound? The Earl of Southwaite is relieved to announce, finally, that his sister, Lady Lydia Alfreton, has married, and to none other than the Duke of Penthurst, thus giving proof that fortune's wheel turns at a whim."

"I am glad our marriage is cause for jokes. I feared you would be angry."

"Angry? *Angry?* It is all I can do to stop myself from falling to my knees and hugging your legs in gratitude."

"Far be it from me to imply that your joy in our nuptials is unseemly, but— Don't you want to know what happened? Do you not care that she was compromised?"

Southwaite waved the notion away much as he might swat at an insect. "She has been doing things that could get her compromised for years. Ask her about last summer and the galley. That episode almost turned me gray, let me tell you. Anyway, it was just a matter of time before it happened. What luck that when she was finally caught in one of her schemes, it was you who was involved and not some highwayman or thief or such."

"What luck indeed."

Southwaite rose and poured some brandy. He came over and held out one of the glasses. "A toast is in order." He raised his glass. "To your happiness."

They both downed the brandy. Southwaite set down his glass and sat in an armchair. "I am very serious. I am glad it is you. I had always hoped, but after that public disavowal of the match—"

"She was a child at the time. I disavowed the arrangement, not her."

Southwaite shrugged. "Your recent presence in her life made me wonder if perhaps—but each time a different, better explanation presented itself. Your letter from Buxton thus surprised me, but it in no way angered me."

"I am glad to hear it. Just so you know, we wed in Scotland. And you should probably be told that she was not happy to find herself with no choice except me or ruin."

That took some of the glee out of Southwaite's expression. "Here I was building a grand, secret romance in my imagination. Perhaps you do need to tell me what happened."

"The only story we will give out is that we eloped. Even to you. As for the rest, as her husband she is now my responsibility. Your duty is well done."

"Done, but not well, from the sounds of it," Southwaite muttered thoughtfully. "There have been some rumors out of Buxton. I paid them no mind, but—"

"Ignore them. Everyone else will soon. In a month she will have been received by the queen, the prince, and the prime minister."

Southwaite smiled, but still appeared thoughtful. Even troubled. "Tell her I would like to see her now. To give my blessing on this marriage she has made."

"I will go and see she comes down at once."

Lydia did not know what to expect when she entered the library to see her brother. She knew Penthurst had held with the plot he had concocted out of the public events in Buxton, however. Southwaite would probably accept that without too much thought.

Upon seeing him, she knew she was wrong about that. His expression could not be called indifferent, or even happy. Rather he looked at her much as he would when she had suffered some slight at a party or ball, with forced cheer and more concern than he knew he revealed.

He held out his hand. "Come and sit with me, Lydia. In the future we will see each other much less, and have little time alone together."

Her throat burned at his words. The last days had been so busy and active, so full of surprises, that she had not considered how her life would drastically change in day-to-day things. Understanding she would live in Penthurst's house did not mean she had fully comprehended that she would no longer be a resident of this one. They would grow apart now, in all kinds of ways.

She went over and took his hand and let him guide her to a place next to him on a divan. He did not release her hand after they sat, but covered it with his other one.

"I am sorry we could not wait until we were back in town," she said, worried that she had wounded him with her precipitous vows.

"It is not unusual for people to be impatient once they make up their minds."

"Impatient . . . oh, yes." She had to remember that a love affair was part of the plot. "The ceremony was very modest, but I found I did not mind."

"I am glad you do not feel cheated of a big wedding. I would not like to think you did." He patted her hand in a slow rhythm, as if he beat out his thoughts. "I also would not like to think you are unhappy about this marriage, Lydia. Penthurst wrote about a compromising situation. There are rumors enough for me to piece together what he meant. That Trilby fellow and all. Of course if you went to Buxton to elope with Penthurst, the compromise only precipitated the event by a few days." Still that soft rhythmic pat. "You did go there for that purpose, didn't you?"

She had never lied to her brother. Not outright, in response to a direct question. If she did not now, however, he would worry and probe and find all the holes in the plot.

She forced a smile, but her heart was breaking. She

wished she could blurt out it all, and he could comfort her. *I had no thought of elopement when I departed for Buxton. Especially not with the duke. I can never be really happy with him, and never considered him in that way. I will not be miserable because I refuse to be, but when I ever dreamt of a man, it was not Penthurst.*

"How can I not be happy? I am a duchess, dear brother. My husband is your good friend, and although my own judgment has been lacking on occasion, yours is unassailable."

He looked reassured. "I will admit I always hoped for this match. I know you will be well cared for. I should probably warn you that he may not be as lax as I have been with you. He is more accustomed to obedience, I think."

"Are you trying to replace the mother I do not have, Darius? Giving me advice on proper comportment and such?"

He laughed. "I would be a fool to try, wouldn't I? When I think of the advice our mother may have given, I think it best to retreat from the subject entirely before it becomes hellishly awkward." He flushed. She was sure she had never seen that before. "Of course, if there is something that you need to ask . . ."

"I expect Emma will answer any questions I have about married life."

"Yes! That is a much better idea." He stood and helped her to rise. "I should return you to your husband, Lydia. I am very happy for you, and very pleased." He embraced her, and kissed her forehead. "I hope that you will visit often here and at Crownhill, without ceremony or invitation. My homes remain yours too, forever, and your presence will be missed."

"That portrait up there is the third duke. Early seventeenth century. It was said he was ninety-one when he died, but perhaps that is an exaggeration. The young woman's portrait below his shows his daughter Katherine, who married the Earl of Hollowcroft. She was a favorite at court. Over here is his son, the fourth duke. No Penthurst has, or ever will, serve in an official government post since him. It is a family tradition. Do not confuse that with lack of influence. My nephew, like my brother did, knows everyone and is consulted about the gravest matters of state. The power of Penthurst is quiet, often invisible, but significant."

Lydia shifted her eyes from picture to picture while Lady Rosalyn gave her a tour of the gallery. She wondered if she was expected to commit all these details to memory right now. She hoped not, because she barely listened.

Penthurst had left the house this evening, to go who knew where. Since he wore that frock coat with the discreet gold embroidery, she trusted he would be among equals. Or perhaps he had a mistress who needed to be appeased about this marriage. She really did not know, although it would explain why they had been back three days now, and he had not visited her bed.

"These miniatures show the cousins," Rosalyn said,

moving down to a glass case. Lydia groaned inwardly. The case held at least twenty tiny paintings. She braced herself for a half hour of biographies.

"You appear tired, Lydia. I hope I am not boring you."

"Not at all. I find it all fascinating. Do go on." And on. And on. No sooner had Penthurst left the house than Rosalyn had announced it was past time to give her a thorough tour of the house.

Very complete it had been, from attics to cellars. And so she had seen the luxurious bower Rosalyn had created for herself. Her apartment, on the other side of the house from the duke's chambers, covered most of the house over there. Lovely damasks and patterns covered the furniture and paint the hue of seafoam brightened the walls. A dressing room of impressive proportions offered seating for private tête-à-têtes. It was the apartment of a woman accustomed to sparing no expense in maintaining herself in the latest style.

Lydia's own chambers in comparison had not been decorated since the reign of Queen Anne, from the looks of them. Since they lay beside the duke's dressing room, she assumed no one had made use of them since the last duchess passed away.

They finished with the cousins. Lydia prayed there would be no more cases or portraits or heirlooms.

"Let us sit a while in the library, Lydia. I would speak with you about your duties."

The tone of voice reminded her of her old governess, who preferred firm persuasion to scolding. It was the voice of a woman who could afford to be generous, because she knew she held the power.

In the library, Rosalyn sat in a straight-back chair. Lydia chose the divan. She tucked her feet up beside her on the cushion. Rosalyn's eyebrows rose a fraction. Lydia pretended she did not notice.

"For the last twenty years, since the passing of the duchess, I have supervised the household. That is now your duty. I will have the ledgers and books brought to you. Mrs. Hill can be relied upon if you keep her as housekeeper. She is honest, at least, and fairly diligent."

"Then there is no reason to make any changes."

"I am not so sure. She has expressed some concerns to me about the changes you have already imposed. In particular, regarding the woman you brought with you."

"Sarah."

"She is not really suitable to be your lady's maid now. For a young girl, perhaps. But for a duchess—" She tsked her tongue, then shook her head in dismay.

Lydia did not mind too much walking for miles through this house while inspecting every piece of silverwork and receiving a full history of its makers and marks. She had tolerated the verbal delineation of the family tree, standing in that gallery until her feet hurt. She had acted demure and grateful for all of the help being given by the duke's aunt, help she never wanted and even found insulting. She would not, however, keep silent while this woman and the housekeeper plotted to deny her Sarah, the only friend she had in this strange place.

She sat up as straight as she could. She smiled as

sweetly as possible. "Rosalyn—you do not mind my
addressing you informally by your given name, do you?
Your use of mine suggested not, and we are family
now—I want to make something very clear. Sarah will
not be leaving. She is suitable because I choose to have
her serve me, and my preference is all that matters.
Please explain this to Mrs. Hill so there is no misun-
derstanding that causes unpleasantness. She is to ensure
that Sarah feels welcomed, and is treated well and
kindly too. The duke promised me this on our wedding
day, you see. I am sure neither Mrs. Hill nor you would
want to involve him in household affairs, but I will not
be gainsaid on this matter."

Lids lowered halfway over Rosalyn's eyes. A bit of
color tinted her white cheeks. She eyed Lydia carefully,
like an animal judging its prey's weaknesses before
attacking.

"Of course, if she is your preference, there is nothing
to discuss," she said with a little laugh. "We only sought
to help you receive the service that would spare you
much time and worry in your new place."

"That was kind of you."

They sat watching each other. Lydia wondered if
Rosalyn would pounce, or bide her time.

"Do you mind that he left tonight?" Rosalyn asked.
"After all, you are so recently wed and just arrived in
this house."

"I do not mind. He will go his own way most evenings, I expect." *And I will go mine.*

"It isn't a woman, if you were wondering about that."

An unexpected lightness entered her on hearing that. She had been wondering, and minding, a little. Stupid of her to bother herself with such concerns. What did she care about that? And yet, the little glow of contentment said she had cared, a little.

"He has gone to his clubs, to face them down," Rosalyn explained. "To silence the talk about this elopement, and the rumors out of Buxton about your rendezvous there, and that magician's interference, and the challenge. He is doing this for you, of course. His own position is unassailable."

"Surely no one will speak of it to him."

"There is no surely to it. Too much drink and some fool may. Let us pray not, however. Should something be said, let us hope others end it before he must. That he might find himself in a duel over such—" She closed her lips into a firm, resolute line and looked away.

Over such as you. That was what Rosalyn almost said. Over the bold girl who had announced mere weeks ago she intended to go to the devil.

"He will not duel," she said, to try to relieve his aunt of her worry. "He knows I do not like it."

Rosalyn's mouth opened in astonishment. Then she laughed. "Do you think you have such influence over him that he cares what you like or do not like? Oh, dear. You are still such a child, and that alone tells me your power is too small to make a difference. He may have done the right thing by you, for whatever reason he felt he must, but he cannot be enthralled enough to ignore a matter of honor for you."

"You really do not know what he thinks of me, Rosalyn, or what he might do at my request."

"I know this. My nephew has never had any interest at all in young innocents. None at all. I suspect he has even less in innocents of more advanced years, such as yourself."

"And yet, he married one."

"Indeed. One wonders why. Let us hope no one else wonders as I do, and looks too closely at the story of this elopement." She stood. "Come now. I will show you your coronet, and explain the ceremony by which you will be received as his duchess at court."

"So?"

The slow, low question came just as Penthurst lifted a wineglass to his mouth at Brooks's. It slid to him from Kendale, who sat to his right. Ambury heard too, and his gaze brightened expectantly.

He drank the wine. "So?" he responded.

"He is waiting for you to reveal the story of your marriage," Ambury said. "As am I. Since Southwaite is not here, you do not have to worry about his reaction. In the event there is something in the tale that he might react to badly, that is."

"I have told you the story. I trust everyone has heard it by now."

"Not that story," Kendale said. "The true story. The one not prettied up for the matrons and bishops."

"You might as well tell us," Ambury said. "Cassandra

is bound to get it out of Lydia eventually. Both she and Emma are very skeptical about what they have heard."

"As are some others," Kendale said. "It does not make sense. Oh, B follows A and C follows B just fine. But there is much that is missing or odd."

Just his luck. Ambury, the investigator, and Kendale, the man who saw only blacks and whites, had mulled over the plot and found it lacking. That meant others had too.

"What is missing?"

"Any indication that she noticed you were alive before a month ago," Kendale said. "Evidence that in the last month she enjoyed your company rather than suffered it."

"You are being overly blunt again, Kendale," Ambury scolded. "What have I told you about that? A little finesse is in order."

"Hell, you are the one who said she looked like riding back in the rain with him was a fate worse than death."

"I did not put it quite that way. I said I would have suspected they went there to meet each other, except that she did not appear happy to have to ride back with him. Perhaps that was not because she did not favor him. Maybe she was afraid someone would start suspecting their secret tendre if she was seen like that." Ambury sighed. "You keep missing the nuances."

"Well, you just touched on another thing to make one skeptical. If there was a tendre, why would it be a secret?" Kendale asked. "Not because Southwaite would not approve. Not because Penthurst has a wife who might complain. Not because she is of low birth and his friends would object. Why would there need to be a secret rendezvous in Buxton, for that matter?"

Penthurst kept his silence and let them make the arguments being made, no doubt, at dinner tables all over town this week.

"I'll not be saying what is missing from this story, but there's those who think they know what it is," Kendale concluded.

Ambury gave Kendale a scowl, then smiled broadly. "More wine, I think." He hailed one of the club's servants.

"What do some think is missing?" Penthurst asked.

Ambury waved the question, and Kendale, away as so much bad air. "He is just being Kendale. You know how he is."

"I do indeed. Regrettably, among his worse qualities there dwell a few superb ones, such as a talent for analysis and incisive deduction. So, Kendale, what is missing?"

"Do. Not. Answer. That," Ambury ordered, firmly.

"He is right," Kendale said. "We can't have you dueling with another one of us. You might end up the one dead this time, and the realm needs its dukes more than its viscounts."

The reference hung there like the dangling sword it was. How like Kendale the Implacable to bring it up casually, as if it did not threaten to slice at all of them, including him.

"I will issue no challenges. I should know what is abroad, however, so I can counter it as best I can."

Ambury appeared skeptical. Kendale just drank his wine.

"What is missing, but some think is implied," Ambury began. "Not by us, of course, and I am sure it has not entered Southwaite's head at all— What is missing is a seduction."

"A ruthless seduction," Kendale elaborated.

"Here in London, with a later secret rendezvous in Buxton, but not for an elopement," Ambury said.

"Of a somewhat addled woman who some think has not been right in the head for years now," Kendale threw in.

"In this thinking, which I repeat none of us believe for a minute—isn't that right, Kendale?—in this thinking, the sudden appearance of Trilby forced your hand. With the Buxton assignation exposed, you had no choice but to marry her fast."

Hell and damnation. He had saved her from ruin, and now he was being painted a scoundrel.

"Who is saying this? Who? I insist you tell me the blackguards' names."

Ambury grimaced. "Ah. Well, see, I can't do that. And I will thrash Kendale if he tries to. If you learn any names, you are going to confront them, and there will be the devil to pay. Then Southwaite will hear it all, and maybe start wondering, and that will be the end of a lot of friendships."

"I thought you should be told, since it involves your honor," Kendale confided. "I was just saying so before you arrived. Ambury convinced me we don't need more duels, however, and I would not want this to get back to your wife and it would if you started killing men over it."

He was not convinced these two did not believe the scurrilous explanation conjured up by malicious minds. They both agreed his own plot did not entirely hold up to close scrutiny, after all.

He looked at them. Honorable men, both. Old friends, for all that had happened and despite Kendale's lack of total forgiveness.

"I will tell you two the true story, and rely on your discretion."

Surprised, both leaned toward him, curious.

"There was no seduction, but also no tendre. Lydia did not go to Buxton to meet me. I followed her there, because I suspected she was up to some reckless scheme, such as she has been known to engage in. No sooner had I arrived than I saw Trilby's attempted abduction. I interfered, issued a challenge in my anger, and brought attention to Lydia's presence in that town, and mine, and Trilby's. Rumors were bound to fly, most of them about her, so—"

"You married her to spare her," Ambury finished.

"Damned decent of you," Kendale muttered. "What was she doing there?"

"She will not say, except to insist she did nothing wrong. I think she went there to gamble, but do not know for certain."

Kendale rolled his eyes. "Make her tell you. Hell, the actual true story may be the easiest to explain."

"Don't be brutish. He can hardly beat it out of her," Ambury said.

"Who spoke of beating? He is her husband. Just demand she tell you."

"You speak as if such demands always result in compliance. That is newlywed bliss speaking. Trust me, Kendale, within a year you can demand all you want, and if your wife wants to keep a secret, she will do so."

"Speak for yourself. Marielle and I have no secrets. At least not anymore."

Exasperated, Ambury threw up his hands and turned his attention away from Kendale. "Your actual, true story is safe with us. He is correct, however. If you can be sure her reason for going to Buxton will not reflect on her even worse, letting it be known may be the wisest course."

He did not relish the notion of trying to pry that information out of Lydia, but he knew he would have to try. In the meantime—

"You can tell whomever you choose the following. If I learn any man has said I seduced Lydia, let alone with dishonorable intentions, I will call him out. If I hear any woman has spread such a rumor, I will see she is not received in any house worth visiting. We fell in love and eloped because we thought it would be romantic. It is not a very dramatic story, and perhaps too simple for minds looking for intrigue, but there it is."

Kendale left soon after, and he and Ambury joined

others at a card table. An hour later Ambury also took his leave.

Penthurst walked out alongside him. "Before you go, take a turn with me outside."

Ambury followed him out of the club. They strolled along the street, shrouded by the mist.

"I have decided to accept your offer to do some investigating for me," he said.

"Do you want me to find out what Lydia was doing at Buxton?"

"It isn't that." Not yet, at least. "It has to do with Lakewood. I need you to find a man for me. His name is Michael Greenly. I believe he is of a gentry family in Yorkshire. He was in the Life Guards for a few years, but is no longer."

"That last bit should help. Why would he give up a plum commission such as that?"

"It was discovered that he bought the favor that had recommended him for it. His choices were selling out, or scandal and possibly a trial."

Ambury paced along a good hundred feet before asking the inevitable question. "Are you saying he paid Lakewood for that favor? That Lakewood was selling commissions?" His tone carried censure. Influence came into play all the time in such things, but should not be sold.

"Lakewood did not have the position to influence commissions. He had friends, however, who did."

"Which friend did he use with this Greenly?"

"Me."

He felt Ambury's gaze peering his way in the night. They turned and retraced their steps.

"Greenly could not hold his drink and spoke of it to a fellow officer one night. How he had paid dearly for his commission, and far more than was known. My word as a gentleman that he had not paid me was enough to silence the matter, but he was invited to sell out at once. I confronted Lakewood, since I knew what must have happened."

"I am seeing the map that brought you to that field that morning, Penthurst. And I find myself scouring my memory for whether Lakewood ever asked *me* to put in a good word for a young man seeking a commission."

"I suggest you do not search too deeply. Just find Mr. Greenly, so I can learn whether I misunderstood the matter in some way."

Chapter 15

Lydia did not sleep quickly that night. She lay abed with the lamp still lit, trying to distract her unaccountable restlessness by planning how she might decorate her bedchamber.

Toile, perhaps. In green. She would not want her apartment to drip with satins or velvet. Better to live in a fresh open garden than a ballroom. She would replace the heavily carved furniture with items showing Roman influence, perhaps in a light-toned wood.

While she debated wall coverings, she listened for the sounds of Penthurst returning. Of course he would eventually. Even if Rosalyn's fears had been realized and he had issued some challenge, the duel would not be fought right away.

She should have asked for a promise he would never

do that again. She doubted he would have given it, but she could have at least tried. She hated duels, and how men resorted to them at the least provocation. Penthurst seemed to do that faster than most too.

She remembered the day she learned about that other duel. The news had come from Southwaite, in a brief note while she was visiting her aunt Amelia in Hampshire. He had been distraught, she could tell, over the death of his friend. His words offered little comfort to her, but then he did not know how she felt about Lakewood.

No one had guessed. Not her aunts and not her brother. No one ever knew how she had cried into her pillow night after night for weeks on end. And when the pain finally receded, it had left her numb and uncaring.

The memories had dazed her. She blinked them away, and saw her bedchamber again. And at the door to the dressing room next door, she saw the duke.

He watched her. She could tell even though he appeared a dark form in a dark threshold. The lamp picked up tiny golden lights in his eyes. How long had he been standing there, watching?

It burned when she swallowed, and she realized she had shed a few tears while remembering. Had he seen that?

She collected herself. She put aside the love-struck, miserable girl and found the woman of the world. She could spend her whole life hating the duke, and hating her fate, but that would be a stupid choice.

"Your aunt told me you went to your clubs to issue

challenges if necessary. I trust we will not be entertaining a line of seconds tomorrow."

"No seconds will be calling. No challenges were issued."

"I am glad."

"For my safety?"

"For the friends and families of everyone, including you."

He came into her chamber. He wore a loose patterned silk robe. She guessed that was all he wore. "Sometime we will have to talk about that. About the friends and families." He reached out and ran his thumb over her cheek. When he lifted it, moisture glossed its skin. "We will have to talk about this too."

She wiped her eyes quickly. "Not tonight, I hope."

"No, not tonight." He turned to go.

An odd emotion prodded her. Disappointment? No, embarrassment. He had come here and found her weeping like some child. *He has no interest in young innocents. None at all.*

She would have to live a lifetime with this man.

"Are you going? I thought you had come to collect on the second debt, the one from Morgan's."

He paused, and turned. "You are nothing if not unpredictable, Lydia. And still a little reckless too."

"I hope so. I would not want to be predictable and staid. Life can be dull enough without being determined to make it so."

He sat on the side of the bed. "It sounds as if your

goal as a woman was excitement, not marriage. That explains a lot of things."

She wondered what things. Perhaps she would be better off not knowing what he really thought of her, since they were stuck with each other. "I will admit that I have preferred experiences that are out of the ordinary. Perhaps it was the excitement."

He gave her hip a little swat, and gestured for her to move over. He drew off the robe and lay beside her, then moved so he lay atop her, his hips settled between her thighs. His physicality startled her as it had the first time. The sensation of his skin on hers, and of his body pressing hers, had her senses all alert and waiting.

Braced on his forearms, he toyed at a tendril of her hair. "At night we will find excitement, Lydia. Whether it is out of the ordinary will be up to you."

She puzzled what he meant, but only for a moment. He kissed her and distracted her from pondering meanings and innuendos.

She knew what was coming this time. Her body relished the pleasure as it began its sly titillation. He let her embrace him, and she held his shoulders, then ventured a little caress that revealed the smooth texture of his skin and the firm frame and muscles of the hard body it covered. He did not appear to mind, so she explored a little further, fascinated by the feel of him, admiring the shoulders tensed above her, gazing past his head while he kissed her so she could watch her fingers play along the hills and ridges of his body.

His lips smiled against hers. He broke the kiss and looked down at her. "You are fairly distracted by something."

"I— That is, not distracted as such, just—"

He rolled onto his back. His hands closed on her waist and with an easy swing he set her atop him, straddling his waist. "Just curious. This will be better for you, then. You can look and touch as much as you want, Lydia. Your hands give me pleasure, just as mine do you."

She assessed her position. "This is not exactly ordinary, is it?"

"Not completely ordinary, but not so unusual either."

It felt quite daring. Exciting. She settled in better. A prod on her bottom startled her. She looked back and realized that the tip of his shaft poked at her, low on her bottom, as if searching for her— The possible implications left her astonished.

He kissed her crown and caressed her breast. She squirmed a bit. That prod responded. She wondered if she could scoot forward just a bit so—

"Do not worry. That is for another night, not this one."

That hardly reassured her. She thought, however, that if she sat up, she might not feel as vulnerable. Once she did, she understood what he meant about this being better. She could see him nicely now, those shoulders and arms and his chest down to where she sat. She fluttered her fingertips over him, to judge whether all of him felt like his shoulders.

Better, she decided. She laid her palms flat against

him high on his chest. She felt his heartbeat, its rhythm pulsing right into her, up her arm and down her body.

Other than a slow caress on her arm, he had left her to her explorations. Now abruptly he guided her head down and kissed her hard.

He held her like that, his hand behind her neck, while he ravished her mouth. She sensed the power of desire in him far more than she had the last time. His kiss did not so much lure as demand. Her body became sensitive all over, alive with anticipation. When his tongue entered her, he held her head in both his hands so she could not refuse, or in any way pull away even a small bit.

He kissed her breathless before releasing her. She pressed her weight onto her arms and hovered, thinking she might fall over.

He dragged the skirt of her nightdress up. "Take this off."

She had to kneel up high to do that. She slid it up and over her head. The cool air lapped at the fine sheen of sweat that passion had raised on her skin. It seemed another tease, one more thing designed to make her think and care about nothing except being touched and kissed and driven to sensual insanity again.

Holding her around the waist with his two hands, he lowered her again. Only this time she landed a little farther back, and on top of his shaft. She felt it beneath her, hard and big, pressing against her softest flesh. Shudder after shudder trembled through her loins.

This position might be better for her to see him, but he also could see her. He watched her reactions when he gently stroked her breasts' tips. He saw how she struggled to contain it, and deliberately made sure she could not. He aroused her until she could barely stay upright, and until her exposure to his gaze undid her. She wanted to hide her madness by cowering beneath him, not show him how he made her die of want.

Finally he guided her down for another kiss, then spoke. "Do as I say now, and I think you will know a pleasure most extraordinary, Lydia."

He rose up and stacked pillows so his upper body rose. He reached for her and moved her forward. "Put your hands here and press to steady yourself." *Here* was against the headboard, a foot above his head. Doing that meant angling forward while kneeling, so she hovered over his torso and head.

He moved her knees farther apart, wide. Her stance alone aroused her profoundly. He took her breasts in his hands and that made it worse. He caressed the tips again and again until she could not contain her cries.

"Some night I will put you like this, but kneel behind you and take you that way. Do you understand? But not tonight. Tonight I want you to accept the pleasure. I want you to weep and cry and scream with it. Obey me and you will be glad for it, I promise."

Then he ensured she cried. Her breasts hung near his mouth and he used his teeth and tongue to push her past all sense of decency. The more he tortured her, the more she felt sanity slipping away. She pictured the night to come, when he would kneel behind her, and her bottom rose and her vulva pulsed as if he were there.

She had no choice but to accept the madness. It claimed her completely all on its own. It brought excruciating desire, however. He slid his hand into the slick damp atop her thighs, where her splayed legs left her open and helpless. He touched again and again, each sure, small stroke sending a sharp shock of pleasure into her chaos.

She cried out, frantically, shamelessly. With each touch she did again. When his caresses stayed on two spots of unbearable sensation, her cries turned pleading. As if learning what he needed to know, long deep caresses shook her essence. She moved to make it better, worse, more, and lost all control when she did.

Soaring now. Aware of nothing but pleasure so intense it was not real. It suffused her, then constricted more and more, increasing in power, frightening her.

Suddenly a shock of sensation burst out of the center of the intensity and shattered it apart, casting her into darkness. Wave after wave of bliss flowed through her while she existed in that unearthly place.

When she found some sense again, he was inside her and she was on her back. His palm now pressed the headboard while he leveraged his weight into a rhythm of thrusts. Not as careful as the last time, nor as gently, he thrust again and again until he too accepted the ecstasy.

He dragged himself back to alertness, and to the tangle of limbs they made. He moved off her and rolled onto his back, still half absorbed by the small death of release. He tucked her close instinctively, to ride out the rest in her warmth.

She stretched against him like a cat and snuggled against his side under his arm. They lay like that until his brain began working right again.

"You were right," she said sleepily. "It was most extraordinary. Was it wicked of me?"

"We are married."

"Yes. But . . ."

But still wicked, because he might as well have been a stranger, he guessed she meant. Wicked because women thought pleasure and love belonged together, unless a woman was a whore.

"What other experiences have you had in your determination to be extraordinary, Lydia?"

She yawned. "Not any this interesting."

"You saw those men naked. That was not predictable for an innocent."

"I can claim no credit. It was an accident, as I said." She pulled the sheet up, and curled on her side to sleep.

"Who were they?"

She went still. She did not speak.

"I know you are not asleep already, Lydia."

She sighed. "If I tell you, do you promise not to do something noble and honorable about it. They cannot be blamed either."

He liked that "either." He suspected Lydia, the aspiring woman of the world, had looked at those bare asses good and long. "I will not blame them or ever speak of it."

"Since you promise—it was Kendale and Ambury."

Kendale and Ambury? Hell.

Very awake now, he glared at her peaceful, contented face.

"Are there any other extraordinary experiences I should know about?" He sounded a little harsh to his own ears. But the mind reeled. He remembered Kendale bringing up male brothels. It would be just like her to be curious, and visit one to see what it was all about.

No, that was a mad notion. She wouldn't ever have done that. He eyed her. Would she?

"It would be best if I knew now, Lydia. For example, your brother mentioned something about a galley—"

She came alive in an instant. Her eyes opened and flashed anger. "I am going to scold him severely. How dare he speak of that. And to you, of all people."

"He probably thought your husband should be prepared for prior adventures that might lead to talk."

"No one knows about that. Except him. And now you. And of course the smugglers."

"And of course *the smugglers*?"

"It was their galley, wasn't it?" She sat up, exasperated at her brother's indiscretion. "It was last summer. Do not tell anyone, but living on the coast as we do, we know some of the smugglers who ply the waters there. You really can't avoid acquaintance with someone in that trade. One in particular we know very well. I think he helps Southwaite with that watching, but we have known Tarrington since I was a child. He is like you that way."

"Except he is a criminal and I am a duke." A small detail to her, no doubt, but one worth pointing out.

"He has galleys that go over to France and bring back wine and lace and such. Such adventure! Again and again he goes. I have never been to France at all."

He covered his eyes with his hand. He knew, just knew, where this story was going.

"So I stowed away. He discovered me halfway over. It was so hot under the canvas pile where I had hidden that I had to come out. Tarrington was not very nice about it."

"He knew your brother would have his head if anything happened to you."

"So he said. Still, he did not have to turn around as he did. He could have at least finished the run so I could see France. He did not have to tell Southwaite either. And he most definitely did not have to make me help row. My hands were blistered for weeks."

He knew Tarrington. His opinion of the man now rose with each of her sentences. "A few blisters on your hands was a small punishment. You were lucky your brother was not the sort of man to give you blisters on your rump for such a stupid and dangerous caprice."

"It *was* stupid. I knew it was even as I did it. But it was still exciting." She smiled slyly, turning their prior conversation back at him.

He hardened at once. He came close to throwing her down and showing her more excitement. Instead he stretched for his robe, threw it on, and left her to her sleep.

She might be nothing but trouble. She might try one outragcous extraordinary thing after another. As a duchess, however, the whole world would hear about most of it.

There was nothing else to do. He would be forced to see that her need for excitement was met in other ways. Duty called.

"I t is very early for you to be going out," Rosalyn said two mornings later. She sat in the morning room drinking coffee and eating the little cakes she kept instructing the cook to make. Her earlier than normal arrival for breakfast meant Lydia had not left before Rosalyn came down, the way she had planned.

Lydia pulled on her gloves. "I am going to Berkeley Square."

Rosalyn considered that while she sipped and chewed. Finally she gave an expression of quasi-approval. "I suppose with your own family, the question of appropriate hours for calls can be ignored."

"I am so relieved you think so. I almost did not dress until I received your agreement that it would not cause a scandal."

Rosalyn's lids hooded her eyes. "You do not fool me, Lydia. Nor will I allow you to make me the brunt of your disrespectful humor."

"Then do not indulge your inclinations to treat me like a schoolgirl, Rosalyn. I do not need a finishing governess."

"Do you not?" Her gaze raked Lydia from head to toe. "Better if you had not dressed before seeing me, I dare say. That dress will not do for a duchess, even if she only visits family."

"Actually, I am going to visit Cassandra."

Rosalyn's brow puckered. Her mouth twitched. Lydia picked up her reticule and left.

It had been naughty to deliberately upset Rosalyn by announcing she would visit the unsuitable Lady Ambury. Very wrong. But each time she saw Rosalyn, Rosalyn managed at least one nasty poke. One criticism or one sigh or one expression of dismay. Under the circumstances, she could be forgiven for poking back. Perhaps in a few years she would become so mature that she would be able to resist doing that.

She instructed the coach to take her to her brother's house. She entered it as he had insisted she feel free to do, without ceremony. She found Emma finishing her own breakfast.

Emma ate faster on seeing her. "I am ready. Just one more bite."

"Has Southwaite come down yet?"

"No, but he will soon."

"Then we should go. I would rather not lie to him."

"And I would? I have already told him you and Cassandra insisted on taking me to some shops so I do not die of boredom. That was not a lie. We will indeed go to some shops before we return."

Emma stood. Rather suddenly in the last week her condition had begun to show. The styles hid it still, but when she moved, the little bulge became visible beneath the muslin.

"It is so good of you and Cassandra to do this," she said as she buttoned her spencer.

"I have been looking forward to it, Emma."

They went out to the coach. It then circled the square to Ambury's house. Cassandra appeared at the door as soon as it stopped. She came down the steps and accepted the footman's help into the carriage.

Lydia took in Cassandra's fashionable blue coaching ensemble. "You can hardly be useful wearing that."

"I brought an apron."

"You will cry off doing anything that might dirty that ensemble, apron or not. If I had to suffer Rosalyn thinking I had no style, you could have worn old clothes too."

"Rosalyn only disapproved. Ambury would have been suspicious if I decked myself out like a servant. Now, let us go. I confess I am very excited, but I do not know why. Perhaps because we are on a secret mission."

"How dramatic," Emma said. "I hope you are as excited three hours from now. I fear you are in for a big disappointment. This will be hard work. I would have brought the servants if I could be sure they would be discreet."

The coach rolled through Mayfair, heading south. It stopped near Piccadilly, on Albemarle Street. Emma led the way into a tall building that housed Fairbourne's auction house.

A chaos of activity greeted them inside the exhibition hall. Men scrubbed floors and dusted high chandeliers. Others moved tables. Two hung paintings on one of the high gray walls.

They followed Emma through it all to a chamber in the back. She paused after she opened the door and audibly groaned. "It is even worse than the letter from Obediah admitted."

All kinds of objects stuffed the chamber. Paintings and rolls of paper. Silver objects and fine porcelains. Small furniture pieces and stacks of leather-bound books.

A new presence hovered behind Lydia. She stood aside so Obediah, a slight, balding man with an avuncular manner, could enter.

"I am distraught that you had to come, Lady Southwaite." He looked around, shaking his head in dismay.

"How long has it been since my brother was here?"

"A week or two. Maybe three."

Emma's eyes narrowed. "None of this is catalogued? The auction is less than a fortnight away. I will *kill him*."

Cassandra patted her shoulder. "Do not become overwrought. We are here and in no time at all we will have dealt with this."

Emma did not appear convinced. Stoic but unhappy, she studied the contents. Then she walked out.

"I will do it, as I usually do, because he does not. Here is how we must proceed. The items should be brought to me in the office, one by one. I will write them up, and you can dust them while I do. The men have too much to prepare and cannot be spared today, but hopefully they can help tomorrow."

Cassandra shed her mantelet and donned her apron. Lydia removed her spencer.

"The silver first," Emma said before disappearing through a door nearby, to the office.

Lydia gripped a heavy candelabra. Cassandra handed her a cloth.

"Do you think your brother will be angry if he learns she is doing this?" Cassandra asked.

Lydia thought about how her brother treated Emma. He was no one's fool, least of all a woman's, but they had a very special understanding of each other. "If he forbade it, yes, he will be angry, but mostly out of worry for her. He understands what Fairbourne's means to her, so that will make a difference."

She carried the candelabra to Emma. She sat at a desk, paper and ink at the ready. Her sharp eyes examined the base for marks, then she scratched onto the paper. Dust flew when Lydia used the cloth.

She returned to the storage room. "We must dust here. She will be the worse for it if we do it in the office."

She and Cassandra found a rhythm that wasted little time. It was hard work, however, especially when they handled the larger items. If Emma tired, she did not show it. The hours progressed in a series of passings, Lydia going one way while Cassandra went the other.

After delivering one of the rolls of drawings, Lydia returned to the storage room to find Cassandra waiting. "After she finishes with those, we must make her stop. It has been more than four hours. She will go all day and all night if we are not firm with her."

"It was a rather thick roll. I expect it will take her some time." Cassandra sat on a chair waiting to be catalogued. "It appears you and I have time for a chat. How do you fare at Grosvenor Square?"

Lydia moved a tapestry and sat on another chair. She had not really spoken to either Cassandra or Emma since her return to London. Oh, they had seen her that first day and showered her with expressions of happiness, but neither one had visited her yet, and no questions had been asked.

One just had been, however.

"I manage not to hate his aunt, although she does not like or approve of me and makes her opinions very clear. She is careful not to go too far, because she fears he will ask her to leave then. Only that restrains her, I think."

"I was not really asking about his aunt, Lydia."

No, she was not.

"I have learned that I like sharing a bed with a handsome, exciting man, even if I do not love him and hold a serious grievance against him. So I fare well, I suppose, in the one thing that could have made this marriage hellish."

Cassandra's smile barely wavered. Her gaze probed, however. "There are not many whose direct speech can startle me, but you have always been one whose words often do. So it was not a love match. I wasn't sure. He always seemed to be around you the last month, and I thought, perhaps— Had you no choice, Lydia?"

"He insisted not, and I saw no way out. A comedy

of coincidences and accidents lined up, leading to that church in Scotland. I wasn't even really compromised. It only thoroughly appeared as if I had been. If that isn't unfair, I don't know what is." She laughed, then sighed. "He probably feels he was trapped into doing the right thing, and I feel trapped into being a duchess. If you sympathize with his plight more than mine, I cannot blame you."

Cassandra took her hand in hers, and looked very sympathetic. "You have found one kind of contentment, you say. Perhaps with time you will find many other kinds."

"I am determined to try, but . . ."

"But you have that serious grievance. Does he know about it?"

She nodded. Cassandra said nothing. Lydia looked at her friend, sitting there patiently, not asking the question whispering in the silence. Cassandra had been more sophisticated at nineteen than most women were at forty. She did not judge quickly, or in the normal ways.

"It is that duel," she blurted. "None of this would have happened if my brother and Ambury had not become his friends again. I was supposed to just accept that they did, and that all was forgiven and forgotten. Only it isn't. Not with me."

Cassandra appeared surprised, even taken aback. "You mean Lakewood. It was almost two years ago, and while he was your brother's good friend—"

"He was my friend too. A real friend, not like

Ambury and Penthurst whom I saw as they came and went."

Cassandra peered intently at her. Curious. Guessing. "Did you spend time with him?"

"On occasion, after I came out."

Cassandra stood abruptly. She paced, her arms crossed, her expression distracted by thought, glancing Lydia's way every few steps. One quick look slid past Lydia's chair and Cassandra strode over and closed the door. She sat again.

"Lydia, I find myself in a dilemma. Forgive me, but I must ask—did Lakewood indicate he saw you as more than a friend? Did he lead you to believe he wanted a life with you?"

Had he? She had picked through her memories so often, even before he died. Had his attention been only friendship, and she built the rest out of air? There had been all that time in Hampshire, however, and a kiss, and the way he wanted their time together to be a secret so her brother would not interfere.

"I do not know," she admitted. "He did not propose, if that is what you mean. Yet—I think he flirted. He did not treat me like Southwaite's little sister entirely. He amused me with descriptions of great adventures we might have one day, but those could have been mere storytelling. I thought there was more, but perhaps he was just being kind."

"Do not blame yourself if you misjudged Lakewood's intentions. If he did not want your brother to know, he had some purpose, whether good or ill. You were simply too inexperienced to see it, and to guess which way it would go."

It was a very Cassandra sort of thing to say—direct, almost cruel, but immediately noting the one part of the story that made the relationship something other than a normal friend-of-the-family one—Lakewood's desire for discretion.

"Lydia, I cannot absolve Penthurst for what happened that day. However, I doubt Lakewood's intentions to you were honorable. He probably planned an elopement, because your brother did not countenance a marriage. Lakewood's fortune had been much diminished, and he sought to marry well, by any means possible."

"You damn him easily, with no evidence."

"Evidence enough, to my mind. He was charming as sin, Lydia, but he was not of good character."

"You still hold whatever happened between you and him against his reputation, when it was years ago. Six or seven, no? Ancient history, but you will speak badly of him and he cannot defend himself." She stood and hurried to the door. "I am sorry I confided in you."

She found Emma cleaning her pen in the office. "You must go home now, or you will become overtired and Southwaite will never forgive me, Emma."

Emma rested back in her chair. "I will not argue. I have made good progress, and am content that the auction will not be a disaster. I will finish with the paintings another day."

Cassandra stepped into the chamber too, removing her apron. "We will visit a few shops on Oxford Street on the way back. We need only step into them to make our explanation for the day's outing honest."

"If we must," Lydia muttered. She had expected Cassandra to comfort her, not tell her Lakewood had planned to use her like she was a young, naïve idiot. Now she longed to be alone with her thoughts at home.

Emma stacked her pages neatly, then looked from one of them to the other. Her gaze lingered on Lydia. "Only a few shops, Cassandra, if you do not mind. I think both Lydia and I are quite done for the day."

After the shops were visited, the coach brought Cassandra home. Lydia and Emma proceeded on to Southwaite's house.

"Did you and Cassandra have an argument?" Emma asked.

"A small one. It was not important."

Emma leveled that frank gaze at her. "It has much affected your mood for something not important."

"She cast aspersions upon an old friend who cannot defend himself."

"Are you speaking of Lakewood?"

"How did you know?"

"I only guessed. His ghost has a way of appearing too often in our lives. You must forgive Cassandra. The man brought her to the edge of ruin, so she is hardly able to see anything good in him."

Lydia turned and stared at Emma. "I know that she refused to marry him after a minor sort of compromise. I always thought that very sane of her. However, it hardly is reason to condemn the man's character."

"There are no minor compromises. She paid a high price for her refusal to marry him, Lydia. She left England soon after, to go on tour with her aunt, and was abroad for two years to escape the scandal."

Lydia recalled Cassandra's words in the storage room. He would do anything to marry well, she had said.

"The gentlemen believed he pined for her to the end," Emma said as the carriage stopped again. "For a long time they thought the duel was about her, but are now convinced not."

This day had held many shocks, but none so big as this one. "Do they know who it was about instead?"

Emma shook her head. "Nor will the duke say. If he did not speak of it at his trial, he probably never will." Emma accepted the footman's hand and stepped down from the coach. Distracted now, and looking tired, she walked toward the house's door.

Lydia stuck her face to the coach window. "Emma, why did they ever think it was Cassandra?

Emma turned back for a moment. "I suppose they thought that because to the end of his life, he kept telling them that Cassandra was the only woman he would ever love."

Chapter 16

"Since he is still here in London, he on occasion sees some of his friends from the guard. Privately, of course. While you spared him public disgrace, they all knew he sold out under pressure and that never is good news."

"You are very good at this, Ambury. I should have hired you for all kinds of investigations in the past. I had asked his old comrades-in-arms for his whereabouts last year, and learned nothing."

"Did you ask as a sympathetic new friend who had just bought them several rounds in a tavern, or as the Duke of Penthurst who wanted to find a man whose career he had helped ruin? Even if you attempted the former, they would have smelled the latter. Men will reveal in confidences what they never will under coercion."

They rode through the City on the streets surrounding Covent Garden. This area of London sported a broad assortment of people of all classes. Whores loitered at corners not far from coffee shops frequented by men of the ton. Items of all kinds overflowed markets large and small. Thousands crammed the old buildings lining the narrow streets.

Ambury removed a small paper from his coat and checked it, then twisted to ascertain the numbers of the buildings. "It should be after the next crossroads."

A few minutes later he stopped his horse and dismounted. "Up one level, I was told. In the front."

Penthurst swung down and tied his horse. "I must ask you to stay here."

"If you like, but I have a personal interest, don't I?" His tight expression indicated he had realized he too had been used by Lakewood. Ambury no longer defended Lakewood, and said he knew far more than anyone guessed, but Penthurst doubted he had escaped scathing disappointment on realizing his friendship had been tainted this way.

"I told you not to think too deeply on it."

"Good of you. The mind, however, cannot always stop its thoughts. As I recall, he came to me twice. Perhaps he turned to you because it would be rash to drink from the same well too often."

"Something like that."

"How much like that?"

He wanted to know it all, of course. He had the ability to find out if left to his own devices. Perhaps half a loaf would dissuade him from doing that. "Lake-wood first exploited Southwaite after you. He then turned to me after approaching Kendale, in the army himself at the time, who insisted on meeting the aspiring officer to assess fitness rather than relying on Lakewood's good word."

Ambury laughed, bitterly. "Well, God bless Kendale. No shortcuts on duty for him."

"No."

"Southwaite too, though. Does he know?"

"I don't think so."

"No reason for him to, it seems to me."

"I agree."

Ambury looked up to the second-level window. "It was said he drinks. It might be wise to have me come with you."

"I think I can still pacify a drunk if I have to."

"Have it your way."

He entered the building. Smells assaulted him. Fish, onions, tallow, and decay mixed with the sour stink of people not given to cleanliness in either body or home. High above a child screamed. He passed a door out of which a hot argument seeped.

At the top of the stairs he found the door to the chamber that would overlook the street. A young man answered his knock. Dark hair ungroomed and slack jaw unshaved, his pasty color said he had not seen daylight in a while.

He had never met Michael Greenly. A mistake that. Kendale would have found him lacking. He was not foxed yet, but halfway there, and his eyes held surly lights that did not speak well for his temperament.

Penthurst felt stock being taken, such as one assesses horses up for auction. Whatever Greenly saw had him backing into his chamber.

There was only one, clearly. It held a bed, table, and a heap of clothes. A bottle of gin stood on a bookshelf not far from the bed.

"Who might you be?"

"Penthurst."

Greenly chewed that over, then his eyes narrowed. "You're the reason I was forced to sell out."

"I'm also the reason you had a commission to start."

"You got your money for that, free and clear, looks like to me. I'm the one who was out thousands."

He resisted the temptation to hit the man, but only because his anger was for another person. He knew Lakewood had used them all. He had not known for certain until this moment that he had also implicated all of them. "Sit, please. I want to talk with you about that."

"Nothing to say, is there. Bled me well, you did, then turned around and—"

"*Sit.*"

Greenly sat.

"I have some simple questions for you, Mr. Greenly. It would be best if you answered them simply too. And honestly."

Greenly glared at him.

"When you bought your commission, to whom did you pay the bribe?"

"I just said. You—"

"To whom did you hand the money?"

"Your friend you used as a go-between. Lakewood."

"Did you ever see anyone else with him during your negotiations? Think hard."

"Not with him, but once I followed him out of the tavern where we met and he was entering a carriage and there was a woman inside. Pretty. Red hair. Not that fire color. Darker. More brown. I remember because he had just told me the price and I was thinking it would be a long time before I could afford such as she."

"Did he ever speak about her?"

Greenly laughed. "Are you worried that your mistress was exposed? I guessed that was who she was. Lakewood told me about her, and how she ran things so you would not dirty your hands."

This was what Greenly had revealed at the start— that he had paid a duke's mistress money for his recommendation. When confronted, Lakewood had denied any woman was involved. It had been a gallant lie. Greenly's description would help, but not enough. "Did he tell you her name?"

"A little late to be trying to clean up, isn't it? Nah, he never said her name. He was discreet, for all the good it did him with you."

Lakewood had told a story, and this man had no reason to doubt it. Much like his own plot to explain his marriage to Lydia, the story fit all the known facts very neatly. Greenly would never be persuaded it was all a lie, but one had to try the truth, despite the long odds against it.

"Mr. Greenly, I never received your money. The amount would not have affected my comfort much, so you should ask yourself why I would risk my good name for it. Nor did I have the good fortune to enjoy a mistress at the time. Lakewood lied to you. He kept the money, and perhaps shared it with conspirators unknown, including that woman. Since I was not involved, I did not betray you when, upon hearing about your accusation while in your cups, I did nothing to save you."

"Like hell."

"Believe what you will, but there it is." He looked around. "How do you live?"

"They let me sell out. I got that much back out of it."

"Be glad. Others did not." He removed twenty pounds from his coat and set it on the table. "Go back to Yorkshire and your family. Nothing good will come to you in this town."

Ambury waited outside. "Did you learn anything?"

"A few things. Not enough." Not enough, and all of it disheartening.

They mounted their horses.

"Are you going to tell me?" Ambury asked.

"To what end? Nothing good, that is certain. I already regret that I told you what I did." He turned his horse. "Thank you for finding him. I am leaving town for the afternoon, so will part from you here."

He rode off and aimed his horse for the river. Two hours later he was swinging an ax on Mr. Gosden's farm.

* * *

Lydia ate dinner with Rosalyn. That was a mistake. Rosalyn quizzed and poked about the day with Emma and Cassandra. It took more effort than Lydia wanted to expend to avoid being cornered into a lie or an indiscretion.

Better to have just stayed in her apartment, where she retreated upon returning from the auction house, and to where she ran after the meal ended. Penthurst had been gone all day and it appeared he might be gone all night. The hours ticked by with silence next door.

She could not escape a melancholy that had entered her after the day's outing. Hearing Lakewood disparaged by women she respected created confusion about her memories. Hearing that he had claimed an unending love for Cassandra made her sick at heart.

She drifted toward sleep in her sadness. Then, abruptly, her senses snapped alert. She cocked her head. All still remained silent next door, but she sensed movement there, as if it came to her through the floorboards rather than through sounds. She listened intently and finally she heard steps on the other side of the wall, in the duke's dressing room. Voices too, she thought.

She padded over to the connecting door. She opened it a crack and heard the duke tell his valet to call for hot water, lots of it. She ventured down the short corridor and peered around the corner.

"What happened to you?" she cried.

Penthurst stood there, absolutely filthy. Mud covered his boots. His cravat was gone and his top shirt button undone. Soiling showed on his coats and shirt, but his face had received the worst of it.

"Were you waylaid and thrown in a ditch?" She went over to him. "Have you been hurt?"

A corner of his mouth curved up. "I am not hurt at all. I have been visiting a tenant's farm."

"And he threw mud at you?"

He shook off his coat and unbuttoned his waistcoat and shirt. "I was working there. I do that sometimes. Think of it as a small eccentricity on my part." He stripped off his shirt and threw it onto a chair.

"I would think of it that way, except you are not eccentric. Well, keeping that queue and the old fashions as long as you did came close to eccentricity, I suppose. Still, you are not odd the way eccentrics tend to be."

"I'm not? And here I was working so hard at it."

Three servants with buckets of water filed in and lined the buckets up on the floor. His valet showed at the door to the bedchamber, but the duke gestured for him to leave. Then he poured water into the bowl.

"I should leave so your valet can serve you."

"Do you want to leave?"

"No. I was bored and could not sleep, but did not want to wake Sarah."

"Stay if you want, although watching me wash will be poor entertainment."

As it turned out, that was not true. She had never seen a man wash before, and found it quite interesting. She also had the rare chance to look at those shoulders and back and chest and arms completely for a long time, not just glimpse them in the little vignettes she saw in bed.

"Why were you working on the tenant's farm? Is he ill?"

Having washed his face and neck, he went to work on his chest and arms. A soapy rag lathered him up nicely. Another rag began removing the soap. "He is not ill. He thinks I am, a little. In the head. I go about once a month, or if I need to think, or bury a hot anger. It is physical and worthwhile and not at all ducal." He looked at her. "You might find something like that too. Something that reminds you that you are human, so being a duchess does not go to your head too much."

"Being an earl's daughter did not go to my head too much."

"It will be different. Believe me. You have seen how duchesses wield power among both women and men. Even if you do not try to do that, you will be treated as a woman who can."

"I will put my mind to finding a way to humble myself. It is a little peculiar that you chose this work for that purpose. I can think of a hundred other ways to be reminded you are human," she said. "Most will not make you so dirty."

He beckoned her with a crooked finger. She went over and he handed her a soaped rag. "It is too late for a bath, so I will need to wash thoroughly this way. Since you scared off my valet, you can do my back."

"I can? What fun." She pushed up her dressing gown's

sleeves, stood behind him, and scrubbed away, reaching high to attend to all of him.

"I first worked a field when I was ten," he said while she kept at it, only now with long, soapy caresses. "A cousin and I had cruelly teased the son of one of my father's tenants. When my father heard of it, he ordered me to work for that farmer for a week. I was angry the first day, indignant the second, sorry for myself the third, and accepting the fourth. By the seventh day I discovered there were things about it that I did not mind and even enjoyed. When that field was harvested months later, I watched, knowing my labor had helped grow that crop." He turned and took the rag from her and handed her one for rinsing. "So I go back and do it sometimes, when I need to think or to escape being a duke for a few hours."

She finished with his back, and wondered why today he had wanted to forget he was a duke.

He sat down and pulled off his boots, then stood and began on the buttons on his breeches. He paused and looked at her. "You may want to go now. I still have washing to do."

She sat in a chair and tucked her legs under her. "I'll cover my eyes so you are not embarrassed." She smiled brightly to hide how the notion of going away and being alone again with all those sad and confusing thoughts dismayed her.

He saw it anyway. He set down the cloth and came over to her. Wet hand under her chin, he raised her face and looked in her eyes. "You are sad about something. Was my aunt unkind to you?"

"I am not really sad. I am just tired of trying to sort through some things that I need to think about. They do not signify to anyone else except me and I cannot see through them clearly tonight."

He did not appear convinced, but he released her. "If you are seeking distraction, perhaps this will help." With that he turned his back on her and dropped his lower garments.

That distracted her very nicely. She admired his bum and decided it was the nicest of all she had seen. What a treat to be able to study it up close like this too. He washed the other side of him while she experienced a profound aesthetic experience. His long, lean legs in particular occupied her attention. She had not realized before how handsome they were. Nicely shaped and just perfect with the rest of him.

He bent to wash them, his muscles stretching and his body angling. Then that soapy rag came around his hip to wash that alluring bum. On impulse, she went over and took it. "I can do this too."

He turned his head just enough to see her out of the corner of his eye. She laid the cloth over her palm for better purchase, but discovered it meant little fabric interfered with the feel of him. The sensation captivated her. Women were soft here, but his rounded swells felt hard and tense, even when she pressed her fingertips to check for certain.

"You probably could use this now." He handed the other cloth over his shoulder.

She took her time, making sure every bit of soap was

removed. He turned before she had finished to her liking, caught her waist, and pulled her tight against him.

"I do not think I have been so clean since I was a baby, Lydia."

"I like to be thorough."

He held her firmly. His gaze, serious and dark beneath his mussed, damp hair, scrutinized her. "But it was only a momentary distraction, I think."

Had she become so transparent to him, so quickly?

He stroked her cheek with his fingertips. "Something troubles you. It is in your eyes. What is it?"

I discovered today that the only extraordinary thing in my whole life had in fact been so ordinary, so predictable, that I am ashamed of my failure to see it for what it was. She wished she could say it. Standing like this, seeing the honest care in his eyes, she almost believed he would find a way to convince her that the conclusions forcing themselves on her were in error.

"Just thoughts that need sorting. I tire of how they plague me tonight, however. Hence my delight in the momentary distraction." She reached around and gave his bum a little tap.

He caught her hand back there. "I cannot stop the thoughts forever, but I know how to for a while. As for your past and ongoing interest in male anatomy—" He brought her hand around and placed it on his erect, enlarged shaft.

That shocked the tiresome thoughts right out of her head. Too curious to pretend she was not, she rested her brow against his chest and inhaled the scent of soap and flesh while she looked down and tentatively stroked. It did not feel at all as she expected. She almost giggled when it swelled more at her touch. She tapped the tip and it moved. He let her play, pressing a never-ending kiss to her crown.

"How interesting. What a very fine momentary distraction. I am understanding why some people give them names, like Harry or John."

"But we will not."

"No?"

"No."

She closed her hand around it and looked up at him. "You are sure?"

"Damnation, Lydia."

The next thing she knew the floor and walls were sliding past. Her legs flailed against air, and her head was very close to that handsome bum. He bundled her under his arm like a carpet, and sped through the dressing room and into his chamber.

With a thump she landed on his bed and he was above her, knee high between her legs, braced up on his arms. He looked down so intensely that she thought she could be absorbed by his eyes. She quickly worked the buttons and ribbons on her undressing gown, so she could open the front and push aside the fabric. His head lowered and his mouth closed at once on her breast, still covered in her thin cotton nightdress.

Her arousal came like an assault. She clutched at his shoulders and pressed against his knee and tasted his skin wherever her mouth could reach. "Yes," she whispered.

"Make it a very long distraction. Take me where I do not think about anything except pleasure."

She was wild in her passion. He responded in kind and ignored the sure knowledge that something drove her besides desire.

His mind clouded as a rare fever claimed them both. With grasping holds and biting kisses they pushed each other further. Her breasts, always so sensitive, stretched the thin fabric dampened by his mouth. Neither of them wanted to waste the time to drag the nightdress off.

Her hand closed on him again. Still tentative and careful, but Lydia was nothing if not bold. She quickly discovered what pleasured him, then turned ruthless.

He contained the ferocious drive that kept building while her caress created luxurious sensations. When he doubted he could control himself further, he knelt back, away from her, between her legs.

The undressing gown, with its ribbons and lace, framed her lithe body. He decided to keep it, and the nightdress that she still wore. He pushed up its hem, uncovering her legs. She watched, her eyes now filmed with desire, no longer so haunted as when he first saw her tonight. She breathed heavily, a series of gasps, each with a high, feminine note whenever she liked his touch.

He lifted the hem higher yet, pushing the dress up to her waist, exposing her mound and thighs. He slid his finger along the soft cleft, being as ruthless as she had been. She closed her eyes and moved into his touch.

Pleasure softened her face to a beautiful, ethereal expression. He watched abandon claim her and branded his mind with her glorious joy.

He bent down and kissed her inner thigh. When he rose, she was staring at him, her eyes wary beneath those thick lashes.

"I am going to use my mouth now, Lydia."

She pushed herself up on her arms. She tried to bring her legs together.

"You will like it. If you do not, I will stop."

"It sounds wicked."

"Many think it is."

She still looked shocked and skeptical. "Is it something most wives do?"

"No."

"But you want me to."

"Yes."

She fell back on the mattress. "Wicked and unusual. Perhaps this will not be such a terrible day after all."

What a Lydia thing to say.

He settled between her legs. He brought her along slowly, using his hand until her cries filled the chamber. He teased with his tongue until she overcame the first shocks. Even when she began moaning he restrained himself, even though her scent and taste sent him to a dark, uncivilized place.

Her release broke abruptly in a long series of quakes that flexed her whole body. He moved up and took her scream into himself with a kiss, then entered her and took her hard until he found his own furious finish.

* * *

He felt her moving, gathering herself to leave.
"Stay," he said. "Perhaps it will provide further distraction."

She reclined again. "Perhaps."

"I thought you were with Emma and Cassandra today. Did they quiz you too closely about us?"

She shook her head. "Each said something, however, that changed many things and confused some others." The night pulsed with silence. Then she spoke again. "Did you know that Lakewood was the man who compromised Cassandra years ago. The one she refused to marry?"

After talking to Greenly today, he had spent hours at the farm getting Lakewood out of his head. If what troubled Lydia touched on the man, he could swallow his distaste for the subject, he supposed. "Yes. We were friends then. His reputation was tainted by it, as surely as hers was. We were unkind to her as a result. Ambury presumably has been absolved, but not the rest of us. Not completely."

"I always admired her for not being bullied into it. I thought she was very brave."

Lydia had not been so brave. Was that what she mulled over so intently? Regrets that she had not been as bold as her friend?

"Did you know that the gentlemen thought your duel with Lakewood was fought over her?"

Hell. "Had they been talking to me, I would have explained they were wrong."

"Emma says they thought this because Lake-wood kept insisting he loved her and would love no one else."

"I always assumed he claimed that to garner sympathy that might spare him the worst assumptions of the gossip regarding that compromise."

"The others believed him, however. Do you suppose they also believed you had an affair with Cassandra, and that was why Lakewood called you out?" She turned and looked at him in the dark. "It is like one of your plots, isn't it? It fits all the publicly known facts."

It did indeed. They probably had believed that. It explained a lot of things. "I never had any affair with her, or even a mild flirtation."

"Yet the duel was over a woman, you said."

"Not a lover." At least he did not think so. "We were not rivals over a woman, is what I mean."

Did he imagine that she lightened suddenly? A dark cloud might have just blown away.

She resettled on her pillow. "Cassandra did not speak well of him today. She implied he would do anything for money."

Even Cassandra did not know the half of it. If he told Lydia that, would she believe him? He could do without that ghost in his life, and even in this bed. "I do not know what she referred to. I do know that he had a talent for using people."

She gazed over at him. A few glints of resentment flashed at the criticism, but he saw much more in her eyes. Sadness, such as he had seen in the dressing room. Disappointment too.

He suddenly realized what all of this had been about. This conversation, and her need for distraction tonight, and even her fury over that duel.

Damnation. He should have guessed. He should have at least wondered. Yet why would he? Lydia may show deep emotion about Lakewood, but Lakewood had never once spoken of Lydia with interest or admiration. Not once.

"I know you think badly of him," she said. "You have to, don't you? There could be no justification for what happened otherwise."

It was the wrong thing for her to say, today of all days. Anger over the day's revelations combined with resentment at how she kept this flame alive for a scoundrel. "I like to think that I am fair to him, and see the good and the bad. I also think I knew him better than you did, and I will tell you that he was not a friend to me, or to anyone else, if it suited his own purposes."

She sat up. "That is not true. I knew him very well, better than you or anyone else knows. He was a friend to *me*. For years, a *good* friend. His death undid me. I grieved such as I have never grieved. You men would have never noticed how he dealt with me, how he was kind to the child and drew out the girl. He made me laugh and we shared confidences. I have never had as good a friend, and probably never will."

It poured out in a furious rush, as if the words had

been dammed for years. The chamber became unnaturally silent when she finished.

"It sounds as if he was more than a friend, Lydia. Was he?"

Her face flushed. She started to leave the bed, but he caught her arm and held her in place.

"Was he? Both your loyalty and your emotion suggest it. If you are going to throw your anger and resentment at me, if that ghost is going to always interfere, you can damned well admit the reason."

She tried to retreat behind the sphinx mask, but the tears in her eyes would not allow it. "He was the great love of my life," she said. "So now you know why you are the last man I wanted protecting me, or obligated to marry me."

"Yes, now I know. But here we both are anyway."

She tried to leave again. He held firm.

"You will stay here tonight, Lydia. Lakewood might be the great love of your life, but you are mine now. I'll be damned if you will go back to your bed and spend the night burnishing his memory."

She said nothing. After a few minutes she turned on her other side, her back to him, and pretended to sleep.

She looked fragile there, her legs drawn up and the undressing gown still bunched around her form. Eventually her breaths lengthened and he knew she really slept. He wrapped his arms around her, tucked her against his body, and fell asleep himself.

Chapter 17

A week later, Lydia made quick work of her morning mail after finishing her breakfast. Rosalyn sat nearby, her sharp eyes missing nothing.

Several of the letters were invitations. Rosalyn knew the senders after merely glancing at the paper and handwriting from across the table, and offered recommendations on which to accept without prompting. Lydia hoped she would make at least one error, but she never did.

A few other letters contained petitions from charitable causes. She read the latter. Most were from large, notable charities taking a chance that a new duchess might want to patronize them along with so many of her peers. One, however, came from a charity that she had contributed to already.

That charity had never written to her before, and the

letter broke her heart. It read like a parting letter. The women who ran it thanked her for her past patronage, and wished her well in her new life. They seemed to assume that she would find more fashionable recipients of her largesse in the future.

Perhaps she would, but not quite yet. Lydia Alfreton would make at least one more contribution, she decided. Soon too. With winter coming, the money would be needed.

She thumbed through the rest of the mail, halting at one. She recognized the hand. Sick with foreboding, she unsealed it.

The letter was not signed. Of course not. She wanted to curse when she read it.

Your Grace,

I am delighted to learn of your good fortune! Well done. Under the circumstances, it might be best if our business is concluded faster than you proposed, since a duke might find your prose even more problematic than an earl. I await your reply.

The despicable scoundrel. The lying cheat. They had an agreement. He already had almost three thousand. She should not even have to think about him for a year.

"Did you receive bad news, Lydia?" Rosalyn peered at the letter while her teeth pierced one of the cakes.

"Not bad news. Just unexpected."

"Then you will not disfavor my plans for the day. I

would like you to accompany me on some calls, so you can spend time with some of your equals. There is much you can learn from them."

"I am sorry, but I have plans of my own. There is the appointment with the solicitor this morning, then I need to call on my aunts. I have neglected them."

"I will join you instead, then. I have not seen Amelia in some time. Let us go there first, then you can visit your aunt Hortense later, on your own."

There was no way out of it without being rude. She excused herself and went up to her apartment so she could stomp and yell and curse Mr. Trilby in private.

By the time she read the letter again, however, she had grown too disheartened for histrionics. Of course he would not honor their agreement. He had no honor. He was a blackmailer.

Sarah noticed her mood, and stopped sorting through the winter wardrobe. "Is something amiss?"

She handed over the letter. "I thought all was settled. Now, he sends this. It is as if he does not know his own mind. He agrees to one thing, then a week later changes what he wants and expects. How am I supposed to buy off a blackmailer if he will not stay bought?"

"He is a bold one, that is sure." She handed back the letter. "He believes he has you well cornered now, with your marriage, I suppose. The price of scandal has gone up."

It certainly had. It had gone up by the price of a duke. The cost to Penthurst of such a scandal had increasingly preyed on her mind.

Two months ago, she might have taken a wicked pleasure in seeing him humbled. She might have considered it delayed justice. Now, however . . .

She might never love him, but she could not deny that affection had grown and not only because of the pleasure. She still grappled with the role he had played in her life, and with the results of that duel, but she found it harder to assume he had done it over something insignificant.

Her thoughts drifted back to that night when she had helped him wash. She had never told anyone except Sarah about her feelings for Lakewood. Penthurst had guessed, however. He had seen her interest in that duel for what it was. If he had not demanded she tell him, would she have done so anyway? The urge to do so had been building ever since they said the vows. Perhaps she had hoped that if she laid that down between them, there was a chance one of them would find a way to step over it.

That had not happened. Yet the revelation had changed how they dealt with each other. Not for the better, but not for the worse either. More honestly perhaps. She only knew that in giving voice to that resentment, she had been relieved of some of the resentment itself.

Now, this stupid letter had come, reminding her in the worst way that she still harbored secrets that could do far more damage than any admission of her girlish love for another man.

"I do not know what to do, Sarah. I picture little letters coming all through my life as he repeatedly threatens exposure and asks for more. I doubt he will ever say I have paid enough, and hand me that manuscript."

"Seems to me you should have agreed to my first idea, that we steal it back."

"Well, I cannot even consider that now. It would be a fine thing if I were caught breaking into Trilby's home."

Considering the story given out for her elopement, that would give the gossips something to talk about! Nor did she think Trilby kept the manuscript where he lived. The mounting evidence said he would be too shrewd to do so, and would not risk her sending someone to find it. For a dull man, Trilby kept making some unexpectedly sharp decisions.

She stared at the letter with increasing annoyance. He had also proved himself unreliable. No agreement would ever be honored. Trilby had not even made reference in this letter to her demand to see proof he still had the manuscript before further payment. No page from it had come with his letter. No promise to provide proof either. For all she knew he did not have the whole manuscript. Perhaps he had only come to possess a few pages, which he had used to lure her in this deeply.

The notion stunned her once it popped into her head. Was he that bold? That cunning? If so, she had been the worst fool.

If he only had a few pages, that did not answer the question of how he had come by them. No one knew about that manuscript, so its theft had always been hard to envision. A few pages, however, might more easily be obtained and passed along. A servant could have found it all, read it, and seen the value of those lists, for example . . .

Something else popped into her head. An old memory emerged from the cloud where it lived—the image of a sunny spring day, and the shade under a tree, and ivy picking at her skirt while a book of poetry was shared . . .

It was not true that no one knew about the manuscript. Lakewood had known. She had told him about it under that tree. She had even brought some of it with her when he next visited her, and amused him by reading a couple of pages.

Surely he had never told anyone else. Why would he? Nor could he have taken it himself. It had still been in her trunk when she received the news of his death.

"What are you going to do?" Sarah asked.

Lydia opened a drawer in her writing table and set the letter under a stack of paper. "I am going to do what I should have done from the start, and try to find out how Trilby came to have that manuscript, if indeed he has it at all."

"It may be wise to put him off for a while with just a bit more money. I'd not want to have to explain all of this to the duke, if I were you."

She rebelled at the idea of giving the scoundrel one more penny. However, Sarah was correct. Another payment might be unavoidable, to keep him at bay.

Two hours later Lydia sat in her brother's study, beside his desk. He sat behind it and the family solicitor, Mr. Ottley, occupied a chair drawn close to the other side. On the desk lay several large, vellum documents written with a flourishing hand.

"As agreed between you and His Grace, Lord South-waite, the lady is to receive a thousand in pin money per annum, paid quarterly. There is also to be an open account for her wardrobe of two thousand per annum, with an additional thousand this year so she might purchase the necessities of her new station." Mr. Ottley handed one of the documents to Southwaite to read and check.

"And this itemizes the settlement you are making on her, to be in trust. This other one she must sign. She gives up her dower rights in return for a lump sum, to be apportioned to her children upon her death. The addendum to it lists the allowances for her household after the duke's death, or if she should at some point live separately from him while he is alive."

She looked at her brother. He ignored her curiosity on that last point while he perused that document too.

More followed. She was to have her own carriage and two footmen at her beck and call. She was to choose her own servants to attend to her personal needs. She would have free use of the family heirloom jewels, but most of them would not pass into her private possession. That page included a few unusual provisions too, such as the duke's acceptance that he would not interfere with her family relationships.

Southwaite scribbled his signature on the stacked sheets, and Mr. Ottley departed.

"I know little about these things, brother, but some of it sounded peculiar to me," she said.

He shrugged. "It is wise to attempt to cover all eventualities. He understood that was all I was doing."

"It will take some effort at extravagance for me to spend three thousand on my wardrobe this year."

"He thought you would need more. I think that aunt of his does not restrain herself at the modistes, and that is his only recent reference, except—" He caught himself. He suddenly decided the inkwell would be more convenient on the left side of the desk. He moved it there with great concentration.

"Except his mistresses?"

Southwaite reconsidered his desk, and moved the inkwell back to its old position.

Her brother would know about the mistresses. He assumed the likelihood there would be more of them, as was so common among peers, especially those who made arranged marriages for financial or dynastic purposes. Or due to being obligated to do the right thing after comprising an innocent. She supposed that was why he included that bit about a separate household in the settlement documents.

Then again, maybe he thought the duke would want to put her in a separate residence if she became the problem wife just as she had been the problem sister.

"Thank you for looking out for me in this matter. It could not have been easy to bargain against a fait accompli."

"There was little bargaining, Lydia. He agreed to

almost everything without discussion." He smiled. "The Dukes of Penthurst can afford to do that."

"How fortunate for me. I am not being facetious. I know that few women have my good fortune, or even a fraction of that settlement. While I did not seek this match, or even want it, I am not so stupid as to ignore its many benefits."

"I hope the day comes when you tell me you are not only fortunate, but happy, Lydia."

She was not sure that day would come. She was not even sure she knew what happiness meant. Something like that time in Hampshire, she supposed. Perhaps only ignorant, silly girls could be truly happy.

"Before I go, please explain how this money comes to me. Do I have to ask the duke for my pin money?"

"It is not an allowance to be given at his discretion. I expect his solicitor will have it delivered to you, or put in a bank account for you to use. In a week or two the first amount should be available."

Two weeks. She needed it sooner than that.

"Do you have an immediate need to buy pins?" he asked. "I am sure Penthurst will give you money, Lydia. He just has not thought about how you are without any funds now."

"I would rather not ask him. I will have to wait."

He pulled open a drawer and flipped up the top of a wooden box. "What do you need?"

"Two hundred and fifty?"

She received a sharp glance for that.

"I trust it is not so you can gamble."

"No, not that." Mostly not, at least.

He handed a small stack of banknotes to her.

She stuffed the notes in her reticule. "I will pay you back when my pin money arrives."

He walked her to the door. "Between not having to buy your wedding wardrobe, and being spared the cost of your keep in the future, I can afford to make this a gift."

"I had not considered that. You are now free of the worry and cost of me. This has turned out very nicely for you."

He grinned. "It has indeed."

Aunt Amelia clearly saw Lydia as a duchess now, and not a wayward niece. Delicacies poised on pretty plates on her tiny drawing room's tables. Expensive tea filled their cups. Lydia knew her aunt could ill afford such luxuries, and felt guilty such money had been spent for this brief social call.

Rosalyn felt no guilt at all. She critically surveyed the plates, and complained that her tea was too hot. She found fault with one of the cakes and advised Amelia on a better shop where, for a few shillings more, superior sweets could be found.

Amelia fawned at everything Rosalyn said. They had a friendship, but poor Amelia was the supplicant in it, not the master. That her aunt now fawned at everything she said too was too odd for Lydia to bear.

"I expect that you will be adding to your wardrobe

now, Duchess." Amelia's soft, round face shined with joy. "It will be exciting to see what you choose."

"I have not begun thinking about that yet. And please do not address me that way. We are family."

"Your niece still does not comprehend her new station, Amelia. Of course you must address her thus, as must everyone. Too much familiarity is unwise. Why, do you call the earl Darius?"

Amelia flushed. "Yes, I do. Only sometimes," she hastened to add. "Not often at all."

"As do I," Lydia said. "You do not address me as Duchess, Rosalyn. If my aunt must, so must you."

Rosalyn's mouth pursed into a kiss of disapproval. "See what I must contend with, Amelia. One would think a marriage made like hers would engender gratitude and humility."

"A sad business," Amelia said, shaking her head.

"I think you should tell the duke to lecture me on gratitude and humility, Rosalyn, although he may not understand why my gratitude should be toward *you*."

Rosalyn decided to ignore her challenge in favor of Amelia's agreement. "I trust you have not been too embarrassed by those rumors coming out of Buxton, Amelia, dear."

Amelia hung her head. "Not too much. Although there were a few cruel things said in my hearing the first few days, the duke's threats have moved that from drawing rooms to boudoirs. I suppose after what happened with the Baron Lakewood, everyone believes he will duel if there is gossip. So sad that was too. I always thought the baron was a nice man, and very kind."

Rosalyn glared at Amelia. It took poor Amelia a good ten count to realize her terrible faux pas. Her face fell in dismay. "Not that I in any way question the rightness of it. Honor is honor, of course." She looked desperately from Rosalyn to Lydia, close to tears. "I am not such a good judge of character. I am sure he was wicked just as Mr. Trilby seems to be."

"There is nothing wrong with liking a man who showed you considerable kindness," Lydia said.

"He did, didn't he? Especially that spring after my dear Harold passed away. You remember, Lydia? You were with me for part of my time at the cottage. He would come to call when he came down from town, and sometimes even brought friends, to draw me out of myself."

"I do remember." Although he brought no friends during her visit, because after he attended to Aunt Amelia, he would spend the afternoon with her niece. "You are not obligated to condemn him just because you are drinking tea with relatives of the man who shot him. Isn't that right, Rosalyn?"

Rosalyn's ire faded. "Of course. Although, Amelia, you are correct about your inability to judge character."

Amelia was quick to agree. In fact she spent the rest of the visit agreeing with everything Rosalyn said, even when Rosalyn opined that Lydia would be wise to place herself totally and unconditionally in Rosalyn's hands while she learned her duties.

Rendered an object of discussion rather than being

a discussant herself, Lydia waited out the hour. At its conclusion she saw Rosalyn into the carriage, but did not enter herself.

"Forgive me, but I left a glove. I will return in a thrice," she said.

"Send the footman—"

But Lydia had already reached the door.

She went back to her aunt. "I need to ask you something. Has there been any trouble at your cottage in Hampshire? Evidence of trespassing, or of theft?"

"Theft! Goodness, why would you think that? All appears in order when I go down. I have not noticed anything missing."

"Has the caretaker ever written of"—Of what?— "anything out of the ordinary?"

Aunt Amelia gave it some thought, shaking her head even as she did. "If he ever did, it was not notable enough for me to recall it now."

Lydia did not know if that was good news or not. How much easier if she learned the house had been ransacked last winter.

After returning Rosalyn to Grosvenor Square, she had the carriage take her to Aunt Hortense.

She heard little of what Hortense said while they sat in her private sitting room. Her aunt never needed strict attention to hold a conversation, since her own voice interested her more than anyone else's. While Hortense pontificated on everything from politics to fashion, Lydia laid some plans.

Perhaps it was time to learn if Lakewood had been

Aunt Amelia's nice, kind man, or Cassandra's scoundrel. In the least, it might be time to find out which he had been with Lydia Alfreton. Unfortunately, the answer lay in memories that she had worked hard to shut away.

They would never come to her here in London. Too many other people here had opinions about him, and each one influenced her. Penthurst's criticisms in particular had shaken her faith badly.

She wished she could claim that she had woken after their night together secure in her own view of the great love she had thrown in his face. Instead she had met the dawn enclosed in his embrace, and spent an hour pretending to sleep so she might remain in that warmth while she doubted herself. Had she been so infatuated with Lakewood that she never really knew him?

It was time to find out about that too. If she really wanted to know the truth, she needed to go where the truth could be found. It lay in her own mind, and in her own heart. And in Hampshire.

Two nights later Lydia jumped out of Penthurst's carriage and strode to the door of the house. She breezed past the servant who opened it, then quickly walked to the library. Empty. She retraced her steps.

"Where is he?"

"The duke is in his study," the butler said.

That meant he dealt with estate business. Normally she would not interrupt, but this was not a normal night. She marched up the stairs, and to the door of the study that sat at the end of his apartment. She did not request entry, but walked right in.

He sat on a chair with an oil lamp on a nearby table. His hounds lulled at his feet. A stack of papers and parchments covered his lap. He concentrated on them so much that it took him a few moments to become aware of her presence.

"Lydia." His gaze swept over her. "You look lovely tonight. Where did you go? The theater?"

"No, I went to Mrs. Burton's for a while. A very brief while. Of course you know what I discovered."

"Unless you went only to observe, I do indeed." He appeared vaguely amused.

She could not believe his calm, but then he had not been the one embarrassed in front of a salon full of people. "Mrs. B said I could no longer game there. She said you had written to inform her of this. How dare you!"

"How *dare I*?" Any amusement disappeared. "Remember that you are talking to your husband, Lydia. I have the right to dare whatever I choose."

"I do not accept that you have the right to do this just because you choose to. Worse, you did not even tell me. I think you wanted me to be turned away. I think you wanted the whole world to see that you controlled me now."

"Only a woman who has never known control would think you now suffered it. Do not try my patience or I will follow my better judgment and make sure you behave exactly as I believe you should."

She collected herself so her anger would not push this into a huge row. She would be calm too, and rational. He was not an unreasonable man.

"You said I could still visit the tables."

"I said until you lost one hundred a year. You have already lost more than that this year. To me alone. So you are done until January."

"That was one wager. I am well ahead for the year. I was even ahead that night."

"With me, you were down. A holiday from the tables is in order, anyway."

"That is not fair. It is how I earn money. The only way I can. I have expenses."

"You have no need to earn money. If you need money, I will give it to you."

"Then it is *your* money. There are things I want *my* money for. So I can do what I like with it, without permission from anyone." He was not looking reasonable at all. Quite the opposite. "Not for anything bad or dangerous or even stupid. Certainly not for jewels or silks. You are welcome to spend your money on those things for me."

"Not dangerous or bad. Not luxuries. Then, what?"

How to explain it? Could any man even understand? Rich or poor, they always had their own money of some amount, to use according to their own judgment. They never had to ask brothers or husbands or trustees, or explain what they intended to do. They did not have settlements that decreed allowances or pin money to be used with their own discretion, but clearly delineated and arranged by lawyers to come from their husbands.

"I should be able to have or do things that are just mine. That begin and end with me. Nothing is like that unless I obtain money on my own. If I use yours, or my brother's, it isn't the same. It is not fully mine. Is that so hard to understand?"

"Nigh impossible to understand. Your objections are only the dying embers of your girlish rebellions. I informed the gaming halls not to accept you, for your own good. If you do not like it, I am sorry. I am responsible for you now, and I have decided that you need a long break from gambling. It does nothing but get you into trouble. Hell, it was what got you stuck in this marriage you did not want."

"My wagers with you did not stick me here!"

"Your visit to Buxton did. Why else would you go there, except to gamble far from the eyes of those who might tell Southwaite?"

Why else indeed? How had his high-handed behavior ended up with her at a loss for words?

She found some anyway. "I do not accept this. I will not have it. As for a marriage I did not want, I was beginning to think I did not mind that so much anymore, but you have convinced me otherwise yet again."

She walked out on him, and ran to her bedchamber. What a pigheaded man. He had no idea how he interfered with matters of importance to her. Nor did he care. His Grace had made a decision, and he expected her to accept it. She should let Trilby do his worst, and let His Grace face the scandal and disgrace that Trilby would cook up.

That notion sobered her. Her indignation cooled in a snap. Any scandal would be horrible for her, but much worse for him. Humiliation could be as bad as a noose for a man.

She pulled out her purse and counted what money she had. Her brother's two fifty would take care of Trilby for a few months at least. She would send it to him tomorrow. As for the other demands on her purse, the one she had intended to cover with tonight's winnings, she could either put them off until the first of her pin money arrived, ask the duke for it, or raise it another way.

She went to her dressing room. Sarah sat, bent to a lamp's light, mending the nightdress Lydia had worn the night she helped Penthurst wash. In the throes of their passion it had ripped at one seam.

"Sarah, we need to take one of our walks tomorrow morning."

"To the park?"

"We can go there first if you like, but I need to visit a shop on the Strand after that."

"All the way from the park to the Strand?" Sarah groaned. "Not far along the Strand, I hope."

"It is not so far that you will faint. The memory of your citizen soldier's smiles should keep your steps light all the way."

Sarah returned to plying her needle. "What will we

be doing, that you don't want to use the duke's carriages or servants?"

Fanning the embers of my girlish rebellions. "Never you mind what. Just be sure to have me awake and dressed before nine o'clock."

The next morning Penthurst dressed early. He expected a full day, and not one to anticipate with joy. While his valet buffed his boots, he reread a letter he had received late the day before. It mostly consisted of a list of names and had been sent to him from the War Office.

He thought about Lydia, sleeping on the other side of the wall. If his queries into Lakewood's activities bore the rotten fruit he feared, she would not thank him. Cassandra's comments on Lakewood's character might have prompted the start of disillusionment, but Lydia was fighting its completion.

The chance existed that nothing more would be found. His instincts did not believe that, but he hoped that would be the case for her sake. While he would not mind ending her memories of her girlish infatuation, he also did not want to see how that would hurt her.

He slid the letter into his coat pocket. When he began this investigation, he had hoped to silence questions that whispered in his head and kept that duel from receding into the past. Now he debated whether his own need to know outweighed her need to believe.

Polished and preened, he walked toward the door to her chamber, to see if she had woken yet. Considering his mission today, he would like to smooth the troubled waters stirred by last night's argument.

"The duchess is not there," his valet said while he replaced his brushes in their drawer. "I saw her and her woman walking out when I was opening the window a few minutes ago."

It was barely nine o'clock. Where could they be going at this hour?

Lydia's penchant for unusual behavior prodded at him as he went down and waited for his horse to be brought around. After last night, she might be deliberately doing something extraordinary, just to prove she could.

He sat in the saddle for a long count, debating. Although still of two minds, and weighing the demands of that list in his pocket, he turned his horse toward Hyde Park.

"Thank you," Mrs. Beattie said. "Your continued patronage will be a great relief to Mrs. Kerry. She feared your change in circumstances might lead to changes in this as well."

"I hope that does not happen." But Lydia could not promise it would not. "I am sorry it is not more."

"As it is, it will feed everyone for months, and allow us to admit a few more guests."

Mrs. Beattie and Mrs. Kerry always called the inmates of this house guests. While they were not family, and were free to come and go, Lydia still thought the appellation charming.

Reformers of the best kind, the two woman served as mothers, teachers, confessors, and guardians to the thirty girls who slept in the beds lining the chambers and attics.

"Two of the girls were taken into service by a family in Essex," Mrs. Beattie reported. "Another has apprenticed with a dressmaker." She fingered the banknotes that lay on the table between their chairs. "Your last act of kindness allowed her fee to be paid."

Lydia asked after a few other girls who had left in the last year. Mrs. Beattie described their success, and in two cases, their failures. "They went back," she said sadly. "It always breaks Mrs. Kerry's heart when that happens, but I tell her to remember the triumphs, not the defeats."

"Back" was to the brothels of the City. Lydia had learned of this house from Aunt Hortense. Buried in one of her soliloquies a year ago had been her outrage that a place such as this was permitted in the decent, solid neighborhood near Hanover Square, where one of her friends lived. It appalled her that Mrs. Kerry, the widow of a merchant, had turned her home into a school for whores.

Until that day Lydia had not been aware that some of London's prostitutes were children.

She began to take her leave. "I do not know when I will be back, Mrs. Beattie. It could be that someone else will bring anything I have for you in the future."

"That might be wise, although Mrs. Kerry will be heartbroken she was not here to see you one last time. Still, with your marriage and new position, it would probably not be appropriate being seen at our door."

Lydia collected Sarah and left the house, thinking how no one had noticed her at the door in the past. It should not matter in the future, but of course it did.

As soon as she stepped outside, the evidence of that greeted her. The last person who should see her here stood beside his horse.

"What a surprise," Lydia said, walking toward him. "It is unfortunate you did not follow me in a carriage."

Penthurst gave Sarah a direct look that had her peeling away at once. When he and Lydia were alone, he spoke. "What is this place?"

"A school."

He peered at the façade. "For girls? I keep seeing their faces at the windows."

"You would attract attention. I doubt they have ever seen such a fine horse before either."

"Let us walk, then, so my presence does not interfere with their lessons."

They paced slowly down the lane. The area was residential, and not far from Hanover Square. No doubt some widow had formed a small school in her home, as happened with some frequency.

"Why are you visiting a girls' school, Lydia?"

She chewed over her answer so long he began doubting there would be one.

"It is not your typical school," she said.

"I am not surprised. If you visited it, I just assumed it was unusual."

"The girls in there are young. The youngest is eleven and the oldest fifteen. The women who own this house and run this school found all of them in brothels. They buy the girls' freedom and bring them here and educate them for another life." She said it in one long, agitated sentence.

"That is very good of them."

"Aren't you shocked in the least? They are *little girls*. I refused to believe it. Then I learned it was true, to my horror. And no one calls out the gentlemen who misuse them. Those men go back to their clubs and estates and lands with no punishment." Her anger rose with each word.

It was the kind of depravity men hoped their mothers, wives, and sisters never learned about. "You do not know they are all gentlemen, Lydia."

"Don't I? I was told by the owner of one of those places that the young ones are very, very expensive."

He took her hand in his. He lifted it to a kiss, then held it. "If I had my way, they would be hanged. Right now, however, I am wondering how you came to speak to the proprietor of a brothel. No, no—do not tell me. I expect you made the most extraordinary morning call that any gentleman's daughter has ever made."

"I had to know if it was true, didn't I?"

"I suppose *you* did." He turned them to retrace their steps. "I have a confession to make. I saw you and Sarah in the park. I thought you had only gone there so she could watch the militia. Imagine my surprise when you did not return home afterward, but walked to a pawn shop on the Strand. I hope whatever you gave the man was not of great or sentimental value."

"No." She gave him a very sharp glance. "You followed me."

"I did. Do not ask me how I dared such a thing. A husband is bound to be curious when his wife walks all over town when there are carriages and horses available."

"It does not anger me that you dared such things. It angers me that I am in a situation where someone has the right to dare such things."

That was a subject best side-stepped, although he guessed they would discuss it plenty in the years to come.

He gestured to the school. "Did you give them the money from the pawnbroker? Was this the thing you wanted your own money for?"

"One of the things. Please do not tell me that a duchess should not dirty herself with such charity. They are only children, and not responsible for their sordid pasts."

"I will not tell you that."

They arrived back at his horse. Sarah stayed two houses down, so she would not overhear. "I should have asked you what you did with your gambling profits. I never even wondered, Lydia. I just assumed you spent it as woman do."

"At first, I put some aside for a tour of the continent after the war ended. Since it looks like the war will never end, I found other ways to use it."

"Generous ways. I misjudged you. Forgive me. But—why did you never tell anyone? It is a good thing you do, and nothing to hide."

"I was not hiding it as such, only keeping it to myself. For myself. It was the one thing I did without any help, and I liked the feeling it gave me."

"Rather like mounting and riding a horse on your own the first time."

"Yes, much like that. You do understand!"

Not entirely. And of course most women never mounted horses on their own.

"You speak in the past tense, Lydia. You do not have to stop. You can do much more for them now if you like."

"If you are offering to fund a larger contribution, I must accept. However, a part of my joy in this is over. I knew it was when I came here today. Even if you allowed me to return to the tables, this can never be how it was."

"I never thought I would feel guilty making a woman a duchess, but you come close to evoking that reaction, Lydia."

She tilted back her head and looked at him thoughtfully. "How guilty do you feel?"

"What do you mean?"

"Do you feel a thousand pounds guilty? Two thousand? They would be secure if they had a trust and a regular income."

"I expect we can do that. It does not change that you have lost a spirit of independence that mattered to you."

"I have to grow up and accept a woman's lot eventually. Since mine is a luxurious one, it would be sinful to complain. Before I don all of a woman's shackles, however, there is something I need to know. For myself alone. It does not concern you at all. I will have to make a journey, however, because I do not think the answers that I seek are here."

How had they gotten from her charity to her leaving him? "Where are they?"

"Hampshire, I think."

He experienced untold relief. He had half expected her to say America or Russia. Then a bit of concern colored his reaction. The questions may not concern him at all, but that did not mean the answers would not.

This was about Lakewood. He just knew it. Felt it. He cursed that he had waited to request the list in his pocket. He should have never allowed his sentimental concern for Lakewood's reputation to compromise his explanation of that duel, or his ferreting out the whole truth.

"I think not, Lydia. Maybe next summer."

"Please reconsider. I want to go there, to my aunt's cottage. I need to think about something, and that will be the best place to do so honestly." She managed to appear helpless and begging and sultry and promising all at the same time. If he did not care about her, it would have no effect, but he did, so he started wavering.

Still, he did not like it. Lydia alone in a cottage half a country away did not suit him at all. His own thought caught him up short. Suit him. He should think what would suit her.

He calculated the journey there and back and the days she might be gone. A fortnight at least. It seemed a long time.

"I may as well give my permission. If I do not, you will find a way to do it anyway. You must take Sarah, however, and the coachman must stay nearby."

Her pleased expression captivated him. He bent to kiss her, thinking that having a husband's right to tell a woman what to do was not worth much in reality.

A muffled, squeaky cheer leaked out of the house. He looked to the building. Ghostly faces showed behind the wavy panes of the windows. A few opened and little hands appeared, clapping.

Lydia looked behind, toward the cheer, and laughed. "We were indiscreet. Now, should Sarah and I ride home and you walk, or do you think we can hire a carriage near here?"

Chapter 18

Lydia stared at the cottage while the coachman carried in the trunks. Sarah had already entered, to assess their lodgings.

She wondered if she had erred in coming. Even now, without so much as seeing one chamber or walking one lane, nostalgia drenched her. Worse, it fell from a cloud that she knew too well and whose power she thought she had finally escaped.

The coachman approached her. "I've carried in some wood and water. I'll take a chamber at that inn we passed in the village a few miles back, Madam. I'll come every morning to see if you'll be wanting the carriage brought to you that day."

"I will not need it tomorrow."

"I'll be coming anyway, Madam. The duke instructed me to do so."

He returned to the carriage. Sarah appeared at the door.

"I always thought this was a charming cottage, milady. I like how the kitchen is built on in the back, so I'll not have to be carrying food from an outbuilding."

Lydia stepped inside, and waited for the cloud to fall.

It didn't. Relieved and emboldened, she wandered through the chambers that she had shared with Aunt Amelia those months. She had come on a mission of sympathy, to be a companion to a new widow still deep in grief, but she had also known that her aunt would be too self-absorbed to pay much attention to her. And she had hoped as hard as any girl ever did that the young man who had stolen her heart might appear at the door.

He had hinted he might. Lakewood had a bit of property somewhere near here. A stamp of land, he had called it, referring to its very small size. He had inherited a title, but not much of an estate. She had always thought he handled that with impressive grace. He never expressed envy of her brother, or resentment of his own lack of fortune.

Sarah skipped to the back of the house. Soon the sounds of pots and pans rang through the cottage. Lydia followed to find her rearranging the place to her liking.

"I will put it all back before we leave," Sarah

explained. "It doesn't make sense to me to have the pots over there."

Lydia gazed out the window to the garden. She saw herself out there, strolling with Lakewood, laughing.

An arm came around her. Sarah rested her head against her own and looked out too. "I hope you did not come here to be sad again, Deea."

"That was not my intention."

"You hardly spoke of it, but I knew you had hopes. Who wouldn't? All those walks together. He visited often enough to raise your expectations."

He had visited too often if he did not plan to fulfill those expectations. Perhaps he had. If not for the duel, maybe she would have eloped with a different man, two springs ago. It wasn't as if Southwaite would have reacted well to an offer for her hand from Lakewood. Aside from his poor fortune, Emma said he had been claiming undying love for Cassandra back then.

She pulled herself out of the memories. "I will help you put away the food we bought, then you can make a pie."

An hour later, while Lydia cut apples and Sarah mixed pastry, Sarah spoke into the silent peace of their camaraderie. "His name is Jonathan Peace. My citizen soldier. Peace with an *ea*."

"That is a nice name."

"He grew up in Kent, like me, but not near the coast."

"It sounds like the two of you have spoken to each other."

Sarah blushed. "He helps with the horses at the

White Swan, and comes around a bit. I've not neglected my duties or—"

"I did not think you had, Sarah. Is the man as nice as his smile?"

"I think so. He wants to court me properly. I told him I would ask you for permission."

"You do not need anyone's permission to accept a man's attentions, Sarah. I will tell the housekeeper that she is to allow him to wait for you down in the servants' sitting room, and not object if you walk out with him."

Sarah pressed the pastry into its pan. "You need to cut those apples thicker or they will turn to mush."

Lydia tried to make the slices thicker. "I am glad a decent man whom you find attractive wants to court you, Sarah. I am happy for you."

Sarah set to grating sugar off the small cone they had brought. "And I am happy for you too. I can say that to Deea, but it would not be my place to say it to milady the duchess."

"You are? Why?"

"Because of the duke, of course. He likes you more than such men have to like their wives. I see it in him when he watches you."

Did he like her? Was their growing comfort more than just two people accommodating the inevitable, or the result of the physical intimacies of marriage?

She set down the knife and wiped her hands. Sarah started heaping the apples into the pastry.

Lydia went to the sitting room and took her spencer

from a peg. "I am going to take some air in the garden, Sarah. I will return soon."

She stepped through the garden door and looked at the familiar plantings. Her aunt had not been here in several months, but the caretaker maintained the property well. She spied the stone bench at the far end of the center path. In summer the shrubbery obscured it more from the house, but those leaves now skimmed along the ground, yellow and dry.

She could do this. She was not that infatuated girl anymore. She would conquer the fear and sadness. She would not hide in the cloud again, not ever. One can't see much from within a cloud, for one thing. Perhaps that had been its appeal.

She strode toward the bench, and toward the past.

Fairbourne's auction house had become known for its grand previews. A crush of notables filled this one. Penthurst attended without his duchess. After drinking good wine with the prime minister and pawing through the books alongside the prince, he turned critical eyes on the paintings.

The event distracted him from the thoughts racing through his mind these days. He had spent the last week seeking out the men whose names were on the list he had received from the War Office. They were all suspected of having bought the influence that garnered them a commission. Five of them had admitted to him that they paid Lakewood for arranging the recommendation of an earl or duke. Lakewood had not limited himself to their circle, it seemed.

Other than those confirmations that the scheme had been larger than guessed, little information had come to him. There had been a few other sightings of some woman, but she had possibly been Lakewood's current mistress. He might have sworn unrequited love for Cassandra, but he had never stopped pursuing other women.

So the threatening scandal would have been bigger than Penthurst had known the morning of the duel. Big enough to cause the despair that would make a man arrange to die?

Southwaite and Emma found him while he peered at a landscape as his mind went over it all again.

"You appeared so interested in that van Ruisdael that Emma felt obliged to come and urge you to bid on it," Southwaite said.

"I do not intend to urge at all," she said. "That is Mr. Fairbourne's duty, not mine." She glanced to where her brother enjoyed the party rather too much, and neglected the duty she described.

"You look beautiful and happy, Lady Southwaite." It was the honest truth. Emma was not the most beautiful of women, but she had always had something compelling about her, and being in the family way enhanced that indescribable quality.

"That is because I am relieved this preview is such a success. Will you attend the auction tomorrow?"

"I expect so. It will occupy me for a few hours now that I am a bachelor again."

Southwaite laughed. Emma did not. She looked to the other side of the large exhibition hall, where Cassandra chatted with Kendale and his wife, Marielle. "Please tell me the truth. Did Lydia leave town so she could avoid us tonight without being bluntly rude? Cassandra and I will be heartbroken if it is true, and if we offended her, we need to make amends."

"I do not know what was said among you, but I do not think she was offended. Her absence from town is not to avoid this invitation, or you, I am sure."

"More likely it is to avoid him," Southwaite quipped, jabbing his thumb in Penthurst's direction.

"I am sure that is not true," Emma said.

He was not sure of much anymore, where Lydia was concerned. She had written twice—brief, empty letters that could have been sent by a passing acquaintance.

Kendale, Ambury, and their wives came over. The ladies peeled away to examine the jewelry.

"Are you enjoying the monk's life?" Ambury asked.

"There are unexpected benefits. I am being reacquainted with my aunt, for one thing. She seeks me out no matter where I hide, to fill my ears with gossip."

"I'm sure you have had a lot of time to read at night too. It is always good to exercise one's mind," Ambury said.

"A respite from the other kind of night exercise in which you have been indulging recently can be reinvigorating too," Southwaite said. "Or so I have been told."

"A bit early for that, I would think," Kendale said. "Early for a separation too, no matter how brief. Did she wear you out as Southwaite says, Penthurst? Or was there a row?"

Southwaite hung his head and shook it slowly in amazement. Ambury grasped Kendale's shoulder with tight fingers and leaned into him. "Southwaite was joking. And we don't ask each other about the other thing."

"You mean the rows with wives?"

"Yes, I mean the rows."

Kendale cleared his throat. "Sorry."

"There was no row," Penthurst said.

"Of course there wasn't," Ambury said. "No one except Kendale ever wondered."

"No one," Southwaite echoed.

"She knows she must start a long round of calls and receptions, and has gone to the country to rest before embarking on those duties." It spilled out, sounding almost reasonable.

When he had agreed for Lydia to go to Hampshire, he had never thought how odd it would look for her to leave so soon after the wedding. If his own friends found it peculiar, the rest of the people in this hall must be spinning all kinds of unflattering suppositions.

"That was probably wise of her," Ambury said. "Resting, that is."

"So, she did not wear you out. You wore *her* out," Kendale said.

Ambury threw up his hands. "Zeus, will you think—"

"I am the one joking now. Penthurst sees the humor even if you do not."

He did see the joke, but not the one Kendale intended. He had been very careful not to wear her out, as Kendale put it. Lydia was a passionate woman, but it had not been a love match, after all. *He* had not been the great love of her life.

Yet, the nights since she had left had been torture. Normally he did not find periods of abstinence hard to bear. This one was driving him mad. He did not just want relief either. He wanted her.

Cassandra gestured for Ambury to join her at the jewelry.

"Uh, oh," he muttered. "This is going to be expensive. Come with me, Southwaite, and pull away your wife so she does not convince Cassandra to bid on half the case."

They walked away, which left him drinking wine with only Kendale.

"Do you miss her?" Kendale asked.

It was another question that men did not ask each other, unless they were the closest of friends, which he and Kendale were not. But then Kendale had even less finesse in talking about women than he had in other areas of conversation.

Kendale's gaze settled on the ladies bent to the jewelry case, and in particular on the willowy, elegant one who was his wife. The look in his eyes said he knew what his own answer to the question would be.

"Yes, Kendale. I miss her."

* * *

The preview was nearing its end when Penthurst saw Ambury standing alone. He walked over. "I have another small way you can help me with my investigation of Lakewood's activities."

"Whom do you want me to find?"

"No one. I only need some information."

"Tell me what it is. If it can be found, I will find it."

"It can best be obtained from one person. You."

Ambury looked at him. "Damn."

"You knew him best, Ambury."

"The hell I did."

"The longest at least."

"Damn."

"If you would rather not—"

"No. Better it be me."

He might as well have said, *Let us not alert anyone else to how much he was a scoundrel. Perhaps something of his good name can still be saved.*

They went out to the garden to have some privacy. The night had chilled enough that their breath showed.

"What do you want to know?"

"Did he ever have a mistress with red hair?"

"You want to know about his lovers?"

"Only the red-haired ones."

Ambury thought about it. "He did not have mistresses as such. Not the sort he would introduce to friends. There were women, of course. I'd see him with one sometimes. About five years ago I saw him in town with a woman with hair more chestnut than red. She was striking, so I looked twice. No way to know if that is what she was to him, though."

It was not much. It might not even be the same woman Greenly and the others saw. A lot of women had red hair.

"Tell me about his estate."

Ambury laughed. "You know he inherited very little."

"So little he never spoke of it. That is why I am asking you."

"He chafed at his lack of fortune. It had to be hard on him, especially with you and Southwaite as friends. I at least had my father keeping me poor for a while."

"Perhaps that is how he justified using us. We had so much, he had so little, surely we would not mind his helping himself to a few pounds with our unknowing aid."

"More likely he counted on our never finding out, and was prepared to lose the friendships if we did."

Ambury sounded more bitter than Penthurst felt, but then the disillusionment was fresh still with Ambury.

"He always hoped to make a good marriage, of course," Ambury said. "After that business with Cassandra, that became less likely."

"Was he in debt?"

"Less than you would think. No expectations mean not much credit."

"He had some property, however. I recall once when he spoke of it in passing."

"A few farms in Derbyshire kept him in cravats and brandy. He could eke out something resembling a fashionable life on those rents, but he had to watch every shilling."

"He used to joke when in his cups about his country manor. I assumed from how he referred to it that it was not a manor at all. Was that house in Derbyshire?"

"You mean Dunner Park." Ambury chuckled. "I knew him two years before I realized the name was a joke. I don't think Dunner Park, whatever its size or condition, was up there. Hampshire, I think it was. He had a spot of property there that he would go down to on occasion. Maybe fifty acres."

Cassandra arrived then to steal Ambury away. Penthurst wandered out to the street amid the remnants of the guests. Ambury's information had not told him much on the face of it. It had added some nuances regarding Lakewood's lack of fortune, but little more.

Unless he wanted to count the information about "Dunner Park." That all but confirmed that Lydia had gone to Hampshire to find answers to questions that involved the man who had been lord of the manor there.

"Now, this is odd," Lydia said upon reading a letter that came in the post from London. "Do you remember how I said that I could not find my trunk? I looked everywhere. The attics and cellars and every chamber. It had disappeared. I wrote to my aunt Amelia asking what had become of it."

"Did your aunt send it back to town, when she knew you were not going to return?"

"Here is what she wrote: *I had the man put it in the barn with the other things, so it would not be in the way.*" She looked over at Sarah. "What other things? What man? The caretaker?"

"What barn? There is no barn here."

"Perhaps she meant the carriage house. Let us go see."

They crossed the garden toward its back portal. Lydia glanced at the stone bench when they passed it. She could sit there now and not be sucked into nostalgia. With effort and sheer will she had banished any ghosts from the house and garden.

The rest still waited. The paths of those long walks, the kiss under the tree deep in Forest of Bere, the words both ambiguous and incriminating. Tomorrow she would start looking honestly at the hardest parts.

The carriage house stood to one side of the garden's back wall, about a hundred feet behind. No carriages lined the left wall. No horses ate hay in the enclosed stalls on the other side.

She walked down the center, looking for the trunk. In the third horse stall she found furniture heaped in a jumble. She recognized some of it as having once graced the house. She peered around and through the pile.

"Help me. I think I see it."

Together she and Sarah moved small tables and chairs. Underneath it all lay her trunk.

"This furniture perhaps holds memories of my aunt's husband, and she had it removed. As long as a man was doing that, she must have decided to move this too." Lydia crouched down and examined the latches on the trunk. She had never locked it. She flipped the top open.

Clothing lay at the top. Sarah shook out and held up each piece.

"Take what you want, and sell the rest for your own purse," Lydia said while she moved aside some books.

"Are you sure? This dress—"

"I am very sure."

She stacked the books on the stall's floorboards. She plucked out a little doll that she had forgotten she had packed. She could not remember why she had brought it. She had not been a child that visit, and had left dolls far behind.

More followed. A small box of jewelry, filled with simple but favored items she had concluded were lost. The sheet music of a song she was trying to learn. A sketchbook. She resisted flipping through it because she knew what it contained.

Long before she hit bottom she knew the manuscript was not there.

She sat back on her heels and surveyed the contents. She knew she had not brought it back to London, but she had searched her apartment in her brother's house anyway, to make sure her vague memory was correct. She had placed that novel in this trunk, and now it was gone. So Trilby indeed had it all, most likely. She had hoped perhaps he did not.

She piled the books and the rest back into the trunk. "Bring the garments if you want. I must write to my aunt again." She needed to know the name of the man who moved the trunk, and whether anyone else had access to its contents after she returned to London.

Two mornings later Penthurst shared breakfast with his aunt. She made sure he regretted it.

"Her absence from town is all the talk. You allowing it is very odd. You must make her return or people will think you are one of those men who indulges his bride to the point of idiocy." She sank her teeth into a cake with a firmness that suggested the cake would suffer what she thought Lydia deserved—a thorough chewing out.

"I doubt my reputation will be affected at all," he said.

"How like a man to believe that. There are names for men made weak like Sampson by a female."

"There are? Enlighten me." He raised his gaze from his paper and feigned curiosity.

She blushed. "It would be vulgar for me to repeat them. They are very rude names. Not something to be said in decent company."

"Yet you know them, and I do not. I suppose that means my company is more decent than yours." He returned to his paper. Tsking and sputtering sounded across the table.

The butler brought the first post's mail into the breakfast room. Rosalyn's big stack would occupy her for a good while. Penthurst's smaller one heralded a week of private meetings while the government considered some secret overtures from France for negotiations to end the war. Not only ministers had written, although the number who wanted a private word was interesting. Two junior treasury appointments and three members of parliament had requested audiences too. He assumed some controversy was brewing and most of these letters came from men wanting him to exert influence, not impart useful information.

At the bottom of the stack, a different sort of letter waited. Thick, and written in a hand he did not immediately recognize, it had been posted in London the afternoon before. He set it aside while he read the others and calculated which he could decline.

"Has she at least written?" Rosalyn asked while pretending to be distracted by her own letters.

"I received a letter yesterday afternoon. I am sure you do not expect her to write twice in twenty-four hours."

"I can guess what happened, and I think you are handling it wrong." Her voice dripped with sympathetic understanding. "Her maid can hardly give her advice. She needs to talk to an older woman with experience in these things. Her aunt Amelia, for example."

The oddity of her new tone and words eventually settled into his mind. He set aside the letter. He rested his chin in his hand. "What do you think happened?"

"Surely you do not expect me to speak of it."

"I do expect it. I am very curious. Your insights are often enlightening. "

She flustered while she avoided answering. He just waited. She found her courage and firmed up her face and tone. "You shocked her, of course. Everyone thinks so. All those older mistresses jaded you and you became too . . . ambitious with her."

"You mean in bed."

His bluntness horrified her so much that he wondered absently if she had her salts on her, should they be necessary.

"By too ambitious, you mean that I made her—"

"There is no need to say what you made her do, thank you very much. I am sure that if you write and apologize and promise to confine such vulgarities to the women who are paid well to tolerate them, Lydia will return and all will be well."

"And everyone thinks this is the reason Lydia went down to the country?"

"Of course. Why else would you allow her to leave?"

He returned to his breakfast. "I am very sorry she was not here for this conversation, Rosalyn."

"No doubt. It would avoid your having to raise the subject yourself. Yet you must."

"I promise to do so, in great detail." That odd letter caught his eye again. Still imagining Lydia's laughter when he described this extraordinary breakfast with Rosalyn, he lifted it and broke the seal.

Two pages fell open. One had been torn from an agenda or diary book. He recognized Lydia's hand. Puzzled, he scanned down the words. It consisted of a list of ships.

He picked up the other page. None other than Algernon Trilby had written.

My Lord Duke,

As you can see, both your and the duchess's reputations are in grave danger. She has put me off repeatedly as to the fair reimbursement for my time and trouble in procuring the documents from which the enclosed page derives. Her last attempt to do so resulted in a laughable amount. I am sure that you will comprehend the seriousness of the situation more than it appears she does, and will want this settled and behind us all.

He read both pages again while his temper grew darker and darker. Two thoughts managed to survive the onslaught of fury. The first was that he was sorry he had not followed through on that duel with Trilby. The second was that he now knew what the hell Lydia had been doing in Buxton. This tiresome man had not been courting her. He had been blackmailing her.

He collected all the mail and strode up to his chambers, calling to the servants to get his horse ready. Appointments with ministers be damned. He intended to find Trilby and thrash him senseless.

Marcus Trilby, artist, lived in an airy loft of an attic, one full of light, canvases, paint smells, and a chaise longue on which his model, a girl who looked to be about fifteen, lay stark naked. She held a broken urn that presumably symbolized her lost innocence. The painting in progress made the most of that urn, to impart a moral context to a sentimental and erotic painting that looked like it would appeal to the kinds of men who favored the girls that Lydia's school sought to save.

The artist bore some resemblance to the magician with his fair hair and thin face. Excitement descended on him as soon as he read the card in his hand. "Oh! Please come in, Your Grace. Whatever I can do for you— Cover yourself, Katy! Uh, unless, Your Grace, you would prefer—"

"Tell the girl to leave, please."

"Out with you, Katy. Take your clothes and dress down in the kitchen." Trilby the artist threw the child out, then offered his guest a seat on that same chaise longue. He began pulling paintings from their stacks and setting them out for view. "I am overwhelmed, Your Grace. That a collector such as you sought me out—it is a dream come true, especially after the Royal Academy disappointment. Did you learn of my art from a friend? If so, I would be grateful to know the name so I can express my gratitude."

"I am sorry that you have misunderstood. I did not come here to add to my collection. I am seeking a relative of yours that I am told lives here. Mr. Algernon Trilby."

He stopped his busy activity. He stood before the paintings, disappointed.

"Algernon is my cousin. He does not live here as such. When he comes to town he uses an extra chamber I have, that is true, but it is not his primary residence."

"Is he using it now?"

"He left just this morning. He said he might return in a week or fortnight."

Damnation. The blackmail letter was burning a hole in his pocket. He had looked forward to making Algernon Trilby eat it, quite literally.

"If this is not his primary domicile, where does he live?"

"At his family home. He came by it when his father died. He and his sister live there, although of late he has been coming up to town. He does these silly little tricks with cards that the ladies think are fun. He has been doing quite well since I made his first introductions." He looked at his paintings and spoke the last sentence with resentment.

"I would like to write to him. Would you be kind enough to give me his postal address?"

"Of course. However he may not be there now. He spoke about going to Brighton, to a house party of some lady who likes his tricks. I expect he will be performing there before going back home." He pushed aside some palettes to reveal a writing table underneath. He found a scrap of paper and a colored chalk stick and began jotting. He stopped quickly, and looked over cautiously. "Say, he is not in some trouble, is he?"

"Do you think he might be?"

"Not at all." He wrote a bit more, then stopped again. "It is odd for a duke to come around looking for him, however. He has not done so well as that. And those magic tricks of his—some men use them for ill gains."

"Does he?"

"If you are here because you think he does, you are wrong. I think he tried, but he became clumsy so he gave up."

"Yet he did try."

Trilby the artist flushed. "Once or twice, I believe. Not so long ago he did again, and failed. He returned here the next time very disappointed in himself. I wondered if he was lying, because he seemed to have a nice amount of money suddenly."

"That is all very interesting, but this is not about his magic tricks."

He waited to hear what it was about. Penthurst gestured to the desk. "The address?"

With a startle, he recalled his intentions. He jotted several lines, folded the scrap so the chalk would not smear, and handed it over. "I will write myself and tell him that you called."

"Please do not. I would prefer that my own letter be a surprise." He rose to go, but paused to examine the paintings. "Your technique reminds me of Claude. Perhaps you should try landscapes."

"Claude? Do you really think so?"

"Absolutely. The best part of landscapes is you do not have to pay models. Which reminds me—that girl who was here—in the future, I would like you to require her mother come with her. If I ever return to look more closely at your art, I would not want to walk into a situation that compromises one so young again, and by association me. Having a guardian present is how it is done in France."

"It is?" Trilby shadowed him all the way out. "Oh, yes, absolutely. I will insist her mother attend too. I look forward to your return, and will try to have some landscapes for you to see."

Once on the street, he opened the scrap of paper to see where he could find the blackmailing rogue. He barely noticed the first two lines of the address because the last word riveted his attention thoroughly. Algernon Trilby's family home was in Hampshire.

Chapter 19

Everything looked different. She could not help remarking on it each day. Fields appeared smaller, buildings less picturesque, light less golden, and paths more rocky.

Had she really experienced the nicer Hampshire, or had her mind prettied up the memories?

It occurred to her as she walked up the path to the cottage, that if Lakewood walked beside her now and she looked over at him, he might not match her memories either. His face survived in a golden glow too, didn't it? Perhaps she would see faults she had never noticed. He might have ears that were too big, or eyes too close together. Her girlish love had made him an Adonis, but she doubted the truth had been even close to that.

She suspected the real Lakewood could not measure

up to Penthurst, for example. The duke did not need some girl's infatuation to make him more than he was. That was true in everything, not only his face and form. Even if he were not a duke, or even a peer, or even a man of property and wealth, he would be formidable. That was not a word that she recalled Lakewood evoking.

For a sane person, weighing things without emotion, there could be no competition between the two men. None at all. Except that Lakewood could beat the duke on one single point. There was the chance that he had loved Lydia Alfreton. It could be a major difference if Lydia Alfreton was your name.

Had he?

She had come here suspecting maybe not. She wondered, as she entered the cottage, if the question still remained open merely because the likely answer would leave her feeling like the worst fool.

She heard sounds coming from the kitchen. She called to Sarah while she removed her spencer and bonnet. "Did a letter from my aunt come in the post, Sarah?"

Sarah did not answer. Curious, she walked to the back of the house to see if Sarah had gone out to the garden.

She jumped with surprise when she entered the kitchen. The duke stood by the window in riding clothes.

In that startled instant when she first saw him there, she had all the answers she would ever need. The joy in her heart told her the truth. So did the stirring in her body.

The real question, she realized, was not who had loved whom in the past, but whom she loved now.

* * *

Lydia jumped as if he had popped out of a hiding place to scare her. Then she did not move at all. He might have been a stranger from the way she examined him.

She looked beautiful and fresh. Her hair poured freely down her shoulders and back and her skin showed a flush from her walk. The contentment he experienced in seeing her astonished him even more than the anticipation had. Within that peace, however, a seed of nostalgia sent down tiny roots. If things went badly the next few days, he might never know this contentment again.

He expected she would upbraid him. *How dare you follow me, as if I need a nursemaid or guardian, after I told you this did not concern you at all. I would think it was clear I wanted to be alone here.*

Instead she walked over, wrapped her arms around him, and laid her head on his chest. He embraced her closely and pressed a long kiss to her crown.

"How did you know how to find this place?" she asked.

"Your aunt was happy to tell me. Considering the rumors about your absence, the matrons of the ton would have forced her to if she had hesitated."

"Rumors?"

"I will tell you later. Right now—" He kissed her. It had only been two weeks but it might have been a year from the way that kiss moved him. His essence sighed with relief and gratitude as her warm, soft lips accepted sweetly, then eagerly. He lifted her into it, closer, and she circled his neck with her arms.

Very soon the kiss was not enough for either of them. She looked at the window. "Sarah—"

"I sent her to the village to see if she could find some wine to buy."

"That should take an hour at least. It is a bit of a walk."

"Sarah is a smart woman. I think it will take at least two."

She hung on him, and smiled up impishly. "You arranged that neatly. Did you ride all this way because you missed me as a lover?"

"That was one reason. The biggest one." The other one was in his pocket, waiting for another day.

Her smile did not waiver, but her eyes turned serious and soulful. "I am flattered. I have missed you too. Badly. I am so glad you came. I need you to hold me. I need your friendship too."

Her declaration of need provoked a fierce arousal. He saw no sadness in her, but her words implied her mission was not done yet. Nor could he see it through for her, or change the truth to protect her. He could hold her the way she needed today, however, and be the friend she sought.

Not only a friend, of course. A lover too. Right now that part of their alliance refused to be denied any longer. He scooped her into his arms. "Where are the bedchambers?"

She laughed, and pointed to the ceiling.

She lost one shoe as he carried her out of the kitchen. Another fell on the stairs. Her arms remained circling his neck all the way up. She distracted him with a kiss on the landing. It did nothing for his control.

"That way." She pointed.

It looked like a girl's chamber, all white and frilled. He set her on her feet and began pulling off her clothes. She laughed again, and pushed his hands away. "A bit of patience, Your Grace. I did not bring much with me, and can ill afford to have you shred this dress."

He left her to it and dropped his coats. While he untied his neckpiece and sleeves he noticed more of the chamber. The furniture was old-fashioned and simple. The bed had an iron headboard and footboard made up of wrought vertical rods, with four long ones at the corners holding up the canopy and the frame for drapes.

He sat down and pulled off his boots. Lydia's own disrobing distracted him. She was down to her chemise and hose. She noticed him watching and teased a long time in removing the chemise. It inched up ever so slowly. She turned, pretending to be shy, and her soft round bottom was revealed first.

He reached for her and pulled her back so he could kiss the dimple at the small of her back, and luxuriate in the sensation of her skin against his caress.

"They think you left because all was not right between us in bed," he said while he kissed her back and slid his hands down her legs.

"Who thinks that?"

"Everyone, I suppose. Perhaps even our friends. It seems husbands would only allow their wives to go away so soon if husbands have imposed so much that their wives are miserable about it."

"Too often, you mean?"

"Too erotically is the thinking, I believe."

She turned around. "I did not leave because of it, but you did say some of those things are not commonplace with married couples."

He kissed her stomach, loving the sensation of her velvet skin on his lips. He watched his hands gloss around her breasts. "You would tell me if you did not like something, wouldn't you? I do not want you to feel obligated."

Desire had already transformed her expression. She leaned into his caresses the way she did when she wanted more. "Of course I would tell you. The *on dit* is wrong at least with me. But you already knew that."

He flicked his tongue at her breasts. She tensed and gasped and stretched her fingers through his hair and held his head closer. "Have you been hinting that you want to show me something else extraordinary?"

"Many things. But not right now." Despite the images crowding his head, he did not want to give erotic lessons now.

He stood, lifted her again, and set her on the bed. He shed his lower garments and settled on top of her so he could feel her totally all along his body. He used his hand to make sure she was ready, then entered slowly, making it last, soulfully grateful for every exquisite instant. Then he did not move for a long while, but lay there in her embrace with his kiss resting in the crook of her neck while he breathed in the reality of her.

Sounds came from below. The light at the window showed the afternoon was waning. Lydia feared losing the poignant beauty if she moved, so she remained where she was, with Penthurst's arm crossing her body in its gesture of protection and possession.

She would not have minded extraordinary in an erotic way if he had wanted that. She found those lessons exciting. She much preferred that he had sensed she needed something quite normal, however. She needed this slow pleasure, with its calmer explorations. It allowed her to never lose hold on the way her emotions gave the intimacy new depths. That had touched the pleasure before, but today had been about little else.

Had he felt it too? Perhaps men never did. Most likely men married under obligation did not.

His arm moved, to her regret. He sat up. "It is late in the day."

"Sarah has started cooking. Will you stay here with us? I should warn you that there is only this chamber and my aunt's that have beds, and I gave Sarah my aunt's."

"We both fit here. The cottage is simple, but pleasant. I will stay, but only if you do not mind."

He got up and looked out the window. "A glorious sunset is forming. Let us walk out and enjoy it."

They dressed and went below. Sarah came out from

the kitchen and curtsied. "I've the wine, Your Grace. Dinner will be in an hour or so, milady. I just put the potted fowl on the hearth."

She led him to a path that would snake through the fields of a neighboring farm. As their legs strode in unity, she thought of another man who had paced beside her on the same ground. There would not be a single place she could take Penthurst that she had not already been with Lakewood.

"You are very quiet, Lydia."

"I am just lost in my thoughts."

"I hope I have not interfered with your plans here, or tainted the nostalgia no matter what you concluded about its source."

Her heart ached. He knew. How like him now to say in his oblique way that if she wanted to keep Lakewood in her heart forever, he would understand.

He deserved better. She did too.

"I have not drawn many conclusions. I see the time I spent here one early spring very differently than my memories had, however. Less golden, and far less perfect. Even my emotions. I was not a young girl, but my head had been turned for the first time, and that can be a powerful creator of illusions. I have spent the last fortnight looking back with more mature eyes. I can see how I might have been manipulated, and how his insistence we keep our alliance a secret probably reflects his dishonorable intentions."

He did not say anything, but after a few more steps he took her hand in his. They strolled toward the west in the crisp autumn air. Red streaks had formed in the sky as the sun hung low. Suddenly all of the light changed as if an artist had added some pink to the tint of the atmosphere.

They stopped and watched while it lasted. Eventually the sun disappeared behind the horizon and deep twilight fell. She turned to him. "I want you to know that all of this, the time and place and person, had been shut in the past. I did not think about him when we— when you—"

"Were intimate?"

"Yes."

"You would have found the word yourself, after you accommodated how bold you were being in looking for one in the first place."

She laughed.

He pulled her so she snapped into his embrace. "That is good to know, Lydia." He kissed her. "I am almost as relieved to hear it as I was when I learned it had not been his naked bum you saw that day."

For all the humor, a stirring bond held them in that embrace. She had spoken the truth when she said she had needed a friend. Not Emma or Cassandra or Sarah either. This one, who now looked at her as the light faded.

Perhaps it was knowing her face became obscured. Maybe it only grew out of the closeness she felt to him, and the mood her confidences had created. She thought, however, that what she next wanted to say might not be so bold as it would have been even a week ago.

She touched his face, then his mouth. "I think that

I may have cruelly misjudged you about that duel. Will you tell me about it?"

The lights in his eyes could still be seen. They flashed anger, pride, and even, she thought, some pain. He took her hand from his face, kissed it, and they walked on.

Only when the cottage came into view did he speak again.

He never spoke of it. He did not know why he did now. Perhaps because of the allusions she had once made to how dukes can murder friends and escape judgment. He wanted her to know it had not been so black-and-white.

Maybe suspecting that the days ahead would tear open the wound anyway compelled him to prepare her with this other story too.

He would have spared her the tale of Lakewood's dishonesty with the commissions, but that was bound to come out soon anyway. He kept it brief, but that hardly changed the truth. What was left of that infatuated girl might not want to hear it, but the duchess took it in stride.

Talking about the actual duel came harder.

"I thought once he calmed, he would stand down from his challenge. Your brother was his second, and tried to talk sense to him. And to me, but he did not know what I had learned. Lakewood seemed to think that if he killed me, his good name would survive. And if he did not, it might survive too. I did not realize how determined he was to go through with it, fully, until I saw him that morning."

"Did he say as much?"

"He said he would silence me. I told him that others knew. That one of his commissions had revealed too much, which was how I learned the truth. He changed then. The belligerence left him." The memory of that change haunted him. More than the urge to fight and kill had left Lakewood in that moment. He had emptied of will right there, and his gaze had turned inward and haunted. "Then he walked away, to await the call to position."

"If killing you would not stop the scandal, why not stand down then?"

Because he decided to walk into the ball from my pistol. "Pride, perhaps."

She took his arm and pressed against his side. "Yet his reputation was spared, despite what you said, about others knowing."

"You cannot bring a dead man to trial. The War Office investigated quietly, and the offending officers were removed, but revelations about his role were not released."

"Perhaps influence was used to ensure that. A few words from a man of importance, or from his important friends, for example."

"Perhaps your brother pled his case."

"I do not think it was my brother. If he had known

about those commissions, he would not have cut you for over a year."

It was dark when they entered the garden. Delicious odors beckoned from the kitchen. Lydia stopped him before he could open the door.

"Thank you for telling me. Although you did not include everything, did you?"

"I told you most of it." Not the shock of Lakewood's sudden movement, or watching him fall. Not the weeks of reliving those few moments, to try to see what had truly happened.

She stretched up and kissed him. "You were a better friend than he deserved. He knew you would be, I think. He knew that if he died, you would protect his name, because you are so good and fair."

He had concluded much the same thing. A self-inflicted death to atone for his sins, knowing his good name would be spared—it was a fine plot. Lakewood's character appeared almost noble and sacrificing in the story it told. It had taken a long time to realize the plot suffered from melodrama.

It would take more than the threatening scandal over those commissions to drive Lakewood to do what he did. He had seen something else in the future, once questions began being asked. Something he would rather die than face.

He followed Lydia into the cottage, wondering if she would think him so good when he found out what the rest of Lakewood's crimes had been.

Chapter 20

First light made her stir. Subtle movements pulled her awake. The bed beside her was empty. She turned to see Penthurst dressed already. He came over, kissed her, and tucked the bed cloths up around her.

"Go back to sleep."

"Are you leaving?"

"Only for a few hours at most. I thought to walk to the coast. It is not far from here. I can smell the sea sometimes."

She threw off the bed coverings. "It is maybe an hour walk if you go through the Forest of Bere, but longer by the roads. I will come too, and show you the shorter way, if you do not mind company."

"It isn't too far for you?"

She slipped out of the bed. "I have walked it often

before. I have walked even farther when I stay at Crown-hill. You should have realized by now that I am not very delicate in constitution."

He waited, sitting in a chair, watching her wash and pull on her chemise and hose and dress.

"Thank you for reassuring Sarah about the militias last night. She was much relieved to hear they are unlikely to ever see a battle," she said.

"There are determined efforts at negotiations at work. I think we may see this war end soon, or at least have a truce so those efforts can be doubled."

"That would be wonderful. I have lived my life with this war, it seems. An end to all the costs and deaths has appeared out of reach."

"After it is over, we will go to France. You did want to once, enough to stow away in a galley."

She pulled on her half boots. He gestured for her to come over. One at a time, he lifted her feet to his knee and worked the side buttons. Bonnet, spencer, and gloves came next. Finally she was ready to go.

"Wait." He opened her wardrobe and poked around. He emerged with an old shawl that she could not remember ever seeing. He unfurled it and wrapped it around her. "It is cold out still and the night's damp will chill you."

"This is very ugly. I think it belonged to a servant who once worked here. If we pass anyone, I will embarrass you."

"If we come upon anyone, you can shed it and I will carry it. But you will wear it now, Lydia. This walk will take enough of a toll that I will not have you get sick too."

"You will see it takes no toll at all on me. Let us go."

Early mornings were the best time for walks, Lydia decided. The whole world still carried the stillness of the night, and the silver light made even ordinary sights magical. They made their way south over the countryside and into the forest while Penthurst described events in London.

They were very close to the coast before that light turned white and the sun showed. Even so she was not sorry to have the ugly shawl. The air held the crisp chill of winter's near arrival.

"You know your way here very well," he said.

She knew her way because she had come here often with Lakewood. Due to the distance, which had seemed far shorter back then, she had not retraced this particular walk during the last two weeks.

Something in his observation and voice made her think twice about completely retracing those steps today. She led him to a spot a little to the west of the harbor, where the view of the ships was lateral and eastward.

He studied the lay of the harbor, and the position of Portsmouth across the way. He pointed to the long stretch of Portsdown Hill north of the water. "Let us walk up that hill and see the fleet."

"There are guards there. They will question us."

"Then we will answer their questions. I do not think they will be suspicious of a gentleman and lady."

Not if the gentleman was a baron. There had been little company on that hill years ago, but a peer could gain access with a few words. She expected even less trouble if she accompanied a duke.

She did not want to trudge up that rise of land, but she followed. Each step reminded her that when she returned to London, she would again be trying to placate Algernon Trilby. They walked to where most of the fleet could be seen at anchor and the busy activity on the docks looked like a swarm of ants. A guard did stroll over to them and question their purpose. Penthurst identified himself, and that ended that.

Penthurst surveyed it all with a thoughtful expression. "You used to come here with him."

It was not a question. "Yes. I would bring food and we would eat *en plein air* here, or on the way back."

"Did you do this often?"

"Several times. It was a favorite walk for a few weeks. Why do you ask? Not jealousy, I know."

"I am not too good to feel jealousy, Lydia. However, this is why I ask." He reached into his pocket and removed a folded paper. He gave it to her. She opened it.

She thought she might faint when she saw her handwriting, and the ships listed. Faint or get sick. She dared not take her eyes off the paper. She could not look at him, but she felt his gaze on her.

"It came to me with a letter, in case you are wondering.

Mr. Trilby decided you had dithered too long and recently sent him too little."

"*Dithered*? I gave that scoundrel almost three thousand and promised more. His demands were too ridiculous from the start, and only got worse."

"There is no winning in negotiations with blackmailers, Lydia." He tugged gently at the page until she released it. "How did you come to write this?"

"It is part of a novel. A bad one, admittedly. I was writing it here, to pass the time when I was alone with my aunt. All kinds of things found their way into it."

"It is very detailed. It looks incriminating as hell, Lydia. You know that. You would not have given him a shilling otherwise."

"We would play games while we ate our meal," she explained desperately. "We would make silly rhymes about the ships, like little school songs. As with any such lesson, it was easy to remember what I had seen."

"The songs were very detailed then, too, if they enumerated the number of men-o'-war and frigates and such."

She gazed out on the fleet. She would not have known a frigate if her life counted on it. Lakewood had pointed all that out, and created most of the silly songs. She had laughed long and hard at how ridiculous some of the rhymes were. She had thought him the most amusing man in the world.

And when next she jotted in her novel, it had been easy to have her heroine walking alone up here, seeing all those ships while she pined for her lover.

A thought came to her. A terrible one. She tried to put it out of her mind, but it stuck there, demanding attention. If she had written down the information memorized through those little rhymes, had Lakewood done so as well? Had that been the whole reason for coming here?

She looked at Penthurst and she knew he had been harboring the same thought. Perhaps he had been for days.

She pointed at the paper. "What are you going to do with that?"

"Burn it. As for Mr. Trilby, I will do what I would have done weeks ago if you had only confided in me. He and I will have a long conversation. Depending on what I learn, and whether he cooperates, I will either pay him off, once and finally, or swear down information and see him sent to the hulks."

They spoke of other things on the way back. The duke did not upbraid her for the stupidity that had led to the blackmail. He did not have to. She knew mortification with every step. Her compromise in Buxton would pale compared with the scandal if Trilby did not cooperate. She did not doubt that Penthurst contemplated how he had gotten a very bad bargain in her.

Her mind also worked through other things. At long last she looked at that early spring with uncompromising honesty. She did not make any more excuses for Lakewood, and she did not shrink from the implications of what she saw. By the time they arrived back at the cottage she was furious.

"It was no accident that he favored the walk to the coast, was it?" she asked while she hung her spencer on its peg.

Penthurst did not answer. He appeared troubled and thoughtful. Not for himself, surely. For her. About her?

"Well, *I* think it was no accident," she said, if he would not. "He would have needed an excuse to spend time where he could study the port. They might let a baron go there, but he could not just sit down and take notes, could he? So he flattered and flirted with a girl heading for the shelf fast, so his visits there could be seen as simple walks to an interesting picnic spot." Indignation poured through her. "And if that were not bad enough, he—"

"Lydia, calm yourself. We do not know—"

"We do know. I know. He used me to do something so dishonorable it cannot be excused or forgiven. Something he would rather die than have exposed. And if that were not bad enough, he then told someone about my manuscript and it was taken and ended up in Trilby's hands. I had even read Lakewood parts of it. He knew what it contained. Who would go to the trouble to steal it unless they knew too?"

He did not appear very surprised, or even sympathetic. He looked like the Duke of Penthurst, who required the world to bend to his liking.

"What you are saying might be correct. I will know soon. I do not think he intended that you be the victim of blackmail, however. The goal may have only been to take your journal so it would not be read by others, and raise questions."

About him, or her? It would be nice to think Lakewood had the decency to try to protect her. "It is not a journal. I told you, it is a novel."

"I assume that will be obvious once I see more than one page of it."

They went in to the meal Sarah had cooked. It proved a quiet and awkward hour. While she picked at the stew, she watched him. She could tell that his mind worked on something.

He did not believe her, she realized. He was not sure, at least. His analysis had left open the chance that Lydia—reckless, excitement-seeking Lydia—had thought it would be fun to at least pretend to spy on the fleet. She could not blame him for wondering, but a deep sorrow saturated her.

He had known everything when he arrived yesterday. It was why he had come. And their tender, soulful reunion in that iron bed may have been so poignant because he knew he would soon never see her the same way again.

"I told the coachman to come in the morning, to bring you and Sarah back to London."

He spoke into the night. Their passion had been fast and unsatisfactory, as thoughts from the day interfered with losing herself in the pleasure. Lydia wondered if this was how it would always be now. She might not have minded had she not experienced better. She would have never noticed a lack of intimacy and closeness if she had never come to love him.

"When did you tell him?" He had not left her side since arriving.

"Before I came by yesterday."

It had all been planned, then. Except her joining him on the walk to the coast. He had intended to do that alone.

"Will you be riding back with us?"

"I have something to do before I return to town. I will be there in a few days."

"Should I close up the cottage, or will you be staying here?"

"Tell Sarah to close it."

He turned toward her. As he fell asleep, his arm came to rest across her in that familiar embrace. She lay there, not doing anything to cause him to move it.

"Did you bring them?" Penthurst asked.

He sat in a tavern in the village not far from the cottage. The man he had arranged to meet had just entered and sat at his table.

Kendale called for some ale. "Your letter told me to bring my army, which made no sense. I have no army, of course. I have not been in the army myself for years."

"Forgive me. I wrote in haste. Did you bring any of those many servants who practice at arms and do your bidding?" It was indeed a little army, much to the government's concern. Had Kendale not been a viscount, he would probably be in prison for some of the things he deployed those men to do.

"Four of them came with me. There is nothing you could need doing that requires more."

Four would probably be more than enough, but there was no way for Kendale to know that, other than his low opinion of the sorts of missions a duke might undertake.

They drank their ale in silence. Kendale asked for no particulars about the letter, or the events to unfold. Penthurst had known he would not. It was why Kendale had received the letter in the first place. The only question had been whether he would come. Since he had, Penthurst did not expect any arguments. When Kendale perceived the true quarry they hunted today, it was unlikely he would voice resentments or judgment either.

"Let us go. It is not far from here."

They went out and mounted their horses. Four men on horseback followed them down the road. After a few miles they turned up a lane. It ended in front of a house of good size. On examination it became obvious that most of the building was of recent construction. The center block and main entrance appeared much older. Its stone displayed the wear of ages, while the additions did not.

"There is no need for you to do anything except line up here and appear forbidding," Penthurst said after he dismounted.

"Are you saying you dragged me all the way here and there is nothing to do?"

"There will be no battles, if that is what you expected."

"Too bad. I brought my sword." Kendale assessed the house. "New money."

"Yes."

"Ill gotten?"

"I think so."

Kendale kept studying the house. "Is this Lakewood's infamous Dunner Park?"

The questions lined up in a way to suggest Kendale, for all of his uncompromising view of that duel, had learned a few things on his own.

"Hell. No, it isn't, but if you ask that question, you may as well come along." Penthurst strode to the door. While he waited for his knock to be answered, Kendale joined him.

A female servant in cap and apron opened the door. Penthurst handed over his card. "Tell her that it is in her brother's interests that she receive me."

The woman let them wait outside while she took the card in. She returned to escort them to a large, high-ceilinged library that looked like something his aunt Rosalyn might have decorated.

A woman sat on a divan, his card in her hand. She had chestnut hair streaked with coppery lights. She possessed the kind of precise beauty that would make Ambury look twice, and lead men to believe she was the mistress of a duke.

"Miss Trilby, it is good to finally make your acquaintance. This is Viscount Kendale. I want to talk to you about the enterprises your brother, you, and Baron Lakewood engaged in to further your fortunes."

She dared a pose of hauteur. "I am sure I do not know what you are talking about."

He turned to Kendale. "Have your men take her into custody. We will bring her to London, and let the agents of the Home Office conduct this inquiry."

She stood, alarmed. "If you would explain yourself, I will do all I can to help. Has my brother done something to attract the government's attention?"

"Blackmail, most recently. Before that the sale of commissions and, of particular interest, a bit of spying. A minor bit, but the word still fits."

Her hands went to her face in dismay. Her eyes brimmed with tears. She turned away. "Oh, Algernon. Stupid, stupid Algernon."

Penthurst walked over until he stood in front of her bowed distress. "Yes, stupid Algernon. So stupid that I cannot see him managing it on his own. Had it all stopped with Lakewood's death, I might have assumed he invented everything. Since it did not, that only leaves you as the mind behind it all."

"Do you think she will do as you told her?" Kendale said while they walked to their horses two hours later.

"It is the smart choice, and that is not a stupid woman."

"I don't like it. Better for it all to come out. The two

of them should suffer the fate they chose when they lured him into this."

Lure was too kind a word. He doubted Lakewood had resisted long, at least not on the commissions. That pretty face in there would have been very persuasive. The two of them had known each other for years, and a man lusting after a woman could fall fast if of weak character.

"It is better this way." He mounted his horse. "She will do as I said. She will make the meeting."

"Because you will have her brother? I would not count on it. She looks the sort to let him swing while she sells out and runs."

She would want to do that, but she would not. Not because of loyalty to her brother either. Greed would move her, as it had all along. He had let her know, obliquely and indirectly so as not to alert Kendale to the reference, that a good deal of money would be waiting at the meeting.

"Will you be needing me for the denouement?" Kendale asked as they turned their horses to the road.

"I think not. There are others in town, should I decide to bring an army. You can return to your bride, although she has probably tired of you by now and was glad to have you gone for a few days."

Kendale thought that was very funny. "Speak for yourself, Penthurst." He laughed as he led his men down the road.

Chapter 21

Lydia thought she would go mad. It had been bad enough to carry an aching heart back to London, and to nurse it for four days now. It had been sheer hell to anticipate the disappointment and anger Penthurst would show when he finally returned too. Now she had information that would add an unexpected layer to the whole plot.

Lakewood and Trilby had known each other.

"You are very sure?" she said to her aunt Amelia. She had paid a duty call, in order to distract herself.

She had not allowed Rosalyn to come this time. Rosalyn had been treating her like an invalid ever since her return. Suddenly it was "poor Lydia" and cooing sympathies that made no sense. Last night she had said Lydia could thank her that Penthurst apologized. Only he hadn't, nor could she remember a reason he should. She suspected this all had to do with those rumors about erotic impositions, but the notion that Rosalyn knew and contemplated that was not to be entertained.

"Oh, yes," Amelia said. Her soft, round face creased into a smile under her gray curls. "The baron brought Mr. Trilby to entertain me. Wasn't that kind? Mr. Trilby does these little magic tricks with cards. I think he accompanied the baron two or three times before you visited. Then Mr. Trilby called after you had returned to town, to see if I needed anything. What a kind man to think of me. He brought his sister, too, and continued to call whenever I went down to my cottage. Last summer his sister urged me to remove some of my Harold's items, so I did not get that bad pang in my heart whenever I saw them. I agreed, and her brother kindly carried them out to the barn while she and I chatted."

The chat would have allowed Trilby to move about the cottage freely. Had he chanced upon that trunk and pawed through it out of curiosity, or had Lakewood alerted him that a manuscript existed? In the carriage house Trilby could examine its contents at his leisure, and find the manuscript. Perhaps he had taken it to be sure it contained nothing that incriminated Lakewood or himself. He had probably jumped for joy when he found pages that incriminated its writer and no one else.

Amelia reached over and gripped her hand. "I will always be grateful that you came to me that spring. I did not think I wanted anyone around, but your quiet presence helped so much. I have regretted how we grew apart afterward."

"That was my fault, not yours. Aunt Hortense is much easier to hoodwink. I knew that once you overcame your grief, I would not have nearly as much fun with you as with her."

Amelia gave her a scolding frown, then laughed. "All is well that turns out well. Since you landed Penthurst after all, who can complain?"

She still ruminated over the discovery about Trilby, and it took a moment for her aunt's last odd comment to gain her attention. "After all? What do you mean?"

Amelia's face fell. "Did no one ever tell you? Hortense and I chose not to, because we did not want you sad that you had lost out on a duke. I thought that surely someone else would be unkind and speak of it when you were older, people being what they are."

"Now that you have spoken of it yourself, perhaps you should explain."

Amelia launched into a surprising explanation of a pact that Penthurst marry her, made by her mother and Rosalyn when she was born. The future duke was not amused, it turned out, and repudiated the arrangement as soon as he inherited.

"He stood in front of that assembly of well-wishers, and said he would choose his own duchess and that he rejected forthwith any arrangements, pacts, or proxy engagements that may have been, or ever might be, made for him," Amelia concluded. "That meant you, unfortunately."

"Of course."

"No more than fifteen, he was then, but you could already see what he would be. When I learned of your elopement, I thought, well, there you are. Celeste got her way in the end. As did Rosalyn, although I believe she had reconciled herself to her nephew's not being swayed by that pact."

"I think so, yes."

"See how everything turned out well, Lydia? It is enough to restore one's faith."

Lydia left soon after that, mulling over the astonishing revelation that her mother had tried to engage her to Penthurst within hours of her birth. How old-fashioned. *Of course* he repudiated the pact. She would have if he had not.

She returned home, to wait and worry and wonder. She tried to stuff her emotions back into her heart, to no avail. Once one acknowledges love, it turns out, it is very difficult to step back into not knowing. She was stuck with it now. If he returned to treating her as he had before that last day in Hampshire, she could just barely live without having her heart broken repeatedly.

When the carriage pulled up in front of the house, she sensed something had changed. The footman who handed her down confirmed it. "His Grace has returned, Madam."

"When?"

"He rode up an hour ago."

"How did he— That is, did he look well?"

"He made a joke and flipped me a guinea, so he looked well enough to me, Madam."

She forced herself to walk sedately up the steps. Once inside the house, however, she ran to the stairs. The whole way up she prayed there would be no strangeness between them. Maybe he would joke with her too, about all those discoveries in Hampshire. He would tease her about including lists of ships in a novel, and tell her that he had used his ducal power to fix everything, and they would fall into bed and she could know the power of loving him at least, even if he only saw her as a troublesome wife he did not mind too much.

Sarah startled when she burst into the apartment.

"Fast, fast," she ordered. "Take off this bonnet and fix my hair. Find me a nicer dress. I should wash my face too."

Sarah ran this way and that, trying to do it all at once. Lydia sat at her dressing table, looked with dismay in her looking glass, and pinched her lips and cheeks to draw out more color. "The new red dress, Sarah. No, the dark green one."

Sarah did not answer. Silence suddenly reigned in the dressing room. She turned to see Sarah standing still with dresses, chemises, and wraps in her arms. Sarah looked at the door to the dressing room.

Lydia turned the other way. Penthurst stood there. He wore no coats and his hair showed damp from washing.

Sarah dropped the garments onto the floor and left. Lydia smiled nervously, and tried to decipher his humor. He did not appear angry, at least, but he did exude a dark aura. She suspected she might not fare as well as the footman.

He came up behind her, bent, and kissed her cheek from behind. "It is good to see you, Lydia." He stroked her cheek. "It is very red now. Perhaps you pinched too hard."

More likely that was the blush she felt warming her face. "Did your journey go well?"

He sank onto the settee behind her. She turned around.

"Well enough. You are not to worry. All has been settled. In two days you and I will meet with Mr. Trilby, pay him off, and that will end it."

She wanted to throw herself on him, weep with gratitude, and beg him to forget any of this had happened. Instead she stayed put. Something about him reminded her of that last day together. Something unspoken hung in the air. "Thank you. If you want to scold me for getting myself into this scrap, I cannot object. I have castigated myself repeatedly for being so gullible and stupid."

"I do not want to scold you for being gullible. I do want to scold you severely for not coming to me, or at least your brother, for help."

"I did, in a way. Go to you."

"I do not mean forcing that wager to raise the money, and you know it. That you did not trust me at first can perhaps be excused. That you did not when he made his last demand cannot be." He looked at her with considerable annoyance.

"As you said, it was very incriminating. You might have thought—"

"That you willingly made lists of ships to be passed on to others? It would have been nice if you had shown a little faith in my trust of you too. I thought there was more between us now, Lydia. If you did not believe my affection for you would make a difference, you might have known my sense of responsibility for you would."

She did not know what to say. She knelt on the settee, circled her arms around his neck, and kissed him instead. "I thought I had it settled in Buxton. I did not expect to think of it again for a year. You are correct, however. I should have known you would not think poorly of me, or suspect the worst, or demand I do some kind of penance."

He pulled her onto his lap and kissed her hard. "You are right on two counts. I would not be so quick to assume the no penance part."

She kissed his cheek and smiled. "You are joking, of course."

"No."

She leaned back so she could see his face. "Why should I do penance when I did nothing wrong? That is not fair."

"In reparation for all the trouble you have caused me since you came here demanding a draw of the cards, that is why. It is very fair to my thinking, and long overdue."

She guessed he included their marriage as part of all the trouble. And a few other things. He had cause for annoyance, that was true. "What kind of penance?"

"First, you will ask Rosalyn to help you prepare for your presentation at court as the Duchess of Penthurst. The queen has expressed impatience, so it must be done very soon."

"I must accept her instruction in this? Please, do not demand this."

"I do demand it. And you must not only accept it, you must *request* it. Go to her tomorrow and ask her, in the gentle, humble way I know you can, to help you."

She almost pushed off his lap. It would kill her to do this.

"Second—"

"I think that is quite enough in itself."

"I do not." He cupped her chin in his hand and looked in her eyes. "Second, you will give yourself to me as you never have before."

A happy, sensual sensation coiled in her at his words. "That does not sound like penance."

"I hope not. But I will still be well paid for all the trouble."

"Why don't I agree to this twice, and we leave off the part about Rosalyn."

"More trouble, Lydia? This is not the day for it."

Probably not, from the looks of him. He appeared very stern. It excited her. "When should I expect this second penance? After the first one?"

He shook his head. "Now."

She waited for him to kiss her again, to start. Instead he took her hand and guided her to her feet. "Get undressed."

He helped with the tapes, but nothing else. He lounged there and watched, his dark intensity making her nervous. She dropped the dress and slid off her chemise. She had donned half-stays for her morning calls. She worked the knot of the lacing, then pulled the laces so she could remove the constricting garment.

He guided her back to his lap. "Leave the hose, I think. Now, do the same for me."

She straddled him, naked except for her hose, and plucked at his cravat. When it was off, he took it from her and set it aside on the settee, next to her chemise. She went to work on his shirt. All the while her arousal increased. He had barely touched her, yet she squirmed against his lap. She lifted his shirt and pulled it off.

He looked magnificent. She could not resist caressing his shoulders and kissing his chest.

"You will kneel to do the rest," he said.

As she slipped off his lap a shudder shook her arousal due to his making it a command to be obeyed, not a suggestion. Leaning into his legs, she reached for the buttons on his breeches. He did nothing to help, but just sat there waiting and watching. Again and again her fingers touched his hard erection beneath the fabric. When she finished with the buttons, she pushed all the garments down to release him. He rose enough for her to pull everything down his hips and off his legs.

He neither moved nor gave more commands. On her own initiative she skimmed her fingertips up his shaft. She had never had quite this prospect on it before. She circled her fingers around the base and used her other hand to stroke.

"Yes, Lydia. Like that." His hand cupped the back of her head. The gentlest pressure urged her to bow. "And like this, if you are willing."

She realized he wanted a similar intimacy to what he did to her. A moment of shock made her resist that slight push. His hand fell away. She looked at the caresses she gave him. She bowed on her own, and kissed.

He positioned his hands below her breasts and glossed over the tips again and again. An arousal, reckless in intensity, broke in her. She kissed again, then caressed with her tongue. When his voice, quiet and low, asked for more, it seemed an inevitable step to take.

It affected him deeply. It affected her too. The eroticism of the act overwhelmed her senses. The titillation of his caresses created unbearable need. When he stopped her, and lifted her to her feet as he stood, she could hardly keep her balance.

He scooped her up in his arms and carried her to her bed. She looked up at him and raised her arms to accept him into her embrace. He did not join her. Instead he flipped her so she hugged the mattress.

His hands closed on the sides of her hips. "Up. On your knees. Hands on the headboard."

She took the position he had requested before. He did not lie beneath her this time. Nor did he leave her thus. Instead he took her left arm and with quick ties of his cravat, bound her wrist to the bedpost.

He went to work on her other wrist with her chemise.

She tested the soft shackles. She could get free if she really wanted to. She decided she did not. The feeling of vulnerability aroused her.

"Is this the penance?" she asked, astonished at how her arms stretched and she hung from the cloth tethered to the posts. It reminded her of— "You do not intend to whip me, do you?"

"No. Inflicting pain creates a crude pleasure. Power, on the other hand—" He moved her knees back and pushed them apart. Now she really did hang from those cloth ties, her arms and body forming a long, slow curve. She stopped trying to fight the effect. She relaxed, and let the bindings support her.

She felt him behind her. She closed her eyes and waited, with an impatience that left her trembling.

He touched her first, in the long, knowing strokes that drove her mad. Control began crumbling. She looked behind just as he lowered his body. She closed her eyes. With the first glide of his tongue, she gave up and abandoned herself to the extreme sensation.

She cried when the pleasure became torturous. She begged. The first tremors of release shook around the edges of her essence. She waited for the violent completion they heralded.

He stopped then, refusing her that finish. She looked back again. He knelt high behind her. His gaze locked on hers while he slowly filled her. He withdrew and entered again. She felt him as she never had before.

Her interrupted release left her deeply sensitive, and the most profound pleasure centered around his deliberate thrusts.

The glorious madness engulfed her, bringing its freedom. She moved her hips, trying to take more, seeking the release that teased with its first shudders. He held her hips firmly so she could only know what he allowed her. Harder he thrust, again and again, while she hung helplessly submissive from the bed, until she shattered inside an unearthly burst of ecstasy.

H e did not have to bring Lydia to the meeting with Trilby. He did anyway. She had a right to be there.

They rode in their state coach with two liveried footmen in attendance. At his instruction, Lydia had dressed in a carriage ensemble trimmed in fur. It was important for Trilby to understand the power that stood against him.

"There he is," Lydia said, looking out the window. They were deep into Hyde Park, far from the areas frequently used in the morning. A few riders dotted the fields back here, but Trilby and his sister stood alone.

The coach stopped. A footman helped Lydia alight. Penthurst joined her and together they walked the thirty yards to Trilby. The footman carried a valise. He set it down when they stopped, and returned to the coach.

Mr. Trilby appeared ashen and cowed. Patricia Trilby did not. She had admitted much in that conversation in Hampshire, as she tried to cast it all as her brother's doing. If necessary, it would all be repeated to a magistrate. A witness had heard everything, but Penthurst doubted he would need Kendale to back him up. Being a duke had its privileges, one being that magistrates were inclined to believe whatever you said.

"Is that the manuscript?" Penthurst gestured to a wrapped package under Trilby's arm.

Trilby nodded, and offered it up. His sister thrust her arm in the way. "Is that the money?" She gestured to the valise.

"It is."

She strode over, grabbed the handles and dragged it back to her brother. Bending low, she opened the valise and pawed through the banknotes.

Penthurst relieved Trilby of the package. "I trust every single page is here. If I find more missing than were given to my wife or me, I will not be pleased."

"They are all there," Trilby said. "You will find nothing untoward. I checked myself before we came, just to make sure." He glanced askance at his sister, indicating who might have thought to take one or two sheets for the future.

"How did you know about it?" Lydia asked. "What made you look for it?"

"Lakewood expressed concerns that you were writing down a record of his time with you. He said you called it a novel, but it sounded like a journal. He worried there was something incriminating there."

"You mean besides his dishonorable behavior toward me."

Trilby flushed. "I had been introduced to your aunt. My sister—that is, *we* decided to try to get it if we could, just to be safe."

"It took long enough," Patricia Trilby said, rolling her eyes. "There were too many boring calls before the opportunity arrived. Imagine our surprise to find that the person incriminated was not Lakewood or my brother, but you." She toed at the valise. "A happy discovery, as it turns out."

"Mr. Trilby, do you understand the particulars?" Penthurst asked, to end the way the woman goaded Lydia. "You are both to leave the country. Go to America, or Brazil. Go wherever you like. If you do not, or if you return, either of you, a damp cell in Newgate Prison waits for you."

Trilby nodded. His sister only smiled, brazenly. Her gaze shifted to Lydia and raked her from head to toe. Lydia stared her down.

"Whose idea was it?" Lydia said. "The ships. Who decided to take that dishonorable step?"

Patricia Trilby's eyes narrowed over that irritating smile.

Algernon Trilby flustered. "That is hard to say. He came by one day and mentioned how from a certain point one could see it all. The notion to see what such would bring just came out of that." He flushed. "It seemed a very minor sort of surveillance, and barely disloyal. Anyone who walked up Portsdown Hill could see the same thing, after all. The size of a fleet can never be a total secret."

"Do you have any other questions, Lydia?" Penthurst asked quietly. An interrogation had not been part of the plan for this meeting, but he suspected she had a lot more she would like to know.

She hesitated, then shook her head.

"Then we are done here," he said. "Take your sister and be gone within a week, Trilby. Do not let her convince you it is not necessary. For once in this sorry business, do not allow her to lead you by the nose."

He took Lydia's arm and they turned back to the carriage.

"She led them both by the nose," Lydia said. "She was the reason Trilby was so inconstant in our negotiations, and kept changing his demands and getting bolder by the week. What a horrid woman. You should have had them thrown in prison. I am sorry my involvement, unaware though I may have been, forced you to be so generous to them."

"I am not sorry. It gave me an excuse to be generous to someone else too, Lydia. A man who, for all his weakness of character, was once your friend. And mine."

Chapter 22

Lydia could not sleep. After tossing under the bed-clothes for two hours, she threw them aside. Pulling on her undressing gown, she padded to the door to Penthurst's dressing room. Opening it, she saw a faint light coming from the bedchamber.

Trusting he would not mind, she walked on bare feet and peered in. He had prepared for bed too, but sat in an upholstered chair reading a document. Caesar and Cleo slept at his feet.

She went in and sat on the side of the bed. He set the documents down.

"Can't you sleep, Lydia?"

She shook her head.

"Are you nervous?"

"A little. The queen does not frighten me so much

as all the others. I expect any mistake I make to be spread far and wide by noon the next day."

She would go to St. James Court tomorrow and be received as Penthurst's duchess. Rosalyn had proven useful, after all. She had seen this often enough in her years, and knew the protocol to the last detail. It had probably been wise of Penthurst to require her aid be requested. And, Lydia had to admit, the time they had spent on planning had made Rosalyn easier to bear in other ways too. She did not irritate as much as she used to.

"Cassandra and Emma will be there. Not all the ladies will be looking to catch you up. Think of it as a day like any other. Whatever happens does not really signify."

That was easy for him to say.

She gestured to the papers. "What are you reading?"

"A manuscript written by a friend. It is not published yet."

"Is it any good?"

"It is extraordinary. Why don't you lie down and I will read you some of it. Perhaps it will help you sleep."

She stretched out on the bed. She heard papers shuffling.

"Here is a remarkable passage. *I knew I should not permit Mr. Beaumont's kiss, but love permitted no denial. I closed my eyes as his lips sought mine. The strict lessons of my governess—*"

"Stop!" She turned on her side and stretched, trying to grab the pages out of his hand. "I thought you burned that two weeks ago."

"I said I *would* burn it. And I will. The dangerous parts have been ashes since the day I got this. I thought I would see what a fifteen-thousand-pound story was like before I consigned the rest to the flames."

She closed her eyes, mortified. "Have you read all of it?"

"Oh, yes. Let me see, where was I— Ah, here. *The strict lessons of my governess faded from my thoughts as the excitement of that kiss stirred my womanhood. I neglected to end the kiss as quickly as I had intended. That must have encouraged Mr. Beaumont in ways I had not intended, because he embraced me and lifted me into a kiss that could never be thought one of mere friendship. 'My dear Christina. I will die from my love for you. How cruel that we cannot marry and know the sweetness of Venus's gifts. Allow me to at least caress your perfect breasts so I once know their sweet softness before I perish.' I did not demur, for the intimacy seemed necessary to my own contentment, and a very small one compared with what we could never share. His hand trembled as it closed on one of my snowy hills and—*"

She groaned. "Please stop. Really."

"It gets better. There is another love scene that is quite naughty, although the author's ignorance becomes apparent toward the end."

She already knew how much better it got. She definitely knew how ignorant the author had been. "Are you enjoying this?"

He laughed. "Very much. My very favorite part is

this description of Beaumont. Did you realize it changes? He starts out with light brown hair but it gets darker. He also grows taller." He cleared his throat. "*Mr. Beaumont was a handsome, overly proud man who looked down on the world. Although his character affected his view, partly it had to do with his significant height. He stood a good head taller than most of his comrades. I found his stature disconcerting. It was a nuisance to be tipping my head back all the time, only to find his dark eyes with their winged eyebrows viewing me with undisguised disapproval.*"

She frowned. She sat up. "I did not write that. You are making it up."

"It is in your hand, I swear. Here." He handed her the page.

She peered at the page. It was hers. When had she written this? It did not sound like Lakewood at all. It described—

"Why didn't you tell me that you dreamt of having my hand close on one of your snowy hills, Lydia? I would have been happy to oblige."

She threw a pillow at him. "You are to *burn it immediately.*"

"Most of it, I promise. You have to let me preserve the description of Christina's brother, however. And that of his friend, the scowling, angry army officer. Since you sharpened your knives to a fine edge before carving up some of the bulwarks of society, it would be a shame to lose those paragraphs." He let the pages fall to the floor and joined her on the bed. "Some of it is not nearly as bad as you claimed. The love story is very compelling. If you ever write another one, you might stick with that and leave out all those lists, perhaps."

"I am being presented as your duchess tomorrow and you are suggesting I might write another naughty novel. I am sure the queen would be amused if I did that."

He lay beside her and took her in his arms. "Do not worry overmuch what the queen finds amusing. Stop worrying about tomorrow's ceremony. I will think none the less of you if it is not perfect. Even if you trip and fall on your face, I will not love you less."

"Do not even joke about my falling. I will never sleep if I start imagining that—" The words died as she realized what he had said. She turned within his embrace so her face almost touched his. "Do you really love me? Has it come to that?"

"It appears I do, Lydia. Unexpectedly, but happily, I find you have stolen my heart. Do women of the world allow their husbands to love them or is that too ordinary?"

"Being loved by you could never be ordinary. Loving you in turn is not either. It is the most exciting thing I have known."

He kissed her softly, then rose on his arm and looked down at her.

"Did you know how I felt?" she asked. "Did you guess?"

"Not at all. I did not expect a declaration from you in return. I spoke of it because I wanted you to know. After how this marriage happened, I thought you should."

"I suppose that is what you meant by the unexpected part. Or were you referring to how you repudiated me when you were fifteen?"

He covered his eyes with his hand and groaned. "Who told you? Rosalyn? I will put her away in a tower house and remove the ladder."

"She is innocent, although her first scold made much more sense after I heard." She gave his side a little poke. "You must have thought fate had ensnared you when you said those vows in Scotland."

"That never entered my mind," he said, gallantly.

"If I had been you, I would have been stunned by the irony."

"It did occur to me that ducal decrees were not worth a lot." He laid his hand on her face, and became serious. "I did not feel ensnared in that Scottish church. The marriage seemed more inevitable to me than ironic. Last week in Hampshire I realized I had been waiting for you to grow up, and that I loved the woman you had become."

She filled with emotion too precious to bear. She stretched up to kiss him. She let her lips linger on his, so she could make an eternal memory of the first kiss they shared after baring their hearts.

"You should probably sleep, so you are ready for tomorrow," he murmured.

"Not yet. I want you to fill me. I want to feel you inside my body and my heart and know all the excitement of being in love with my husband."

He did as she asked, until they were joined so totally

that she felt him in her soul. He moved, then closed his eyes and moved again. "It is perfect, Lydia."

It was perfect. She bent her legs to take him in deeper. She opened her heart, and allowed her love to be free and reckless.

As the power built and they melted together, she whispered declarations of love into his ear, so he would know how he astonished her, and how his love made her life extraordinary.

Keep reading for an excerpt from

The Surrender of Miss Fairbourne

by Madeline Hunter

Available from Jove Books

MAY 1798

The final sale at Fairbourne's auction house proved to be a sad affair, and not only because the proprietor had recently fallen to his death while strolling along a cliff walk in Kent. It was also, from the viewpoint of collectors, comprised of very minor works, and hardly worthy of the reputation for selectivity that Maurice Fairbourne had built for his establishment.

Society came anyway, some of them out of sympathy and respect, some to distract themselves from the relentless worry about the expected French invasion for which the whole country had braced. A few flew in like crows, attracted to the carcass of what had once been a great business, hoping to peck a few morsels from the body now that Maurice did not stand guard.

The latter could be seen peering very closely at the

paintings and prints, looking for the gem that had escaped the less experienced eyes of the staff. A bargain could be had if a work of art were incorrectly described to the seller's detriment. The victory would be all the more sweet because such oversights normally went the other way, with amazing consistency.

Darius Alfreton, Earl of Southwaite, peered closely too. Although a collector, he was not hoping to steal a Caravaggio that had been incorrectly called a Honthorst in the catalogue. Rather, he examined the art and the descriptions to see just how badly Fairbourne's reputation might be compromised by the staff's ineptitude.

He scanned the crowd that had gathered too, and watched the rostrum being prepared. A small raised platform holding a tall, narrow podium, it always reminded Darius of a preacher's pulpit. Auction houses like Fairbourne's often held a preview night to lure the bidders with a grand party, then conducted the actual sale a day or so later. The staff of Fairbourne's had decided to do it all at once today, and soon the auctioneer would take his place on the rostrum to call the auction of each lot, and literally knock down his hammer when the bidding stopped.

Considering the paltry offerings, and the cost of a grand preview, Darius concluded that it had been wise to skip the party. Less explicable had been the staff's failure to tell him of their plans. He learned about this auction only through the announcement in the newspapers.

The hub of the crowd was not near the paintings hung one above another on the high, gray walls. The bodies

shifted and the true center of their attention became
visible. Miss Emma Fairbourne, Maurice's daughter,
stood near the left wall, greeting the patrons and accepting their condolences.

The black of her garments contrasted starkly with her
very fair skin, and a black, simple hat sat cockily on her
brown hair. Her most notable feature, blue eyes that
could gaze with disconcerting directness, focused on
each visitor so completely that one would think no other
patron stood nearby.

"A bit odd that she is here," Yates Elliston, Viscount
Ambury, said. He stood at Darius's side, impatient with
the time they were spending here. They were both
dressed for riding and were supposed to be on their
way to the coast.

"She is the only Fairbourne left," Darius said. "She
probably hopes to reassure the patrons with her presence.
No one will be fooled, however. The size and quality of
this auction is symbolic of what happens when the eyes
and personality that define such an establishment are
lost."

"You have met her, I expect, since you knew her
father well. Not much of a future waiting for her, is
there? She looks to be in her middle twenties already.
Marriage is not likely to happen now if it didn't happen
when her father lived and this business flourished."

"Yes, I have met her." The first time had been about
a year ago. Odd that he had known Maurice Fairbourne
for years, and in all that time he had never been introduced to the daughter. Maurice's son, Robert, might

join them in their conversations, but never Robert's sister.

He and Emma Fairbourne had not spoken again since that introduction, until very recently. His memory of her had been of an ordinary-looking woman, a bit timid and retiring, a small shadow within the broad illumination cast by her expansive, flamboyant father.

"Then again . . ." Ambury gazed in Miss Fairbourne's direction with lowered eyelids. "Not a great beauty, but there is something about her . . . Hard to say what it is . . ."

Yes, there was something about her. Darius was impressed that Ambury had spotted it so quickly. But then, Ambury had a special sympathy with women, while Darius mostly found them necessary and often pleasurable, but ultimately bewildering.

"I recognize her," Ambury said while he turned to look at a landscape hanging above their heads on the wall. "I have seen her about town, in the company of Barrowmore's sister, Lady Cassandra. Perhaps Miss Fairbourne is unmarried because she prefers independence, like her friend."

With Lady Cassandra? How interesting. Darius considered that there might be much more to Emma Fairbourne than he had assumed.

He did not miss how she now managed to avoid having that penetrating gaze of hers connect with his. Unless he greeted her directly, she would pretend he was not here. She surely would not acknowledge that he had as much interest in the results of this auction as she did.

Ambury perused the sheets of the sale catalogue that he had obtained from the exhibition hall manager. "I do not claim to know about art the way that you do, South waite, but there is a lot of 'school of' and 'studio of' among these paintings. It reminds me of the art offered by those picture sellers in Italy during my grand tour."

"The staff does not have Maurice's expertise, and to their credit have been conservative in their attributions when the provenance that documents the history of ownership and supports the authenticity is not clean." Darius pointed to the landscape above Ambury's head. "If he were still alive, that might have been sold as van Ruisdael, not as follower of van Ruisdael, and the world would have accepted his judgment. Penthurst was examining it most closely a while ago, and will possibly bid high in the hopes the ambiguity goes in van Ruisdael's favor."

"If it was Penthurst, I hope it was daubed by a forger a fortnight ago and he wastes a bundle." Ambury returned his attention to Miss Fairbourne. "Not a bad memorial service, if you think about it. There are society luminaries here who probably did not attend the funeral."

Darius *had* attended the funeral held a month ago. He had been the only peer there, despite Maurice Fairbourne's role as advisor to many of them on their collections. Society did not attend the funeral of a tradesman, least of all at the start of the Season, so Ambury was correct. For the patrons of Fairbourne's, this would serve as the memorial service, such as it was.

"I assume everyone will bid high," Ambury said. Both his tone and small smile reflected his amiable manner, one that sometimes got him into trouble. "To help her out now that she is alone in the world."

"Sympathy will play its role in encouraging high bids, but the real reason is standing next to the rostrum right now."

"You mean that small white-haired fellow? He hardly looks to be the type to get me so excited I'd bid fifty when I had planned to pay twenty-five."

"He is astoundingly unimpressive, isn't he? Also unassuming, mild-mannered, and unfailingly polite," Darius said. "Unaccountably it all works to his advantage. Once Maurice Fairboune realized what he had in that little man, he never called an auction in this house again, but left it to Obediah Riggles."

"And here I thought that fellow over there was the auctioneer. The one who gave me this paper listing the things for sale."

Ambury referred to the young, handsome man now easing the guests toward the chairs.

"That is Mr. Nightingale. He manages the exhibition hall here. He greets visitors, seats them, ensures they are comfortable, and answers questions regarding the lots. You will see him stand near each work as it is auctioned as well, like a human signpost."

Dark, tall, and exceedingly meticulous in his elegant dress, Mr. Nightingale slithered more than walked as he moved around the chamber, ushering and encouraging, charming and flirting. All the while he filled the chairs and ensured the women had broad fans with which to signal a bid.

"He seems to do whatever he does quite well," Ambury observed.

"Yes."

"The ladies appear to like him. I expect a bit of flattery goes far in helping the bids flow."

"I expect so."

Ambury watched Nightingale for a minute longer. "Some gentlemen seem to favor him too."

"You *would* mention that."

Ambury laughed. "I expect it causes some awkwardness for him. He is supposed to keep them coming back, isn't he? How does one both encourage and discourage at the same time?"

Darius could not swear that the exhibition manager did discourage. Nightingale was nothing if not ambitious. "I will leave it to you to employ your renowned powers of observation and let me know how he manages it. It will give you something to do, and perhaps you will stop complaining that I dragged you here today."

"It was not the where of it, but the how. You deceived me. When you said an auction, I just assumed it was a horse auction, and you knew I would. It is more fun to watch you spend a small fortune on a stallion than on a painting."

Slowly the crowd found seats and the sounds dimmed. Riggles stepped up on a stool so he showed tall behind the rostrum's podium. Mr. Nightingale moved to where the first lot hung on the wall. His perfect features

probably garnered more attention from some of the
patrons than the obscure oil painting that he pointed to.

Emma Fairbourne remained discreetly away from
the action but very visible to everyone. *Bid high and
bid often,* her mere presence seemed to plead. *For his
memory and my future, make it a better total than it
has any right to be.*

Emma kept her gaze on Obediah, but she felt people
looking at her. In particular she felt one person
looking at her.

Southwaite was here. It had been too much to hope
that he might be out of town. She had prayed for it,
however. He went down to his property in Kent often,
her friend Cassandra had reported. It would have been
ideal had he done so this week.

He stood behind all the chairs, dressed for riding,
as if he had been heading down to the country after
all, but had seen the newspaper and diverted his path
here. He towered back there and could not be missed.
Out of the corner of her eye she saw him watching her.
His harshly handsome face held a vague scowl at the
doings here. His companion appeared much more
friendly, with remarkable blue eyes that held a light of
merriment in contrast with the earl's dark intensity.

He thought he should have been told, she guessed.
He thought it was his business to know what Fairbourne's was doing. He was going to want to become

a nuisance, it appeared. Well, she would be damned before she allowed that.

Obediah began the sale of the first lot. The bidding was not enthusiastic, but that did not worry her. Auctions always opened slowly, and she had given considerable thought to which consignment should be sacrificed like this, to give the patrons time to settle in and warm up.

Obediah called the bids in his smooth, quiet fashion. He smiled kindly at the older women who raised their fans, and added a "Quite good, sir" when a young lord pushed the bid up two increments. The impression was that of a tasteful conversation, not a raucous competition.

There were no histrionics at Fairbourne's auctions. No cajoling for more bids, and no sly implications of hidden values. Obediah was the least dramatic auctioneer in England, but the lots went for more than they should when he brought down his hammer. Bidders trusted him and forgot their natural caution. Emma's father had once remarked that Obediah reminded men of their first valet, and women of their dear uncle Bertie.

She did not leave her spot near the wall, not even when Mr. Nightingale directed the crowd's attention to the paintings and objets d'art near her. Some of the people in the room would remember that her father stood here during the sales. Right in this spot where she now was.

As the final lots approached, Mr. Nightingale

retreated from his position to stand beside her. She thought that odd, but he had been most solicitous today in every way. One might think his own father had taken that fatal fall, from the way he accepted the condolences of the patrons during the preview, almost losing his composure several times.

As soon as the hammer came down on the last lot, Emma exhaled a sigh of relief. It had gone much better than she had dared hope. She had succeeded in buying some time.

Noise filled the high-ceilinged chamber as conversation broke out and chairs scraped the wooden floor. From his place beside her, Mr. Nightingale spoke farewells to the society matrons who favored him with flirtatious smiles and to a few gentlemen who condescended to show him familiarity.

"Miss Fairbourne," he said while he bestowed his charming smile on the people passing by. "If the day has not tired you too much, I would like a few words with you in private after they have all gone."

Her heart sank. He was going to leave his situation. Mr. Nightingale was an ambitious young man and he would see no future here now. He no doubt assumed they would just close the doors after today. Even if they did not, he would not want to remain at the auction house without the connections her father had provided him.

Her gaze shifted to the rostrum, where Obediah was stepping down. It would be a blow to lose Mr. Nightingale. If Obediah Riggles left, however, Fairbourne's would definitely cease to exist.

"Of course, Mr. Nightingale. Why don't we go to the storage now, if that will suffice."

She walked in that direction with Mr. Nightingale beside her. She paused to praise Obediah, who blushed in his self-effacing way.

"Perhaps you will be good enough to meet me here tomorrow, Obediah? I would like your advice on some matters of great importance," she added.

Obediah's face fell. He assumed she wanted advice on how to close Fairbourne's, she guessed. "Of course, Miss Fairbourne. Would eleven o'clock be a good time?"

"A perfect time. I will see you then." As she spoke she noticed that two men had not yet left the exhibition hall. Southwaite and his companion still stood back there, watching the staff remove the paintings from the walls in order to deliver them to the winning bidders.

Southwaite caught her eye. His expression commanded her to remain where she was. He began walking toward her. She pretended she had not noticed. She urged Mr. Nightingale forward so she could escape to the storage chamber.

From *New York Times* bestselling author
MADELINE HUNTER

The Counterfeit Mistress

A refugee from the war, Marielle Lyon is in London to save her father's life. Gavin Norwood, Viscount Kendale, believes Marielle is a spy and will do whatever it takes to unmask her—even if it means playing into a game of seduction…

PRAISE FOR THE NOVELS OF MADELINE HUNTER

"Hunter's books are so addictive."
—*Publishers Weekly*

"Madeline Hunter is masterful."
—*Booklist*

"A sparkling gem…Will keep you dazzled!"
—*Fresh Fiction*

madelinehunter.com
facebook.com/MadelineHunter
facebook.com/LoveAlwaysBooks
penguin.com

M1426T0114